A wedding can bring out the best and worst in people and families, something I have experienced first-hand on many occasions. It seems that there is some kind of chemical reaction that changes people when they have a wedding or participate in a wedding. It can be hilarious or extremely sad, but, rarely, any wedding goes down without some drama. My name is Russell Green, and this is my first book. I wrote this book during the lockdown, and what started as a challenge and something to keep me busy became something much more. I caught COVID at the end of 2020, and the first three months were hell. I spent all that time in bed not able to bend my joints, I couldn't even put my feet on the floor without excruciating pain. When this passed, I developed a severe case of brain fog, unable to concentrate on anything, I lost the ability to read or write, I could see words but they made no sense.

When this passed, I found my memory started to get worse and worse, I completely lost all memory of my work, which for 30 years, I was in the art business, and it seemed as though someone had sucked all my knowledge out of my brain, and this has never returned. I was unable to return to work. My memory is stuck, and now I cannot remember anything that happened on my previous day, it's like Groundhog Day. I record messages every night of my activities of the day and listen to the notes in the morning, but by that night, my memory had been erased. You cannot imagine how many things it prevented me from doing. I needed to find things to do to keep me busy and stimulated. Someone suggested why don't I write a book, something light and not something that needed my short-term memory. The idea came when thinking about one of my business partners and my mentor, who tragically died a few years ago. Often, I would think about him, and it made me smile when I thought about his napkin ring story (this will make sense later in the book). So that's what I did. I made myself a short recording that I listened to every morning telling myself about the book, why I am doing it and where on my computer I could find it. It became a very long process as I could not start writing any day unless I had re-read what I had written, otherwise I would not remember it at all. I am the epitome of living in the moment or the day. Once I had written 30 chapters, it got harder as I had to read all the chapters before I could write the next chapter… but I did it, and here we are.

I'm married and have an incredible wife, daughter, grandson, stepson and stepdaughter, and a father of two grandkids. I am very lucky, they have helped me through some very dark times, and I have been blessed for sure. I really enjoyed writing this book and harbour a dream of renting an apartment in Florence for a year. Picture this: writing on my balcony, overlooking a bustling square, walking my dogs, cycling, and indulging in a nightly ritual of a bottle of red wine with a bowl of pasta. I playfully remind my wife about this dream regularly. It's my way of giving her advanced notice, considering I've been sharing this aspiration with her every month for the past three years. The time to turn this dream into reality is approaching rapidly.

I want to dedicate this book to my wife for showing me the importance of family and turning our house into a real home.

Also, I would like to thank anybody who invited me to their wedding as I'm sure in this book are characters or stories they might relate to.

And, of course, to my kids, because they have given me the golden ticket.

Russell Green

The Trauma of Making Our Wedding

Austin Macauley Publishers

LONDON * CAMBRIDGE * NEW YORK * SHARJAH

Copyright © Russell Green 2024

The right of Russell Green to be identified as author of this work has been asserted by the author in accordance with sections 77 and 78 of the Copyright, Designs and Patents Act 1988.

All rights reserved. No part of this publication may be reproduced, stored in a retrieval system, or transmitted in any form or by any means, electronic, mechanical, photocopying, recording, or otherwise, without the prior permission of the publishers.

Any person who commits any unauthorised act in relation to this publication may be liable to criminal prosecution and civil claims for damages.

This is a work of fiction. Names, characters, businesses, places, events, locales, and incidents are either the products of the author's imagination or used in a fictitious manner. Any resemblance to actual persons, living or dead, or actual events is purely coincidental.

A CIP catalogue record for this title is available from the British Library.

ISBN 9781398484771 (Paperback)
ISBN 9781398484788 (ePub-e-book)

www.austinmacauley.com

First Published 2024
Austin Macauley Publishers Ltd®
1 Canada Square
Canary Wharf
London
E14 5AA

Table of Contents

Synopsis	9
1. Meet the Cohens and the Andersons	12
2. Will It Be a Yes or a No?	29
3. Grow Some Balls	44
4. Motherly Intuition	48
5. The Lull Before the Storm	54
6. Roz's or Claire's	59
7. Andy Goes to See His Parents	62
8. She Knows!	68
9. Friday Night Dinner	71
10. It's a Small World	82
11. Old Blue Eyes	86
12. Please Excuse Me	88
13. Never Assume You Know Someone	92
14. Ding, Ding, Round One	95
15. Swallow Your Pride	103
16. Friday Night Dinner	106
17. Roz Had Lunch with Her Mum	109
18. Xmas Together	112
19. Who Knew a Wedding Had So Many Parts	117

20. Family Updates	125
21. The Operation	129
22. Who Knew a Wedding Could Cost This Much	135
23. Fred Delivers	139
24. The Napkin Rings	142
25. Claire Takes Her Parents Out	147
26. The Results	150
27. David Takes His Dad Out	154
28. Friday Night Dinner (16 Days to Go)	156
29. Family Update	160
30. Tami's Exhibition 13 Days to Go	163
31. Five Days to Go (Baby Is Ready)	165
32. Four Days to Go Tami Struggles	168
33. Three Days to Go, Where Are the Napkin Rings	170
34. Two Days to Go, Andrew Comes Home	172
35. Family Updates	176
36. The Arrival at the Hotel and the Barbecue	179
37. Day of the Wedding	185
38. The Day After the Wedding	197
39. Roz	201
40. Family Updates Two Months After	212
41. Family Updates Nine Months Later	214
42. Friday Night Dinner	217
Summary by the Author	221

Synopsis

Two families becoming one.

Weddings bring out the best and worst in us. When two families come together, it's like a chemical reaction; something happens that's unexplainable as they try hard to become one family.

Dealing with complicated personalities with complex lives, some with powerful secrets that, for the sake of their family, should remain a secret.

There is real humour at times as well as deep sadness, and as my wife would tell me, there is no such thing as a 'normal' family, these families are for sure anything but normal, anyway, what is normal?

The story is set just outside London; the Cohens and the Andersons could not be more different, they live 3km from each other. In their formative years and as they navigated the journey of raising children, the two families had several chance encounters. Fleeting moments occurred, and in some instances, the dots connected. However, it was a wedding that endeavoured to bring them together.

They could not be more different or lead more different lives from each other. The Andersons are extremely wealthy and from a non-practising catholic upbringing, and the Cohens are a working-class family with a Jewish practising upbringing.

Both sets of parents have one boy and one girl each; both girls were born one day apart and both boys two weeks apart.

This story captures a period of 18 months in their lives, and it's astounding what can happen and how so many lives can be opened up and changed for good. The wedding is the catalyst for the majority of this change.

Below, I have given you a very brief description of the eight members of these two families.

The wealthy family consists of...

Husband Andy...Flash, loud, selfish man, born with a silver spoon in his mouth and does not want to get old, has no relationship with his children and has a huge secret to try and conceal, he shows glimpses that there could be a good person in there somewhere, but he continues to press the self-destruct button time and time again.

Wife Claire...Extremely self-absorbed, adores her husband and turns many blind eyes, she has not yet realised the freedom she has due to being wealthy in her own right and that, actually, the life and person she has become is not who she is deep down. This wedding brings out her motherly intuition, love and respect for the family.

Son Michael...He is getting married. He's a follower, not a leader, and until he spreads his wings and leaves the family business, how can he really escape his father's genes and take control of his own life? There is something about him that makes people wary, but no one discusses it.

Daughter Tammy...A very talented artist but a tortured young lady with severe mental health issues. She just wants to be loved and taken care of, everything she never experienced as a child. She grows closer to her mother, the more problems she has.

Working-class family consists of:

Husband David...An unhappy taxi driver, he works hard to support his family, a moaner and a drama queen. He has a secret he has hidden for his entire life from everyone, and he keeps exceeding everyone's expectations of him as time passes.

Wife Roz... The family matriarch relinquished her profession to dedicate herself to raising her children. A skilled cook, she serves as the glue holding the family together. Loved, confided in, and relied upon by all, her wisdom is a guiding force. Unfortunately, her health takes a downturn, casting a shadow over her life and affecting everyone around her.

Son Stephen…A bit of a geek with no friends. He has a fantastic job earning a lot of money that seems to really bother his father; he has hidden the fact he's gay and is living with Abraham, whose parents arrived here as refugees from Ghana. Stephen and Abraham met at university and now are more than just roommates; how does he tell his family?

Daughter Becky…Very pretty, smart, has a great job, she is the bride to be, a very loving daughter, who struggles with her mum's illness, she hasn't yet discovered her true identity, this will come as the story develops, she's really at her most comfortable when she's working, she loves being around academics as she is one herself. Is she getting married for the right reasons, and is she prepared to give up her profession to raise children and run a family?

There are many moments throughout this story that will make you laugh and some that will make you cry, but they all go to show that what goes on behind closed doors is never as it seems and where families are concerned, there is room for pandora's boxes bursting to be released.

1. Meet the Cohens and the Andersons

Welcome, and thank you for deciding to join me on this roller-coaster of a journey, following two families through the highs and lows and traumatic times of planning a wedding. They could not be more different or lead more different lives. One a very wealthy catholic family and the other a working-class Jewish family. The stories that emerge from making just one function are quite astounding, and sometimes it makes you wonder whether, without a wedding and two families trying to become one, would so much have come out or would it still be buried? For sure, with these two families, everything came out.

For some reason, a wedding brings out the best and the worst in people, and I know from my own experiences weddings can make or break a family. When two families combine, something happens. It's like a chemical reaction that's hard to explain unless you have experienced it yourself. So, join me as we experience it together.

It's unusual to start a story with book number three of four, but I wanted to share with you a hilarious and yet sometimes incredibly sad story as these two families come together. I hope over time, you will join me in looking back at how it all started for both families and also where it ended up going later in life.

Being Jewish myself, I've observed that while Jewish families share commonalities with families worldwide, there are unique experiences that I've personally encountered…

We are very good at coming together when there's a death or a health scare.

We like holding onto things. I don't mean objects, I mean grudges.

We worry about everything, if things are bad, we fear they will never get better, and if they are good, we worry about when the bad times will come back.

We worry about our kids at whatever age they are, and we always want to keep their bedrooms just in case, that's normally the mother. The father, wants them gone when they have a job.

Food and family dinners are the centre of family life and bring home everyone at some point.

Mothers and sons go through rocky times when there's a girlfriend involved.

Fathers can't cope when their daughter brings home a boy.

Jewish men cannot do DIY, but worse is that they try.

I hope to give you an insight into two families with very complicated lives…

The Cohens live in a middle-class area, and it also happens to be the centre of a very large Jewish community. They live in a semi-detached three-bedroom house, which Roz, the wife, keeps spotless. She never has any help cleaning the house, the one time she tried having a cleaner, she hated it, and when she left, Roz went around and cleaned everything again.

The Andersons reside a few miles away in a picturesque, leafy area. Their six-bedroom house, nestled in about five acres, reflects a lifestyle far removed from domestic concerns. Claire, the wife, maintains two cleaners every other day, a full-time gardener, and a live-in chef with his wife in a small cottage on their land.

They almost crossed paths on countless occasions over their early days, and actually did on a few, as you will find out. Although they live very different lives and mix in very different circles, yet only living two miles apart, the wedding comes along and entwines them for good.

I have not based these families on any one person I have known, but they are a combination of many traits in people I have known over my life.

I dedicate these books to my amazing wife, Viv, because throughout our life so far, she has taught me the importance of family, and through all the crazy highs and lows, they are always there, and coming home to the noise of a family laughing is the best most comforting noise in the world, and it makes you feel safe.

Let me start by introducing you to the two families so you can get a mental picture of all of them. You can decide for yourself which ones you fall in love with or can relate to, and have fun on this journey with these two meshugana (crazy), families. Oh, by the way, throughout the book, I have used old Yiddish slang words for fun, and I have tried to explain them as we go.

The Cohen family

Husband David is 55 years old, the head of the family (or so he likes to think). He's of small to average height, jet black hair all swept back with a little help from some hair gel and some men's hair colour. It's starting to go a little thin now, bless him, he has a bit of a borch (fat belly), he gave up exercise when he was 30 and started eating more. He has tried to grow a beard, but even at 55, he has a bit of a baby face with sensitive skin, and beards just don't work. When he goes on holiday and returns, he never looks like he's left his house, stays in the shade the entire holiday.

He has had a mixed career, left school at 17, he was a bit of a nabech (sad case), he had a very small group of friends and was very quiet at school, he wanted to be a singer although he never ever told anyone or sung in front of other people. He has managed to keep this secret his entire life, it gets harder as he gets older. Back then, he just wanted to get out, earn money, and get a job that involved singing somehow.

He ended up working for an uncle who had a small jeweller in the local high street. He hated this job; selling was not his thing, nor was having to smile or be nice to people all day. Also, every Jewish person he knew came in to buy their jewellery from him, and all thought they had the right to a big discount, but his uncle always said no deals for family or friends. They pay the full price or they can kishmere touchas (kiss my arse). Anyway, it earned him enough money to fund his social life and, in secret, for him to pursue his dreams of being the next Sinatra.

He liked motorbikes (little man syndrome) and bought one so no one could recognise him whilst he was travelling around singing in small clubs and bars. Everyone knew everyone where he lived, and Jewish teenagers went to youth clubs rather than night clubs or bars, talking about other people and eating food were more important than meeting new people and drinking. Jews never really drunk that much, boy has that changed…

He found it difficult at times and got very despondent, and he really hated working for his uncle, there were no prospects, as his uncle had a son who was a complete shmendrik (fool), but he would take over the business soon.

He wanted to leave, and one of his friends said to him why don't you learn 'the knowledge' and get your green badge to become a taxi driver? You're halfway there; you've got the bike to learn on. At first, he dismissed the idea until he realised it would give him the freedom to tell his family and friends, he was out working the knowledge whilst he was singing as much as he could and trying to get that all-important break. In those days, he was a very optimistic young man and really believed his time would come.

It took three years, but he got there eventually (his green badge, not his singing break) but life does not always go the way you want it to. He ended up getting less work in the clubs and working more on the cabs, and that was how he became a taxi driver. With that green badge, he could always make a living and support a family no matter what.

He enjoyed the loneliness of being in a cab but also loved being on a stage singing, the next Sinatra he would never be, but never stopped dreaming about.

He met Roz in his early teens, it was a bit of a whirlwind romance, and they were both the sort of people that would not date loads of people when they found each other, it did not take more than six months before they were talking marriage/kids etc. And before he knew it, he was married with a mortgage and having to work six days a week just to pay the bills and give his family a good life.

A golf enthusiast, he frequents a local club with three lifelong friends he met at the local Jewish youth club in his teens. Despite his perpetual golfing struggles since the age of 17, he relishes the time spent with his friends. Additionally, he's an ardent Spurs fan, holding two season tickets—one for himself and one for his son. He's also a bit of a drama queen when it comes to illness, spends a lot of time at the doctors with all sorts of complaints, he's a person with diabetes which millions of people are, but his diabetes is terrible of course and not like anyone else's.

When he came home to tell Roz he was diabetic, he walked in with a very sad face and said, "Roz, sit down, I've got something to tell you." She raised her eyebrows which would drive him mad. "Please sit down, I need to talk to you. You know I've been feeling a bit shvach (unwell) for a while. Well, it turns out I am type 2 diabetic, and my diabetes is so close to being type 1, I'm right on that borderline. I'm in a small group of people who are right on the edge." – As he pinches his thumb and first finger together, showing the tinniest of gaps – "It could change at any time, so I need to make many changes to my life."

He waited for Roz to faint or scream or cry, but she just said, "You've got pills?"

"Yes, of course."

"Good," she replied. David was amazed at her reaction, and he wanted to call a family meeting to announce it. Roz said, "Don't make such a mishegus (big thing out of nothing), millions of people are diabetic; maybe now you will start eating better and lose some weight."

I think by now you have a picture of David...

Rosalind, his wife, 51 years old, came from a very froom (religious) background. Her parents were very strict with her as a youngster. She never had brothers or sisters but kept herself occupied when she was at home and loved school. This really brought out her strong personality, and she had this desperate need all the time to take control and look after people. This was for sure because she felt a distance between her and her own parents as they never showed any affection in public and she never wanted to be that way. She adored her grandmother very much and went to see her every weekend and stayed with her. She was devastated when she was 14 when her grandmother died of pneumonia, and this loss was so hard for her to understand; she was really affected by this.

She went from school to university. She was very, very bright and became an accountant, went to work for a firm in London and worked her way up to partner. She was a real social club girl in the days when everyone went to youth clubs with all their friends (of which she had many).

She has blonde hair that went to her shoulders. It had quite an old-fashioned look to it with those flicky back sides, a bit *ABBA* from the '70s. She was thin, too thin, and lately always looked tired. When David was younger, he was an old-fashioned young man, they made a good couple back then, and he sort of swept her off her feet with his weirdness. He wasn't part of the in crowd, but she quickly fell for him. Roz, always destined for family and kids, carried regret later in life for giving up her career. It wasn't a choice; it was an expectation to stay home, raise the kids, and manage the family home. Now in her 50s, she contemplates that decision as the years seem to fly by.

Roz had what you call an under-her-breath comment she used all the time. I think all Jewish wives have this. My mother's was, "Ach, you're not for my nerves," Anyway, Roz, her under-her-breath comment is, "Ach, he used to be so good looking and funny what's happened to him."

Roz learnt to become a good wife and mother. She was also a real bulerboster (old-fashioned cook), loved her cupboards being full of food all the time just in case, especially when the kids came over. She gave away their food in the cupboards, saying, "I bought too much of this, that, and, oh let me check the freezer." It drove David mad. The kids were working and could afford food. "I understand leftovers from a family dinner, but my spaghetti, my biscuits, my juices from the fridge..." Whenever David complained, she always said, "So tell me, when was the last time you went hungry?" She baked like a pro and made chicken soup to die for. On the odd occasion, she would make chulent (a very heavy stew) with dumplings, potatoes, butter beans, gravy and beef. It cooked for about two days, weighed a ton and also had thousands of calories in every mouthful.

Roz was the real matriarch of the family. David, he…was there if she needed things done or moved around, and David relied heavily on Roz, she was only happy when he was working, and the fact he worked nights on the cabs was perfect. She got a good night's sleep and never had to worry that he fancied some rumba as they never spent any time in the same bed together, and when she got up, he came in and went to sleep. The only thing was, they got used to saying "Ssssshhhhhh, Dad's asleep" every day, they all learnt to whisper very well. Roz was getting less content the older the kids got, and she had itchy feet to go back to work as her days of being a mum to grown-up kids were not enough for her, and she always wanted to have her own money and work.

I hope you have a picture of Roz now.

Their oldest was their daughter, Rebecca. She was 25 years old, very tall (not from her father), had golden skin (not from her father), was a strong character (not like her father), a bit of a drama queen (like her father), liked to be called Becky.

She was an easy child. She came out into the world quickly, the birth was easy, she hardly cried and had a real Punim (sweet face) with bright blonde hair. She was going to be a stunner. She was very smart at school, passed all her exams and was a big shot at the youth club she was at, a real guntza muchu (a manager, busy with everything going on there); she had many friends. In university, she studied the history of art, pursued a master's degree, and landed a job as a museum researcher. Mindful of her well-being, she frequented the gym for spinning, yoga, and Pilates, practising meditation and spirituality. Despite her mother's constant plea to wear less makeup, she turned out stunning. The boys admired her, yet she remained focused on her girlfriends and work throughout her late teens and early twenties.

When she got into her early twenties, most of her friends were with someone or married, and that's when she went on a few dates through a website. There she met Michael but after a quick date nothing happened. Of course, Becky still lived at home as she loved all the comforts and could not even turn on a washing machine, she may be smart at her job and runs a team of five researchers and has been asked to guest at other museums because she is so knowledgeable…but she's not street-wise at all, and Roz worries every time she leaves the house. She loses her keys every week, and has even called the police once because her car was stolen at a shopping centre, only to realise she left her car at home and got dropped off.

Marriage to her was the ultimate positive sacrifice, and she was ready to make that commitment. Her religion was very important to her. She went to the synagogue on all the festivals, was not what you would say very religious but she liked a lot about being Jewish. She loved the fact that when she went abroad with her job, she was on her own, the Jewish people always seemed to seek her out, and the connection of meeting a Jewish person in another country was very strong, not like meeting another English person. That's something she would normally avoid, but she also loved a bacon roll.

She met Michael again at a weird party she had gone to (or was forced to go to) with one of her friends. It was at the house of an artist who was doing an exhibition at her own home. In fact, she turned her entire home into an exhibition. It was a bit like taking Tracey Emmin's bed and expanding on it to make an entire house the exhibit. It was a bit unusual, but hey-ho, the art business has many facets, and that's what she loved about it. She never really had that much in common with Michael, but when six of them started talking politics, of which Becky was way out of her depth, Michael came alive, and his knowledge was amazing as he fought an amazing argument. In the end everyone realised he would keep going forever so they all said they needed a drink and left the two of them sitting. They got chatting, and he invited her to his home after the party. She went there, and they sat up all night talking rubbish and drinking coffee, wow, what a house!

The rest is history. They've been dating for three years, two quietly under the radar as Becky grappled with concerns about his non-Jewish background. Despite these reservations, she loves him deeply. Their public relationship of one year seems comfortable, lacking fireworks but exhibiting a remarkable ease with each other.

Many people were unsure that she and Michael were a good match, but they seemed to work, and she really loved him, and he would do anything for her.

They had both met each other's parents, but the parents had never met, it just never seemed to come up, and Roz and David were not sure how serious she was about Michael. Andrew and Claire (Michael's parents) never discussed anything going on in Michael's life, especially if it meant having to spend proper time with him, he always believed he was adopted as he had nothing in common with both his parents. Oh, by the way, one last thing about Becky, she had OCD.

I hope you have a picture of Becky now.

Then we have Stephen. He is 23 years old, Stevey to everyone except his mother; to her, he was Stephen before he was born, during his birth when he was born, on his birth certificate it said Stephen. What's the Stevey thing. Why does every name have to be shortened and then a 'y' added to it? She never understood.

So, Stephen he was a long, painful birth, and he cried a lot. That's why David started working nights so when he came home from work, he could look after Stephen and Roz could get some sleep.

Stephen was the computer nut in the family. He was very short and chubby, he had dark brown hair which he wore high on the top and shaved on each side, his crowd of friends were very geeky and into computer clubs, and they played games for hours and hours on end. He never liked the Jewish social club as it was not his scene. He liked heavy rock music and was in a band and went to festivals and concerts all the time. He was very bright like his sister and breezed through school and through university and got a brilliant job in the city as an analyst for one of the big banks. He moved to Docklands, bought a small flat, and never came home enough for Roz, and she never really liked that. He struggled to connect with his Jewish roots despite Roz's efforts to instil them in him. His clothing style was rather unconventional, and he embraced a somewhat hippie-like, spiritual outlook on life. However, thanks to his substantial income, he had a strong passion for his job and enjoyed the finer things in life. While he may not be the quintessential family man and could appear distant, his shared love for football with his father provided a bridge for their conversations. This common interest was a source of comfort for Roz, who worried about her husband's distant relationship with their son.

Stephen had no girlfriends, or if he did, he never brought any home. He was best friends with a guy he met in uni called Abraham. His parents arrived here as refugees from Ghana and made a life for themselves, and Abraham also worked in the city at the same firm, different department and shared a flat with Stephen.

Stephen was a very conflicted young man, a rock hippie at heart, but he enjoyed working in the fast-paced banking world and loved going to good restaurants to buying expensive but odd clothes. Life was pretty good, but he always looked uncomfortable at family dinners, especially on a Friday, but would never not come as his mum lived for those evenings.

He never played any sports or looked after himself, he had several gym trainers over the years, but they never lasted. He does meditation every week and occasionally yoga and thinks the weight will fall off him during a yoga session.

I hope you have a picture of Stephen now.

Roz and David had two dogs, a brown Cocker Spaniel called Sandy and a black Labrador called Candy (each one of the kids got to name them), and they treated them like one of the family. When Roz got up to let them out for a wee, she would make her tea and toast. Sandy and Candy had their places at the table and shared breakfast with her. They loved tea and toast, Sandy slept in the bed with Roz and David, and Candy slept on the floor right next to Roz, and for sure, they were real family members.

Sandy would happily sleep all day, and Candy just wanted to have a ball thrown for her to catch it all day. They were walked four times a day, and everything revolved around them.

I hope you have a picture of Sandy and Candy.

The Anderson family

Husband Andrew, 57 years old, or Andy as he's known (see there's that 'y' again). Andy was very tall and had brown hair. His hair was quite messy and long, definitely done on purpose to look cool. He loved a spray tan, wore very good quality clothes and loved a knitted polo with a zip which was his signature; with light-coloured jeans and white sneakers, he definitely wanted to stay young.

Andy went to a local private school, which led him to have a lot of very wealthy friends. He was very social at school and school for him was a club where he met his friends. He was not particularly bright and was always being groomed for the family business, so he thought, why bother with an education. On his 21st birthday, his dad gave him 250,000 to invest in no more than three things. One of Andrew's friends' dad was a trader in the city, so Andrew spoke to him. He invested the money in shares and over the next five years, he doubled his money and bought two apartments in a new block that was being built up the road from the family house. He rented them both out, and the income provided him with great social life and clothes.

He was very flashy and there is nothing worse than a flash boy. It irritates the majority of us and is a very unpleasant characteristic.

He had many girlfriends, and none of them lasted as they all saw right through him. It took him a long time to grow up. He kept putting off joining the family business and said he was not ready and needed more time…which was spent travelling, taking drugs and plenty of alcohol. In Thailand, he crossed paths with Claire, who was travelling with friends. Surprisingly, they discovered that they lived relatively close to each other and began travelling together. By the time they returned, their connection had deepened, leading to their marriage. Andrew sold his two flats and invested in their first stylish apartment in East London.

His father owned a stone masons/funeral parlour business, and if you needed a stone for a grave, his father's company was the only one that everyone used. Andy was not very academic and went from a few years of travelling straight into the family business and Andy to his credit learnt the business and took it over when his dad got sick and he never looked back. He has a beautiful home and a villa in Italy that they go to every July/August, he supports Arsenal and has a ten-seater box. That's his real love and he also plays golf like David, but he's really very good. They go to completely different clubs, although they live in the same area.

He's a real flirt, and none of Claire's friends like him. They all think she should have left him years ago, and they were convinced he had affairs. Andy had a shock when he reached fifty. He was diagnosed with cancer, which devastated the family, and he went through a tough year of chemo and now he is in remission. Every time he does something wrong or disappears for a few hours, he always tells Claire that he nearly died, stop being such a (nijer) annoying woman, leave me alone…which most of the time she did.

Andrew was very well-liked by those that never knew him. He had tons of charisma and lit up a room. He was a bit cocky and, having always been fairly wealthy from a young age, never really worked hard and now only works a couple of days a week as the business almost runs itself.

There are two businesses that people love owning: the food because we all got to eat and the death business, as for sure we are all going to die.

He never trusted Michael, his son, to run the business. He had a brilliant manager who looked after things. In fact, Michael was more of a problem. However, he was in charge of the very lucrative and simple part of the business, which was maintenance, upkeep and cleaning of the stones. They had thousands of families on monthly contracts, and Michael ran the cleaning teams. He was out of the office most days, which suited everyone.

Andrew and Claire have had a fiery relationship. They split up no less than three times, but for some reason, he always came back to her, and she always forgave him. They are similar in a way. Both a bit self-centred and hated anything or anyone messing around with their own routine (including the kids). Andrew initially came across as a straightforward, uncomplicated person. Little did anyone know, this was a grave misjudgement, as you'll discover later in the story. He had previously wrestled with a gambling problem, but the threat of being cut off by his father forced him to quit. Andrew couldn't simply go out and find a job, so he addressed the issue before it escalated.

I hope you have a picture in your head of Andrew.

Then there was Claire, 57 years old. Her parents owned a very large group of bakeries that they sold out to a big hedge fund. They were multi-millionaires, so Claire led a very privileged life, went to private school, had a new car on her 17th birthday. She was showered with stuff by her mum and grandparents.

She was for sure the favourite, never really worked, she was too busy doing things. She was on two charities' boards, played tennis, and went to her club most days. She was small with dark hair, very tanned, wore a huge diamond on her finger, was too thin and was always on a diet. She has had quite a lot of work done to her face, which started to really show now. She never ate much, drank loads of coffee and liked a glass of wine.

She was a nightmare and had a habit of telling the truth. She was a good person at heart, loved her family, and can't cook. That's why they have a chef that lives on the grounds in a small cottage. She is very charitable and raises lots of money.

She absolutely adores/idolises/loves her husband very much. They are both busy people and almost run separate lives, and they have sex rarely. Andy seemed to have lost his mojo, and even when they go to their villa, there are always guests of the kids staying over, so it's busy, but she liked it that way. She was only pleased to do things for Andy and have him with her for two months all the time. Or at least when he wasn't playing golf, which she had no interest in.

Oh, she has her nails/hair/reflexology/spiritual readings taken every week and has three very close friends, and that was really it. She didn't like hangers-on, she liked real friends, but they never mixed in the same circles, as Andrew and their husbands never got along. Claire always made time for them, and once a year they would go for a week to the villa in Italy, and Claire paid for everything and took them shopping. It was her pleasure to do this, and she spoke to them pretty much every day; money never affected these relationships.

Claire had no interest in school and never went to uni. Private school was wasted on her; although she was super smart in other ways, she was very street-wise, and if you wanted advice that involved people or relationships, she was very intuitive and could judge someone and get it right very quickly. She loved Andy, although deep down, she knew what he was like, and decided that splitting up her family and giving up her lifestyle was never going to happen, so she turned a blind eye a little.

I hope you get a picture of Claire.

Then you have Tamsin (or Tammy, there's that 'y' again), 25 years old, in fact, there was one day apart between her and Becky being born. Tammy was like an English rose, had a very white skin and long flowing red hair, big green eyes and was the perfect child well-behaved which is what private schooling does. She was not academic but very creative, loved art, and was always top of her class, she went on to take art at a level at university and decided to become an artist. She had her first exhibition at a local gallery. It turned out to be a huge success, and she is now represented by a much larger gallery and has turned it into a successful career.

Growing up, she never showed much interest in family life, and that was really shown when she changed her name to 'Tami Phoenix' she described herself as an unusual and unique character and, like the name Phoenix, a mythical bird that rises from the ashes. She moved away from home and shared a flat with another artist. They lived in a very cool, arty area in a warehouse in Bethnal Green. She seemed to love her life very much, getting up at about 11, painting in her studio staying up until 2/3 in the morning as there always seemed to be people in their apartment.

Although she and her mother had few common interests, they made an effort to meet up once a week for coffee. Claire's persistence sometimes bordered on nagging as she continued to reach out until her daughter agreed to meet. Claire acknowledged their differences and tried to take an interest in her daughter's art exhibitions, even though her father was less supportive and didn't see art as a legitimate profession.

Tammy suffers badly from anxiety and depression and was on medication for this. Her mum never really knew about it as Tammy was not big on opening up to anyone. She had a therapist whom she saw every week, and had become a crutch for her as she relied on the therapy more and more. She struggled with the pressure of life and work and dreamed of leaving it all behind and going somewhere east to live, maybe India.

Tammy was always very grown up from a young girl and loved being around Claire's friends. She would choose to stay in if they had friends over and loved getting involved in their conversations. She had no time for childish behaviour or, for that matter, young boys or even boys her own age. Most of them, she felt, were useless.

Tammy does not keep friends for long. She has many acquaintances but very few real friends; she mixes in a very different circle and has drifted away from her parents, which makes Claire very sad, but she believes Tammy is happy and healthy and leading her own life.

I think you have a picture of Tammy now.

And then we have Michael, age 23. He shaved his head, not completely, but it was very short, he had bushy eyebrows and he was super fit. Thank goodness he didn't shorten his name to Mikey. Michael was born premature and spent three months in an incubator, and it was a bit touch and go for some time. Thank goodness he pulled through. Both his parents treated him a little differently because of that, and I think Tamsin always felt the second child syndrome even though she was the firstborn. Michael was a bit of a dreamer deep down inside, he was super smart, but getting him to concentrate in school was very difficult as he never seemed to be quite in the same room. But whenever he got into conversation with Andy and Claire's friends, Michael seemed to know a lot about everything from politics to sport and economics, none of which he put to good use. He did, however, get into university, which turned out to not be the right thing for him as all he did was drink, take drugs and play the guitar.

Even though he was taking a degree in economics, he knew he would never follow a career in that field. Michael got a job in a café after uni, and that didn't last long as he then decided to take a year out and go travelling. After he returned, his dad finally convinced him to come into the business, which he did. Not that he was interested in it. He was more interested in it funding his social life and drugs. Michael still lived at home, but to be honest, he was never there, always crashing at a friend or being out all night. He always told his parents where he was, so they never really worried. He had been seeing Rebecca for three years now. It seemed to work as they both had their own stuff going on, but there was chemistry on a different level when they were together and they never went out with each other's friends. They just enjoyed being on their own together. They seemed so different from the outside.

Michael profoundly understood that his job was primarily a means to earn money, while Becky took her role at the museum very seriously. She lived each day as it came. Although Michael had little interest in his religion, it held significant importance for Becky. They had discussed their different views and their plans for their future marriage.

Oh, I forgot to mention that Michael had a drinking problem that was finally under control, and he sees a counsellor weekly.

I think you have a picture of Michael now.

So that's it, that's the families. I hope you can visualise them in your mind, who they are, and maybe which ones you can connect with. As I said at the beginning, we will follow the deep trauma, hilarious and incredibly sad events that took place in one emotional time in all their lives.

My wife is always telling me that's a family for you, there's no normal, who do you know that's normal? Anyway, what is normal? I always thought I was, until my wife convinced me otherwise.

2. Will It Be a Yes or a No?

It was Friday afternoon at the Cohen house; David was asleep after working nights on the taxi, Becky was working as was Stephen, but they all knew to be at home by 7 p.m. sharp. Dinner was at 7.30 p.m.

Roz was just getting back from shopping and was running around preparing the dinner. She liked this time on her own, mainly so no one would interfere as she cooked, and it also gave her a chance to wander into her head and dream about her career and why she had this need to go back to work and hang up her mother and wife boots for a while and focus on her for a change. She loved her family, but maybe she would go back to work; she craved being around people, the buzz of London life.

She was cutting the potatoes and adding the salt to her chicken soup she made yesterday, as she always preferred serving it the day after it was made.

She starter by preparing a chopped liver, followed by chicken soup with matzo balls. Despite sounding unappetizing, matzo balls are delightful dumplings with meat inside. The main course consisted of roast chicken from the kosher butcher and roast potatoes, baked rice, butter beans, broccoli, peas, and her homemade stuffing. While she didn't maintain a fully kosher home, she tried to uphold certain traditions. For dessert, she had made a cheesecake during the week as normal and always made her husband's favourite bread and butter pudding.

This was every Friday, and it was very rare the kids were not there as they knew what it meant to Roz. They loved their mum very much, and one night a week got them a free pass to do what they wanted to do the rest of the week.

David had woken and was in the shower. Roz had not seen him since yesterday and hated asking him how his evening on the cab was as he always had a bad day even if he had a good day. That's just a Jewish man of a certain age who is unsatisfied with life generally.

It was 5 p.m., and everything was on track for dinner, so she sat down to get a quiet hour reading her book-club book and waited for everyone to start arriving. Becky called to say Michael was coming as well, and Stephen called to say Abraham would be coming. She laid two more places, and as you would expect, Roz did not need to start preparing more as she always made enough for ten. She always said better to have too much than not enough.

Two miles away at the Andersons, it was a very different scene. Claire was home, having finished her day at her club, having a tennis lesson. Andrew was finishing his Friday round of golf, Tami was meeting some friends for drinks and dinner, and Michael was in his room as he always finishes work early on Fridays. His dad would not be too pleased but was always out, so he would never know or maybe care.

Claire was going to make herself some soup, Michael was going to Becky's house for dinner and Andrew… who knows what time he would be home, probably have dinner at the club. Claire just got a text message saying, "No need to worry about dinner eating with the boys be home about nine." She replied, "No problem, I love you" and waited with her phone in her hand for Andrew to come back and answer, "Me too." She was happy and didn't care about anything else. That's all he needed to do to make her smile; she got back home, and the chef was there waiting to see what the family were doing tonight. Claire told him to go be with his family. "We are OK tonight, but could you make sure we have breakfast tomorrow at 9 maybe, as it's Saturday, we could have pancakes and some crispy bacon. Don't forget, Andrew loves that honey with it. I hope we have some, if not, could you make it your final job of the day and pop to the store to get some?" He left for the store, and Claire went upstairs to put away some things she had bought as she went shopping with her three best friends. She spent a little too much but felt OK as she convinced them to let her go mad on them, it was like therapy for Claire and Andrew just paid the credit card bill when it came in and never once questioned how much it was, which she found strange that he never questioned it.

Claire had never needed to think about anything that she wanted. She just bought it and also remember; she would inherit half of a huge fortune from her parents. Her brother, whom she hardly ever spoke to, would inherit the other half.

At 6:30, David returned home, venting about his challenging day. He had to endure an unpleasant airport run, with the added discomfort of a cab making odd noises. David needed to get the cab checked in the morning, ensuring it was ready for his plans to attend the Spurs match with Stephen. They were facing a major London derby against Arsenal.

Roz had zoned out by this point and was more interested in the potatoes, not overcooking, than anything else; time was marching on.

The door opened, and it was Stephen using his key, and he was followed by Abraham. David met them at the door. "Why do you use a key? You don't live here anymore; why can't you knock like anyone else?"

Stephen replied, "Good, Shabbas, Dad, nice to see you too."

He marched in past his dad and gave his mum a cuddle and Roz replied, "Don't be such a grump, this is still his home, and he can come and go as he pleases." David went and poured himself a drink and sat in the extension watching Sky Sports. Roz hugged Abraham and said, "What have you two been up to?"

Stephen looked a bit shocked and said, "What do you mean, Mum?"

She said, "Don't be so touchy, I just want to know how your week has been." Stephen turned to Abraham and rolled his eyes.

"You know, Mum, not much, just been working hard going to the gym." David said, "I don't know why you have to pay such a crazy price for that club, what's wrong with the one near here? It's half the price, and you obviously don't go often," he shouted. "Thanks, Dad, that's really a shitty thing to say, and it's nowhere near where I live. There, I can come out of work and be in the gym in five minutes, then home in two minutes.

That's why," Stephen replied. "Oh, and I can afford it. I have more money than I could spend" (Stephen knew that would really hurt his dad). Then no response from Mr Grumpy.

The doorbell rang. "See," David shouted, "At least one of my children respects whose house this is and does not use her key." Roz goes to the door, and as they come in, Michael's carrying a beautiful bunch of flowers and a very expensive bottle of malt whiskey for David.

"You don't have to do that. Must have cost you a fortune," said Roz. David comes in, says "Hello," and says, "Thanks, Michael." I wonder what he wants and laughs as he walks back to his Sky Sports. Michael nearly turned very pale green and started to sweat and quickly excused himself for the toilet. Becky comes down the stairs.

"Where's Michael," she says.

"Oh, he went to the toilet."

As he comes out, she sees the colour of Michael and says, "Are you ill?"

"No, I'm just really nervous, don't be such a pussy. It will all be OK."

"Just say it when I give you the sign (she's definitely picked up that no-nonsense attitude from Roz)."

"How are you, Mum?"

"I'm OK, darling, just a bit tired, and your dad is driving me mad. Sometimes I wish he would lighten up a bit."

"Don't start, Mum, we want to have a really nice evening tonight."

"OK, OK, anyway, get Michael a drink. Dinner will be ready in a few minutes. Go and say hello to your brother. He's in the front room with Abraham."

"OK, I will, Mum, don't you think it's a bit strange that Stephen never seems to have a girlfriend? He's always with Abraham, you don't think they are?"

Roz says, "Don't be so stupid, he's just a busy boy making lots of money at work. He will meet someone when he's ready."

Roz momentarily turned away to the sink, seizing a brief moment of solitude as if a light bulb had illuminated her mind.

She rolled her eyes and announced, "Alright, everyone, let's sit down for dinner. Becky, can you assist me in serving?"

Michael chimed in, "I'll help as well," his willingness to assist hinted at an ulterior motive. Michael masked his underlying anxiety as he joined the family at the dinner table.

"So, who do you think will win tomorrow? It's a big day." "I don't watch football," says Abraham. "Of course," says Stephen. "I can't wait." "What about you," says David, looking at Mr Goody two shoes, Michael. "I don't really care, to be honest, my dad makes me come on occasions with him to Arsenal, and I find it really boring." "Becky, how come I never knew Michael and his dad are Arsenal fans?" shouts into the kitchen. "Who cares," says Becky. "I do," replies David, "Can't have a Gooner in the family…" by this point Michael is so green he could camouflage in the garden, and you would never see him. Becky grins at Michael and mouths to him. "It's fine chill out."

David can't let it go and says, "so, Michael, how big a fan is your dad?" "Huge" he replies. "He goes to every home game and every week. It's such a complicated thing." "Who's going to the game, how do we get them the tickets, where do they meet, is it friends/family or business people? and he makes me take care of it every home game." "How many seats do your dad have?" "Oh no, he has a large box at the stadium and for away games, he takes five people, and they get to travel with the Arsenal team. Blimey," says David. "I never knew that, Becky. Did you know Michael's dad has a box at Arsenal?" "Yea, I did. What's the big deal? It's only a game." "Only a game; tomorrow is not only a game. It matters. Its tradition goes back many years; it's enough," says Roz. "Can we drop it? It's not really important." Roz says, "Right," and then she lights the Friday night candles. There is silence in the room. You can see the candles light up Roz's face as she waves her hand three times over the candles and says the prayer, and then she smiles so brightly it out shines the candles. "Good Shabbas," she says, which everyone answers together, even Abraham, who has become such a regular. Roz looks at him out of the corner of her eye as she thinks, "I wonder, it can't be, and if it was, is it such a bad thing as long as my kids are happy and healthy? Who cares? I was never supposed to have a straight forward family." She wonders. She has a daughter in love with a lovely non-Jewish boy who cleans gravestones for a job and a son who may be gay with a very tall Ghanaian boyfriend...life is not simple.

Chopped liver is over as they clear the plates. Becky says, "Mum, can I talk to you later with Dad? Is that OK?" "What's wrong?" she says, "Omg, are you? have you been hiding something from me? I knew it; you've been looking a bit off-colour the last few weeks, and we haven't had coffee for two weeks. Which hospital? What's the name of the specialist? We will get you the best treatment possible, whatever it costs." "Mum, Mum, Mum, stop; why are you driving yourself (serdrayt) mad?" "It's nothing like that."

"Thank God you got me worried. Don't do that to me again, making me go (Meshuga) crazy and putting terrible thoughts in my head." "I'm absolutely fine, good, good." "Sure, after dinner and when we've cleared away." Becky nods at Michael as they drink their soup.

Stephen began to share details about his new role at the bank, and Abraham interjected with his thoughts. As Roz observed Abraham's involvement, she couldn't help but think, "That's something a girlfriend would say." David, on the other hand, was enthusiastic and supportive, saying, "That's fantastic, Son! How much are we looking at per week?" Stephen responded, "Dad, that's private, and it's not the point. Why does everything have to revolve around money?" David retorted, "Well, everything does revolve around money. It's how we afford all this delicious food, after all." "Put a roof over your head and fund your education." "OK, OK, Dad, I know I've thanked you a million times. What more do you want?" "Maybe you could treat your mum and me occasionally; that would be a start." Roz says, "Shut up, I don't want a penny from him; it's his money, and he should spend it how he likes and on who he likes, she says, a little quieter." Then there's a silence. "David says, OK, OK, I'm only joking. Let's drop it and talk about something lighter." He looks across to Michael. "So, what have you been doing today, Michael." He says, "We had two funerals, and I had to help clean two graves as we were short-handed." There is another silence, and then everyone starts laughing and thank God, they see the funny side of Michael's day compared to the family rubbish.

After dinner, as they finished cleaning up, Becky turned to Stephen and said, "Let's head upstairs; I need to have a conversation with you." They ascended to Stephen's former room, which David had transformed into a veritable shrine to Spurs. The walls were adorned with an array of programs, flags, and enlarged images from the final match at the old White Hart Lane stadium. As they entered, Stephen couldn't help but remark, "If this room were featured on 'Through the Keyhole,' they'd probably guess it belongs to a ten-year-old boy." "What's so important? Can you leave now and take Abraham with you now." "What's the rush? Why do we need to go? We haven't had coffee and the (kearchals) biscuits that Mum makes." "Oh, take them with you, with all the other food she will give you. Just go now." "Why? I'm not going until you tell me why." "I need to talk to Mum and Dad." "Why can't you say it in front of me? I am your brother." "I can't," she says. "…please I don't ask you for anything; we need to talk to Mum and Dad." "OK, OK, just…shit, omg, you are pregnant, aren't you?" "No, she replies don't be stupid, OK." "Then it can only be one other thing: you're getting married." She smiles, "Please don't say anything." Stephen screams into his pillow and then hugs Becky, "Wow, that's amazing." "You can't let them know anything." "OK, OK, what will you do about the ceremony? Where will you get married? You know how much Mum would want you married under a chuppah by a rabbi." "I've discussed it with Michael, and he's happy to have it under a chuppah and by a rabbi, maybe have a blessing by a vicar from their church as well. No reason why that is not right." "Of course," Stephen says a bit sarcastically and leaves his old room and takes Abraham. "We will go. I just need a wee; hurry up anyway. Mum's starting to put two and two together about you and Abraham. What are you talking about, Becky?" "Stephen, I've been your sister for over 25 years now. Don't you think I would know if my brother is gay or not?" Stephen looks at her stunned and says, "OK, OK, I'm going now, this is too much for me in one day to deal with, but we will need to talk and soon." She smiles, and he smiles as if they have both just unloaded a huge weight off their shoulders, and everything is still OK. It's a great feeling.

So, Stephen and Abraham say their good byes and leave.

"Anyone for coffee?" says Roz. "Lovely," says David. "OK, I'll make it. Let's have it in the lounge." "Blimey!" says David, "Must be a special occasion; she never lets me eat in here."

Michael is green again. Becky smiles, and Roz goes to make the coffee. Becky thinks, "My mum and dad are so oblivious; how can they not know."

Roz brings the coffee in, and they all sit down. David has the telly on sky sports: it's a game between Man City and Watford. "David, turn it off. We have guests."

"It's only family."

"Turn it off," shouts Roz.

"OK, your bloody dad would watch a game of football if it was on tv between two teams of rabbis and get excited."

"You are right; seeing rabbis playing football, I would pay for that."

"Mum, Dad, we wanted to talk to you, there's something we want to ask you, or I want to ask you," said Michael. "You see, I've been with Becky for three years now." Roz says, "How long I thought it's only been…" then she stops and thinks, "OK, I say nothing. Go on, you were saying." David is oblivious. "Well, me and Becky really love each other, and I want to know what you think about me marrying your daughter. David, we would really like your blessing, and as I have no interest in my religion and I know how important it is to Becky, we intend to have a Jewish wedding under a chuppah, with a rabbi…." There was a silence that seemed like it was forever, and David, being David, looked at Roz, at which point Roz started to cry. David went to the garden shed to get a cigarette, although he was supposed to have stopped smoking years ago and lit a cigarette, returned to the back sliding doors, opened them and said, "You mean you want to marry Becky…." "Mastermind, I think that's what they are saying," says Roz, as she got up, hugged Becky, still crying and then hugged Michael. David still hasn't said much, but it seemed like, from Roz's reaction, he was going along with it, but it was hard to tell, there was a lot of screaming/crying, and Becky then showed Roz the ring and it was some ring Roz just (cvelled) no idea how to translate that except to say she was happy, David still not really with it or so, it seemed so, he kissed Becky walked over to Michael and said, "By the way, yes, you can have my blessing." Roz looked at him and said, "Like it's your decision…" David and Roz hugged like two fellow workers who did not like each other but were saying goodbye; Roz cried again. Becky wanted to phone everyone, but they thought they would go and see Michael's parents in the morning for breakfast. Michael knew now it would be a car crash; Saturday morning is pancakes and bacon day, with both Andrew and Claire together. Roz suggested they phone no one now it's late and, "Michael, your parents would want to know after us, not after Becky has been on every social media site showing off the ring."

So they agreed Becky walked Michael to his car they stayed there for a while laughing and Michael said Becky I really do love you and can't wait to be your husband Becky smiled and kissed him and then he drove home seemingly very happy although as he pulled up he realised he couldn't say anything and tomorrow would be a cross between one flew over the cuckoos next and meet the fockers, Becky went to her room she looked exhausted from the pressure and Roz said to David cup of tea? Yes, please he said but I just need a minute I need to go and see Becky Roz smiled and said OK don't be too long.

He knocked on her door, "Becky, can I come in?" "Of course," said Becky. David sat on the bed, took her hand and said, "I want to say something and I want you to listen carefully. Firstly, I love you so much and although I don't say it enough, I love you more than you could ever imagine." "I know, Dad…" "I said listen, let me finish. I always knew this day would come and I was not sure how I would feel or react. Please remember, to me, you will always be my little girl and that won't change. I have always dreamed of walking you down the aisle, watching you get married by a rabbi and under a chuppah." "Dad, I know where this is going." "No, you don't, it's not about that. I've already spoken with Michael and when I gave him my blessing, I told him this is my only small stipulation, under a chuppah and by a rabbi. Michael never told me you two had already discussed it a few days ago, good he wasn't supposed to and as none of his family are particularly religious and this means so much to Roz. He agreed he would do whatever He needed to (except have the chop). He just wants to marry you, so he has my blessing ten times over; even if Roz thinks she wears the trousers in this marriage, sometimes I get to wear them for a few hours. Anyway, that is not my point."

"I know we are only very average people, and everyone thinks I'm a bit of a (shmok) dumb arse. We can't really afford much."

"Dad, you don't have to, Michael's parents…"

"I don't want to hear what you will say next. You are my daughter, and it's my responsibility to make my daughter a wedding. I put away a policy for this the day you were born, and it turns out it's worth a few quid now. So, I think I can make you a wedding you will remember for the rest of your life, and it's my honour, duty and pleasure to do this for you, it might mean I have to spend more time in the cab but probably better as your mum is better at organising things than me."

He coupled his right hand to her left cheek and smiled and said, "you know your grandmother who you never met would have adored so much about you, this would have been such a proud day for her, it's so sad she won't be there."

At that moment, a tear rolled down David's face, and he allowed it to come down his face to his chin and drip onto his shirt and said, "Remember what I always told you."

"Yes, Dad."

"Never wipe away a tear as whoever you are crying about is in that tear."

"Yes."

"And you can bet your wages; your grandmother just popped in to say hello. Now get some sleep."

David kissed her on the head and said, "I love you and am so proud. You are so very special, and you turned out exactly the way I dreamed a daughter would be before you were even born. I can't wait to hold your hand down the aisle."

David left, shut the door and went down to see Roz, to whom she asked, "Did you have that moment with your daughter you've told me for 25 years you would have?"

David just smiled, rubbed his hands together and said, "Right, let's have tea and a bit of honey cake." That would be nice as they spent the evening together, actually talking for the first time in a long time, and Roz knew it was the wrong time to talk weddings, I'm sure.

"Bless him, he has no idea what a wedding costs, but let's enjoy today before he starts to use the fact, he is a diabetic type two so close to type one he can't handle (Tsuris) aggravation."

Tonight, they were closer than they had been in many years, and they both liked it very much.

It was 8:30 in the morning, and Becky was already dressed and prepared to drive the short five-minute distance to Michael's house for breakfast. David was still fast asleep while Roz sat at the kitchen table, enjoying her tea and toast with her two pets, Sandy and Candy. When Becky entered the kitchen, they embraced, and Roz's eyes welled up with tears. She asked, "Did your father have that conversation with you?" Becky inquired, "What conversation?" Roz replied, "The one he's been planning for 25 years." Becky nodded and said, "Yes, he did have that conversation. It caught me by surprise, but it was a moment I'll cherish forever." Roz smiled and remarked, "I think that was your dad's intention. Anyway, good luck today, and let me tell you, the Andersons are about to receive the best news they could have hoped for – their son is going to marry you." "All his lottery numbers came in at once. I don't think they need to win the lottery," says Becky. "Whatever, who cares? They get you as a daughter-in-law, and don't you forget it." "Thanks, Mum; I will call you when I leave there."

Becky arrived at about 8:45, and Michael must have been looking out the window. He rushed to the front door shouting, "I'll get it," he looked his usual shade of pale green as he greeted Becky, "What else did they say last night?" he said, seeking further approval, "Actually it was all good, in fact, better than good, they were both amazing, especially my dad, he had this whole speech he was waiting 25 years to say." How did it go? "He smashed it out of the park." "No pressure then from my parents. Let me say sorry already for what they might say." "It will be fine; let's go have pancakes and have round 2."

"Omg, the chef prepared all different chocolate pancakes. I mean not chocolate on top of the pancakes; I actually mean chocolate pancakes. He made gluten-free ones with coconut, and he made special ones for Andy, small round fat ones." You could smell the bacon cooking. Romero said, "Yes, please sit down, where are Andrew and Claire?" "Andrew is in the shower, and Claire is just finishing her early yoga class. They will be down shortly." 20 minutes later, they came down together, and at that point, Romero started cooking the pancakes, which Andrew loved, choosing what he wanted from the assortment, but always choosing small fat ones with bacon and honey.

"Nice to see you, Becky," Andrew greeted, and Michael replied, "Yes, well, we're off to an art exhibition today, and apparently, it's a two-hour journey." "Relax, Son, I didn't inquire about your plans for today. I've never quite grasped that art business; it all seems like the emperor's new clothes to me. I mean, how can a canvas and some splashed paint on a piece of wood be worth so much?" Andrew commented. Claire interjected, "Bricks and mortar, that's what I say. Anyway, let's have breakfast without discussing business. In fact, let's keep the conversation nice and light. I've got a terrible headache, and I imagine you have got a bit of a hangover." "I'm fine." says Andrew, "Can we just have a calm breakfast?" Romero serves up all the different variations of pancakes with about four different sauces to pour on them, two plates of beautifully made crispy bacon, A big pot of fresh coffee and an amazing fruit salad with fresh pouring cream. His job is done, he said to Andrew, "I hope you enjoy it, call me when you're finished, and we will come back and clear everything up." "Thank you so much," said Claire. "You are such a darling," and he left. "He gets well paid for doing that. You don't need to thank him." "Oh, shut up. I like thanking him, and it always feels weird having our own chef." Anyway, they all chose their pancakes fillings sauces, and Claire poured the coffee. "So, what are you two doing today? said Claire. "Mum, I've just told you we're attending this art exhibition." "Oh yes, I must've forgotten. I had a terrible migraine last night and didn't really get much sleep. What are you and Dad up to today." "I'm going to have my nails done, then reflexology, and probably try and squeeze in a game of tennis." No guesses where your dad is going today." "What's that supposed to mean. I haven't played since Thursday, whatever," replies Claire with a bit of sarcasm. "It's only Saturday; what are you worried about by missing playing for one day? It's a hard life for you."

"Anyway, I need to be going tee off soon," Michael said. "Dad. Can it wait? I have something I want to tell you." "Tee time waits for nobody or nothing, my son. You should know that." "Dad. please sit down." Andrew, looking puzzled, sits down. "OK," he says, then it dawns on him, "You stupid boy, I can't believe you; we brought you up better than that. You got the poor girl pregnant," Claire screams. "Michael, really…" "Don't panic, don't panic, let me call my gynaecologist. He will do it. Trust me, Michael, a smart woman always has two things: a great lawyer and an even better and more trustworthy gynaecologist." "Mum, for god's sake, stop. I don't want to hear any more, and no, she's not pregnant. We went over to the Cohen's last night and asked for their blessing. We want to get married."

Claire sat back and said calmly, "Are you both sure? I mean, you've only been dating 1 year, actually." "It's three, Mum. I just wasn't ready to introduce her to you, pair of nutcases."

"That's excellent news." Andrew shakes Michael's hand, kisses Becky goodbye, and leaves, saying, "Tee time waits for nothing, even the announcement of your son getting married." Claire swears and tells him to f—k off and not come back. Andrew smiles and says, "See you later."

Now, it was Claire's turn. She shed a few tears, then composed herself and said, "Are you both absolutely certain? Why not try living together first? What's the hurry? You're both so young." Michael replied, "Mum, you had Tami by our age, but times have changed. Living together was not common back then. Nowadays, it's different. The average age for getting married has gone up from 23 to 28, and it keeps rising. We don't want to wait until it's too late."

"Mum, we've been seeing each other for three years. David and Roz are so happy for us it was really nice."

"Well, they are entitled to. Look who they are getting: a fine young man with a job in a business worth a fortune that he will inherit. Becky, I don't mean to be rude."

Then Claire stops and says, "I hope you will be sensible and sign…"

"Mum, if you are about to say what I think you are going to say, quit. While you are ahead, OK, OK," she says.

Then she walks over to her son, couples both hands on his cheeks and kisses him on the forehead, saying, "I knew, I knew this was going to happen in my reading last week," she said, "I would get good news at some point."

And she was right.

"Oh yea," said Michael, "you would get good news at some point."

Could she be more vague? Maybe she meant that Dad had finally gotten rid of his piles.

"That's good news."

"Don't be so facetious, you're still my son."

She walked over to Becky and held out her hand. Becky stood up and Claire looked at her from head to toe and twirled her around, saying, "Very, very nice, she will make a beautiful bride. I can picture white with lace no sparkles fitted at the waist."

"Mum, give it a rest, can't you just be happy for us? I am, I am, but there is so much to do and so little time, venues get booked up, band you can never get a good band unless you plan three to four years ahead and there's only one band, Mum please stop."

"OK, OK, I will. I'm not saying another word."

Then she started to cry. "My little fat chubby son turned his life around, got all those drugs out of his system, and all that travelling everywhere around the world trying to find himself. I could have told him to look in a mirror. It would have saved me so much heartache."

"Now he becomes a husband and a father; ooooh, I get to be a grandmother." "Mum, it's enough now we have to go." "Is your mother allowed to tell a few close friends? I want them to share in our good luck." "Of course," says Becky. "Mum, we need to go. We've got this exhibition to get to." And as they leave, Claire turns around and whispers in Becky's ear, "I hope you love him as much as I love Andrew. You will be OK."

3. Grow Some Balls

David and Roz were having dinner. It was Saturday night, it was David's turn to choose, and he went for Chinese. The good one was a twenty-minute ride, so Roz went to collect it as David had been in the cab all day. Roz had spent the day on the phone telling everyone whom she had never managed to reach last week about her news, even a few people who had to think twice about who she was; she didn't care she wanted everyone to know, she even started to look like the mother of the bride now, and it's only been three weeks.

After dinner, Roz reminded David that Stephen was coming over for lunch tomorrow with Abraham at 1.30 sharp. "In the morning, I need you to go to the bakery on angel road for the bagels, then pick up the salmon from Sharon's on the high road opposite the library. The chopped liver comes from Rothstein's, the butcher, and the egg and the cream cheese comes from mitzvah deli, opposite that greasy. If you like, and if you can get some new green…"

"And where do I need to go for those? don't tell; let me, let me guess, Israel where they were pickled."

"Oh, shut up, just do it. What else are you going to do? it's important that you don't buy everything from one place. You find the best and get it where you can."

"OK, OK, just give me the lists and postcodes for all the shops. What about some Vorsht?" David says.

"Yes, OK, you need to get that from the other butchers: levy brothers in the Broadway."

"Of course, it is."

"OK, tomorrow I'm off on my intrepid journey to many places to collect food; just get what I've asked, your no longer funny."

Sunday morning comes, it's peaceful. David's on his treasure hunt for lunch and Roz is hoovering up and getting the lunch table set up early so she can relax for a few hours and catch up on some tv she has missed out on. Stephen is still not up and neither is Abraham!

Further up the road, Andrew had to head to work. Sundays were particularly hectic at the funeral parlour, with numerous appointments to attend to. He asked Michael to accompany him for assistance. Claire, on the other hand, returned for an emergency reading with her clairvoyant. Tami, having the day to herself in her studio, decided to invite friends over for drinks and lunch. Meanwhile, Becky and Michael were planning to meet friends for a picnic.

There was a knock on the door.

"Get it," shouts Roz.

"I'm in the kitchen."

"OK, OK."

David gets up and goes to the door, and it's Stephen and Abraham, "Ah ha, finally, he learns it's not his house and stops using the key. What a breakthrough."

"Don't get excited, Dad, I just forgot my key."

Stephen and Abraham come in and Abraham presents Roz with some flowers, "Thanks for the invite," he says.

Roz smiles and says they are beautiful. "I get them from the flower market. I love it there."

"A home is not a home without flowers," Roz smiles and hurries into the kitchen to finish preparing lunch.

"Can you all sit down, please. David, turn off the Sky Sports. You are glued to that bloody television."

"One minute, they are just showing the Spurs goals from the Arsenal game. I need to see them just once more."

They all sit down and Roz starts bringing in the food, "I'm sorry there's not much choice, but it's been a crazy couple of days."

She lays out the salt beef with potato Latkas and peas, some freshly made chicken schnitzel in bread crumbs some coleslaw and a mixed salad. David says, "What the hell is this? where's the bagels/salmon/chopped liver/cream cheese and the cucumbers?"

"I changed my mind and wanted to do a hot lunch; it's a bit chilly out."

David looks at Stephen and says, "Your mother is completely (Meshuga) crazy. I've driven thirty miles to five shops to get lunch and she changes her mind."

"Shut up," says Roz, "it won't go to waste. The boys will take it home." David just rolls his eyes.

Stephen says, "Mum, you are joking. There's enough food to feed ten."

Roz always takes that as a compliment. David moans about why she spends so much money on food. "There are starving children around the world, don't you know?"

"Yes," shouts Roz, "And if I could feed them, I would."

"So, Abraham, how are you, my darling? How's work?"

"Work is fine, really busy. Did you get the same rise as Stephen did?"

"No, I didn't. He's in a different department from me."

"Shame," says David, "my boys are earning big bucks now. It would be nice if you looked after your parents a little."

"Shut up, David, I've told you I don't want his money. We do the looking after."

David just shrugs his shoulders, "So Abraham, how are your parents?"

"They are great, thank you, Roz."

"And how's that little sister of yours?"

"She's all grown up now, nearly 18."

"That's nice, you are both so busy at work that you never seem to have time for girls. Aren't there any nice girls at your office?"

"Mum, leave him alone with the questions."

"I'm just asking such a tall good-looking boy with a good job. He must have girls throwing themselves at him."

Abraham laughs nervously, "I don't have time for girls anyway between work and looking after our flat that keeps me busy…"

"What about you, Stephen?" says David, "you must have a different girl every night with your cash to throw about."

"Dad, it's not all about girls. I'm very happy, thank you," and he mistakenly looks across at Abraham and smiles.

"Of course," that is picked up by Roz, who sighs.

"Oh, yea."

"Mom, what about Becky and Michael?" Stephen inquired.

Roz beamed with excitement as she responded, "Isn't it just wonderful? We finally get to plan a wedding! I'm thrilled. And you, Dad, how are you feeling, especially since you get to cover the expenses?"

David chuckled and replied, "Don't you worry about me, Son. We've got it all sorted. Just bring home a girl, and we can have a double wedding."

Roz intervened, "Come on, everyone, I've prepared pavlova for dessert, but you need to have seconds first and help clear this brisket."

They finished the meal, bid their goodbyes, and left Roz to tidy up while David, for the tenth time, rewound the highlights of the game where Spurs triumphed over Arsenal with a 3-1 win.

On the car journey home, Abraham says to Stephen, "Well, that went really well. You really took control and told them about us, didn't you…?" "I couldn't find the right time with Mum asking about girls, Dad expecting me to be screwing girls every night, it was really hard, hard!" "You don't know how hard I've got to tell my mum, who has been in the church choir her whole life and is already planning my wedding, and my dad, who is the reverend of the church, that their black son is gay, oh and by the way, he has a white Jewish boyfriend and is getting married in a synagogue by a rabbi, that's the definition of hard."

"Stop being such a pussy and grow some balls, you must do it very soon." "OK, OK, I will find the right time. Maybe I will tell Mum on her own and let her handle my dad, whatever, just get it done."

4. Motherly Intuition

It's that time of the week when Tami meets her mum for lunch. It has started to feel like a bit of a chore for Tami, but she understands that it's a way for Claire to stay connected with her daughter. Tami arrives at the cafe first. It's a popular spot with both outdoor and indoor seating. Tami selects a table outside and orders a coffee. Claire, as usual, is running late with some kind of drama, but Tami is more focused on her own work. She's been putting in long hours to complete her collection of paintings for her upcoming exhibition and is facing some challenges. Finally, Claire arrives, pulling up right in front of the cafe in her open-top Bentley convertible, painted in a striking, vibrant blue… Tami sinks her head into her hands as Claire gets out and walks the six feet to the table. She loves making an entrance; Tami hates that stuff, but she needs to be nice. Claire is giving her money every month to help pay the mortgage on the apartment she bought in Bethnal Green (her dad put down half the value of the flat as a deposit gift), so Tami is well looked after, I think it's compensation for her not having a good relationship with her parents, but as we all know money doesn't buy you a good relationship with your kids, it just makes them want or expect more.

"You look too thin," says Claire.

"You can talk, Mum, you don't eat."

"I'm fine, don't worry about me."

"I need to see you are eating better and maybe if you put some weight on, you will attract a man. Everyone is going for this huge touchus (arse) look."

"Mum, I'm fine. I don't need a man or a big arse."

"You do, and I'm also worried. You are working too hard for the exhibition. Why does it have to be called 'inside my own inside'? It doesn't sound very exciting."

"Just make sure you have the date in the diary for the opening. I want you and Dad there."

"Of course, we wouldn't miss it for the world."

"Good."

"What else is happening? Are you taking your meds, and how was your session this week?"

"It was OK, and yes, I'm taking my meds. I'm feeling really shit this week; I just can't get my head around painting at the moment I have this horrible sick feeling in my stomach, and I have butterflies all the time. It's driving me crazy I feel really rubbish."

"What can I do to help?"

"Nothing, thanks. I will be fine."

"What about you, Mum, what's going on?" "I'm good, very busy getting ready for the fundraiser coming up soon, your dad is your dad, and we have a wedding to make." "That's great, Mum, but remember you are not making this wedding. It's not up to you." "I know, but I'm going to make sure it's fabulous, you know me!"

Claire is eating her lunch and watching every move her daughter is making; she's playing with her food; she has a slight shake in one hand, and she looks like she has the weight of the world on her shoulders. It's not good, and Claire doesn't like it.

They finish lunch and leave together. Claire says, "Let me give you a lift home." "Maybe I can come in, and we can watch a movie like we used to do when you were younger." "Mum, we never watched movies together. You were always too busy." "Well, I'm here now. What do you say?" "That would be nice. That's the sign to Claire that something is wrong. She doesn't want to be alone. She would never normally want to spend this amount of time with me. It's a mother's intuition."

They go back to Tami's apartment, which is amazing. It's part of a converted school, it's the old gym with huge high ceilings with a mezzanine, which is the bedroom, and it still has the tram lines and basketball net from the school-built into the design.

The open-plan lounge diner seamlessly flowed into the hidden kitchen. They settled down, and Tami asked, "Mum, what would you like to watch?" Claire responded, "I don't mind, you choose," as she walked around the apartment, trying to gauge how her daughter was doing. "I'll be right back, just going to the loo," Claire mentioned. While in the restroom, Claire couldn't resist peeking into the cupboards, searching for clues to understand Tami's well-being. Unfortunately, she came across various medication bottles. Tami was taking pregabalin to manage anxiety, centreline to combat depression, and Zopiclone to aid her sleep. Then she sees a row of deodorants, as she moves them, she sees a little plastic bag with a white substance in it and she panics, picks it up marches into the lounge and says, "What the f—k is this?" as she holds up the bag, "Mum!" she screams. "Why are you going through my stuff? don't worry, I have it under control. It's just for the occasional party and to keep me feeling OK." By this point, Tami is really shaking and she sat down in a chair and just started to cry. Claire went to comfort her and she just collapsed into her arms and cried and cried, she started to tell Claire how she can't cope anymore, she can't take the pressure of this exhibition she feels so low and so lonely she just wants to die. "What do you mean?" says Claire. "I just don't want to be here anymore. I'm no good at my job. I've got no friends and no boyfriend. I can't get rid of this awful feeling in my stomach. It's making me so low," as she stops crying looks at Claire and she can see fear in her eyes. Claire jumps up and says, "Right, you are coming with me back to my house and then I'm calling my psychiatrist to come and see you now. This can't carry on any more." "Mum, I can't. I need to finish the paintings for my show." "Screw your show, that can wait. Nothing and I mean nothing is more important than your health." For the first time, Tami says nothing and just goes with her mother.

They get home, and Tami goes up to her room, which looks exactly the same as it always looked when Tami was growing up. Claire puts her to bed, gives her a sleeping pill, and she quickly falls sleep.

Claire calls her man, and he says he will be around in one hour. After a bit of gentle persuasion and the fact, Claire raises money for his hospital. Claire makes herself a drink and, sits down and thinks, *If I have to look after her, what about my fundraiser? What about my routine? It will all go out of the window.*

Claire shakes her head and says, "Maybe she will be OK, and she can go home, I will pop in every day to see her."

Claire just can't show maternal instincts. What she did for Tami at her apartment was not maternal. That was just Claire taking over a situation and making things happen, but there is no mothering to Tami in her, sadly.

Her psychiatrist arrives, and Claire explains what has happened and wants to come into the bedroom. He says, "No, leave it with me." The conversation with them both went on for at least two hours; it was ridiculous, or at least that was what Claire felt as she was not involved.

Eventually, they come down together. Tami is now looking like a child and very withdrawn, looking at her feet the entire time. He says, "Look, Tami and I have been talking; she is extremely low and seems to be very, very anxious and depressed; she is also having very bad and dangerous thoughts, firstly she cannot under any circumstances be left on her own and I feel she needs to be admitted to the right hospital to help her." "Whatever it takes." says Claire. "Get her into the best private clinic you can get her into." "No need, there is one very close to here, and I work there two days a week. She will be under my care." Jeremy sits down and starts making calls. Within two hours, everything is organised, Claire has paid for a week, and Jeremy heads off with Claire and Tami to the clinic straight away.

Tami was just looking out the window the whole journey and never uttered a word. She was happy at this point to let other people make decisions for her. She just wanted the feeling to go away. It was so overwhelming. It governed her entire thinking she was in trouble and new she had reached rock bottom.

When they arrive, Jeremy says, "Please wait here; you can't come in, Claire. I will hand her over to the team, and they will look after her."

Claire is just holding Tami very tightly and saying nothing. Then, after a few minutes, Jeremy walks outside and waves for Tami to come in.

Tami stepped out of the car; her words were temporarily silenced. She walked towards the front door, then paused to cast a meaningful glance back at her mother. In that fleeting moment, a profound connection passed between them. Tami mouthed the words, "I'm scared," and Claire responded with, "I love you very much." Claire felt like her heart had been ripped out, and all she wanted was to hold her daughter and make all the fear vanish. As Tami waved and entered the clinic, Claire couldn't hold back her tears. She cried like a child, overwhelmed with emotion. Jeremy returned about fifteen minutes later, allowing Claire the time she needed to compose herself, repair her makeup that the tears had smudged, and regain her composure.

Maybe Claire did have those maternal instincts after all. She just lost them somewhere along the road.

"Where did I go wrong? What did I do to contribute to my own flesh and blood being in such a terrible mental state? Am I a bad mother? Was I not there for my daughter? How many times was she looking at me for help and I never saw it? How selfish have I been wrapped up in my own life? I know I can't let it continue. I will change; she will become my priority now."

Jeremy respected that Claire was deep in thought and the journey home was very quiet, but he didn't assure her that Tami would be fine. She just overcame the biggest hurdle; she accepted she needed help, and she let us help her.

When Andy got home, Claire was already in bed and when she got up, she found a note saying, "Got suppliers meeting today will see you tonight, don't worry about food I'll get something on my way home." No kiss, no nothing, and she hadn't even told him about Tami, he won't get it at all and will just tell her to pull herself together. I will tell him, she thinks, but only when he comes home and I get to see him. This lunch turned out to be a significantly defining one for Tami and Claire.

Claire was having coffee and wondering how Tami was coping. While she was thinking about that, Tami was in her room curled up on the bed. Walking into the clinic last night was the scariest moment of her life. As she closed the door and entered, a young guy came over to her and said, "Hi, my name's Glenn; just remember we are all here to help each other, I hope you have a peaceful night, I will find you in the morning to see how you are settling in." She never really acknowledged him, but he never seemed bothered. He probably remembered what he was like when he arrived. She passed a room on the left, which had about 12 people inside, all watching tv and in their pyjamas, as she walked down the hall with the nurse. She passed a bright light on the right and it looked like a treatment room or a pharmacy. Then there was a kitchen with a few people making drinks, and this led to a big room with a table tennis table with two people playing. This led to a door and a hallway with about six rooms. She entered one with the nurse. I don't think whatever the nurse was saying, Tammy could not really hear. She was so scared she just wanted to get into bed. The nurse assured her that she would be stationed right outside her room throughout the night. She emphasised that if Tami needed anything, all she had to do was call out, and she would also check in on her every twenty minutes. Tami took the prescribed medication and settled into bed. Whatever they had given her that night must have been potent because she fell asleep rapidly, with little recollection of anything until the following morning.

She did not want breakfast the next day and was scared to leave her room, but she knew that she would need to throw herself into the programme. For now, she wanted to be on her own. Claire called the clinic just to check on how Tammy was; at least she could rest that she was in good hands.

5. The Lull Before the Storm

The next few weeks were really quiet…for both families or so it would seem!

David was working hard, moaning about how quiet it was and who knows where all the tourists were. "No one tips nowadays how come you go to a restaurant a waiter writes a few things on a pad, walks a few feet with a few plates and puts them down and then picks them up and takes them away again, at the end you tip him, I take people in my own vehicle pay for the petrol, take them wherever they want to go and sometimes I'm taking them to places in the choom (middle of nowhere) and have to drive back to where I was and what do I get (gornisht) nothing."

Roz continued cooking for everyone, and two Fridays passed without too much problem.

Becky was very busy as the museum had a new exhibit and she really had no time to think about the wedding.

Stephen went away for a few days to Greece with Abraham.

Andrew was also away for a few days at a funeral director's conference. It was a bit morbid talking about death for three days and looking at new lines of designer coffins…lucky for him, he never sold coffins to Jewish people as they all go out in a wooden box.

Claire was busy preparing for a big gala charity ball she was holding for the local children's home.

Tami was going through a very painful time at the clinic, but she seemed a little calmer and was in her third week with no immediate signs of coming home yet.

Michael was agonising over who to choose as his best man and where he would like to go on his stag weekend.

While in Greece, Stephen sent several messages to Roz, including pictures of the two of them, perhaps unconsciously preparing her for the upcoming conversation. However, Roz was feeling unwell and didn't give the messages a thorough look. Had she taken a closer look, there would be no doubt about her son's sexual orientation. Stephen would still need to have the conversation with Roz when he returned from Greece, and Abraham was growing increasingly frustrated.

The hotel they were staying in was really small but beautiful, and the pool area was amazing. As they sat there having a drink in the pool, they heard this really loud and brash Englishman trying to explain to the waiter what a mojito was, "are you simple? Lime juice/sugar/a handful of mint/soda water and white rum comprende! Now go and make me my drink and the glass of champagne for the lady." "What a moron, rather too loud," Stephen says to Abraham, "See a typical English flash rich boy, they give us all a bad name when they act like that. You can tell, don't you think so, Abraham? I've no idea. Did you forget for a minute I'm from Ghana, and you and your family are the only English people I know."

The guy calmed down, and apart from attempting to talk to us when we were swimming, he kept trying to carefully glide over towards us, and every time he did, we moved carefully somewhere else. This went on for maybe 15 minutes, and I think he realised we did not want to talk, so he swam quickly over to us and jumped out of the water, saying, "Enjoy your holiday but take it from me, don't order a cocktail, they have no idea."

I nodded and smiled, I thought, *If I respond and say thank you it will be his chance to say, 'ah you're from UK where about?' then we would never get rid of him, especially if he found out I was English. He would never leave.*

A week later, Becky had a Sunday off from work and was invited to lunch at Andrew and Claire it was a hot day, so Andy decided to put the barbecue on just the four of them; cooking a barbecue was about the only thing he did well nowadays, and he laid on a lovely spread.

Claire said, "Well guys, have you had any thought engagement party, wedding when? Where? come on, tell me, well, we don't really want an engagement party." "We hoped to just have a party here for our friends; when you go to the villa, we don't need a big family thing." "Oh, that's a shame. It would be nice to get together with all the family," says Claire. "Do me a favour; our family are like an episode of the soap, all complete misfits, all crazy, all dislike each other or fell out with each other over money," replies Andy.

"I think you're making the right decision: who needs to see them anyway?"

"OK, OK, well, what about the wedding? When? Where? We've got so much to do," Claire says.

"We are thinking about the bank holiday last week of August. The next year, the weather will still be good and everyone will be back from their holidays by then and we need to sit down with my dad first for obvious reasons,"

"Don't you worry," pipes up Andrew. "Whatever he wants, tell your dad I will pay the difference. Money is not an object for this wedding."

"Thanks, Dad, but I don't think Becky means that."

"Oh, well anyway, the offers there. I have enough money to pay for the wedding. I think it's about time we meet this David and Roz. We are going to be extended family very soon. Claire, let's get them over for dinner and get Romero to make something really special."

"I agree," says Claire. "Becky darling, check with your mum and dad and let's put a date in the diary."

"Of course, I will talk to them."

That was the last talk about the wedding until just before they left.

Andrew says, "Becky, please tell your dad what I said about the money. It's not a problem. Ady and I will be delighted to make the wedding."

"Who's Ady, Dad?"

"What?" as he looked at Michael, shocked for a second, "how did he know that name?"

Then he realised what he had said and responded, "What…sorry…"

"It's a big company I'm trying to land for the business and they are called A.D.Y funerals. It must have been on my mind," Claire admitted. "Anyway, please talk to him."

"I will, for sure," Andrew assured her. For a change, they had a pleasant afternoon with Andrew in a good mood, and Claire wasn't as critical when Andrew spoke. However, Michael found himself puzzled. He had never heard of this company, and it was starting to bother him.

Michael decided on his best man and went for the one he knew the longest, even if he had closer friends now. He thought it was the right thing to do, "So Ben was the man…not a good choice he's a bit of a drip, I can't imagine his best man speech will be funny or heartfelt, and as for the stag, probably dinner in a restaurant and a west end show will be his limit." But Michael was not silly. He appointed ushers and asked them all to chip in on everything from the speech to the stag, "I'm not sure who was more relieved, Michael or Ben? Ben was about six ft four inches tall and spoke with a high pitch voice, and he had a lisp. It now seemed like he had six best men, which was good and bad. Let's see how that one turns out later."

David had received an offer to perform at an upcoming major event. It wasn't typically his kind of thing, but the pay was three times what he usually earned. So, he made the decision to accept the gig and dedicated some time to compiling a playlist for the band. He needed to send it to them for preparation. It was rather remarkable that he had cultivated a career in singing, a talent he had kept well hidden from both his family and friends. None of them knew about his passion for singing.

Claire was only a few weeks away from the function and was very busy still trying to sell out the last two tables. this was the most difficult as most of the people had taken a table, but she still had two tables of ten left. She was trying to sell them to couples and make up a mixed table, but it was tough at £400 per couple. She was on her way to Andy's golf club to put up some leaflets and see if that got any response. Andy was away with a client who owned a cemetery, and he was thinking of buying it from him. When Claire got to the golf club she bumped into an old friend from school days, Simon. She never realised he played golf, and they chatted for a while.

Simon said, "How's Andy? I haven't seen him for ages, he doesn't come here much anymore."

"You must just be missing each other. He's here all the time. In fact, he's here more than anywhere else."

Simon just smiled, and Claire said, "Can I interest you and your wife in two tickets for my gala fundraiser for our charity that we sponsor?"

Simon said, "Give me the leaflet, and I will check with my wife. I would love to come."

They said goodbye, and it never dawned on Claire to query Andy about what Simon said. She was so blind to everything that Andy did. It was crazy or very sad.

Roz was spending a lot of time at home; she seemed to be very tired all the time and just never felt well. She called the doctor out, who gave her some medication and told her to rest as it was just exhaustion, but this was more than what Roz felt. But as always, no one in her family really asked about her, as she was the invisible strong one who was always OK, most Jewish families have a Roz, And the more religious they got, the more the role of the Roz grew and grew.

There seemed to be some things bubbling under the surface that could cause some issues, a few paths being crossed relatively closely, and some embarrassing moments to deal with. However, for both families, they were dealing with life with all its ups and downs.

6. Roz's or Claire's

Becky was at home with Roz; they were getting ready to have lunch together. Roz, at the last minute, says, "Let's do it here. I will make some toasted bagels. I've got smoked salmon and those hamisha cucumbers you like." "Mum, I thought we were going out." "No, let's stay here and chat. I'm a bit tired and would rather just stay here." "Are you feeling OK, Mum?" "Yes, darling, I'm just tired and can't be bothered to get dressed." "OK, Mum, you sit. I will prepare the lunch." "Sounds good." Becky is surprised her mum has never let her make a cup of tea, "Something must be wrong; I will keep a close eye on this." she thinks.

"I think it's about time we had Anthony and Claire here for dinner, don't forget we will be mishpokhe (Family) soon. Let's do Friday night dinner."

"Oh, I meant to talk to you about that. They want to invite you for dinner and let Romero prepare something."

"They don't need to get a restaurant to deliver. I'm happy to cook."

"No, Mum Romero is their chef."

"What do you mean their chef?"

"They have a chef that comes over and cooks."

"Why can't Claire cook Mum?"

"Firstly, Claire can't cook and never cooks, and Romero is their live-in chef. They have a chef that lives in their house."

"Is there a room?"

"Yes, there's plenty of room, but he lives in another house at the bottom of their garden."

"He lives at the bottom of their garden?"

"Mum, it's more like an estate," Tami explained. Claire appeared puzzled, asking, "His parents live on an estate, and they have a live-in chef at the bottom of their garden?"

Tami clarified, "No, Mum, they own an estate. I mean, they don't live on one the way you're thinking."

"I'm sorry, darling. I didn't mean to imply that you think they're stupid. But when you say they own an estate, do they have more than one flat on the estate, and one is for the chef?"

Tami replied patiently, "Mum, listen, I'll explain slowly. They have a lot of money. They live in a huge seven-bedroom house with an outdoor pool. Romero, the chef, lives in a separate house at the far end of the estate. They also own a villa in Italy right on Lake Como."

Understanding finally dawned, and Claire said, "Ah, I see. So, they're unga (loaded)?"

Tami confirmed, "Yes, Mum."

Claire mused, "Why didn't you say so in the first place?"

"Anyway, even more, the reason why they must come here, can you imagine if we go there and they start talking about the wedding. Your dad will feel terrible being surrounded by all that money and knowing he's only a cabbie, you know what I mean." "They are not like that, Mum." "So, why does Michael work for a funeral parlour? Can't his dad let him work in the family business?" "He does." "You know Anderson's the stone mason and funeral parlour." "No, why would I know a non-Jewish funeral home." "Well, they own it, the whole thing! Yes, the whole thing."

There's a pause, and you can hear Roz's mind ticking over, then she says, "I pay 24 pounds a month to look after Papa's grave. I have to tell you it's never as clean as I would make it."

"Mum, what do you want me to do? Speak to Andrew?"

"No, don't be silly. I will get your dad to speak to Michael."

"OK, why don't you tell Michael to invite them Friday this week for dinner with their daughter and I will get your brother and Abraham," says Becky.

"OK, they came for lunch last week. He's not gay, although I think it's possible Abraham is. He was telling me about the flowers he bought me and how a home is not a home without flowers that's talk of a gay man."

"Mum, you can't go around saying things like that anymore."

"OK, OK, but my Stephen is not gay. He just is maybe confused. He needs to meet the right girl."

"I'm doing something about that right now…MUM."

"You can't; it will end in tears. Just leave him alone; he will be fine, but don't do whatever you are thinking, OK."

"I get it, but invite them, that's final, they come here Friday week for dinner."

When Roz said that's final, it was her way of saying conversation over now that's it.

7. Andy Goes to See His Parents

Andy's parents live on a small island near Bournemouth called sand banks, they retired there ten years ago, having built up an amazing business, and his father owns lots of properties that he rents out. They travel a lot but only cruise as his mother hates flying. They spend six months cruising a year and six months in sand banks.

Andy has two younger sisters; one is a nurse and lives in Birmingham with her husband, who is a real Brummie with a full accent, the other sister is a fully blown hippie, and after experiencing a year in a monastery in India, she never came home and has lived there her entire adult life.

His mum was very sweet and his dad was hard, miserable, and always moaning about something. He should never have retired, his mum always said, as now he's just trying to do stuff to be busy, and it drives his mother mad. "We bought a new toaster the other day, and no matter what setting you put it on, it burns the toast, instead of taking it back and swapping it over. No, not him, he finds out who made it, some company in China and writes to them in English and pays a translator to send it in Chinese and that's his mission this week, as you can see, he has no hobbies and no friends." Anyway, Andrew arrived, and it was strange as he never gets invited there. When he arrived, he was even more surprised to see both his sisters, straight away he thought, "One of his parents must be dying or why would we be here?" Anyway, he greeted his sisters, whom he had not seen for at least three years, and they were all suspicious of each other and never really got on. They hugged each other, but there was no love what so ever in the hug or how they felt about each other.

It was late afternoon, and Andy's father, Maurice, affectionately known as Mo, had a penchant for a glass of wine. He extended an invitation to everyone to join him on the terrace. Their garden stretched down to the waterfront, where he had a private mooring for a charming little boat. The weather was splendid, and they all gathered, sipping wine and engaging in light conversation. As they settled down, Andy's sister, Joanne, who had come from Birmingham, spoke up right away, saying, "It's nice to be here, Mum, Dad, but we all have busy lives, why exactly are we here?" "That's lovely," said his mom. "We haven't been together as a family for over three years and that's what you've got to say?" "She's right," said Mo, "One thing our kids are not idle, we brought them up well in that regard," they all smiled, Mo continued, "OK, yes, there's a reason why you are here, you see your mum and I, we are not getting any younger and we decided it was time to take a look at our lives, what we have achieved and we didn't want to wait until, we were both dead to see our hard work get some pleasure. So, I decided to fast forward all that and split our assets with you, whilst we can watch you and our grandkids enjoy it." The whole atmosphere changed. Now they were interested in the conversation.

Remember that Andy had been given the business and Joanne had been bought a beautiful house in a lovely area just outside Birmingham, and Mo was financing Joanne's husband Steven, who had two hairdressers and was in the process of opening a third. Karen still had the money in the bank her father had given her when she was 21 and hardly touched it as she was very happy living a single life in India, now working in a school in Kerala.

Mo continued, "So we have much to discuss with you over dinner. I've arranged a private room at a restaurant not too far from here, so enjoy the afternoon, and we'll head to the restaurant around 7 p.m." Andy's sister chimed in, "Dad, do you think it's a bit too public to discuss this in a restaurant?" Mo replied, "That's precisely why I chose a restaurant. I wanted to ensure none of you would create a scene." It was clear that Mo didn't quite comprehend what his children had become. They had a knack for making a scene wherever they went.

They all sort of did their own thing in the afternoon. Andy and his sisters ended up taking the boat out for a spin around sand banks for a couple of hours; they moored for a while, opened a bottle and started to talk for the first time in many, many years, as always Andy took control and started to tell them about Michael getting married soon. He was about to meet her parents, Tammy, well, he held back on her mental health issues. He just boasted about her artistic career. Karen asked after Claire and Andy opened up a little and told them things were not great between them. He couldn't understand why, so obviously he was not going to tell the whole truth. It sort of makes these conversations very false as none of them wants to take any responsibility for what's not working in their own lives, it's always someone else fault, you know the saying "When you point a finger, be careful look where all the other fingers are pointing" really applied to them.

Joanne unfortunately can't have kids, so her input was all about the hairdressing business her Steven was running. She held back the fact Steven was a gambler and basically had gambled away her house and most of the business, and Mo had bailed him out one last time. He was walking on very thin ice. Joanne was very unhappy in her life but was so busy looking after the business as a qualified accountant that she had no time for herself, which was crazy, especially after today. She could leave Steven and have a fantastic life with someone who was not with her just for her father's money.

Karen seemed to be the happiest or the calmest; for sure, she loved her life and wanted very little except to meet someone which was not easy living in India, and she was considering moving to Israel as she had friends whom she met in India that live in Tel Aviv, the lifestyle is great for youngsters, and she thought about opening a cafe, she was at an age where she fancied a change, and was very excited about the future, she loved living in India, she loved being surrounded by all that history, and she loved the weather, she just wanted to meet someone, and India was not the place for that, she had no real possessions no real aggravation, she looked the healthiest and was at peace with herself, she just wanted to meet someone and enjoy the next part of her journey.

They all left together for the restaurant, which was a very busy place, but they had a private dining room at the back of the restaurant with glass doors on all sides. It was like sitting in a fish bowl, but they had privacy. But anyone could see if anyone got upset or an argument would take place. It was a perfect choice for Mo.

Now, they all knew why they were here. They wanted to hear what their father had to say, so after a starter of some wine and the mains had been served, Mo began, "Well, you know why you are here, so I won't waste any time; over the past forty years your mother and I have been very lucky and very successful, we have built an amazing business which Andy has taken over, and we have built quite the portfolio, we now have 45 properties all rented out and managed by a company, we have three homes, sand banks one in Spain and the apartment in London.

"We have worked very hard for our money and want to make sure it's not blown on rubbish and, most importantly, it gets passed down the generations.

"I know I've been hard on all of you, but it served you all very well. This is not a discussion; this is what we have decided, and we will not change our minds."

"Andy, you don't really need anything else from me," straightaway Andy stands up and starts to speak, and his father bangs his hand so hard on the table everyone jumps as he very sternly says, "Sit the fuck down and listen to me." There were a few glances from outside the fish bowl, as I'm sure everyone in the restaurant heard Mo shout. Andy stared at his father and sat down, "I intend to leave you the London apartment, although why I don't really know, Joanne, I intend to give you the Spanish house and Karen sand banks, the property business I want to give to my grandson Michael and Tami, I leave her four million in cash the rest of the money after all the death duties when we have gone will be split between three charities specified in our will and the jewellery is split between Joanne, Karen and Tami, my car collection, will go to Michael," Andy knew straightaway that was his father's way of punishing him as Andy was the car enthusiast.

"That just about sums everything up except, for one more thing, your mother and I have decided to move to Italy, I have bought a house in Florence, and that is where we wish to live out the rest of our lives, all of this will be dealt with by my accountant and lawyer who will be in contact with you to sign the necessary paper work." Andy responded, "I don't agree with you giving Michael the property portfolio." Mo retorted, "Lucky I'm not asking for your blessing, then." Andy inquired, "How do you know he wants out of the family business?" Mo explained, "Firstly, he told me. Secondly, if you had any sort of relationship with your own kids, you would have known this." It was clear that Mo was the only person who knew how to handle Andy, and this marked the end of Andy's objections on the matter.

Mo continues, "There is only one stipulation: we all meet as a family, children and grandchildren once a year in Florence every Easter."

"For how long?" asks Andy.

"Until we are both not here anymore." Again, there is no response from Andy.

Lisa, who has been sitting there quietly throughout the meal, says, "All I ask is that you be nice to each other and we get to see you once a year together. It's not a lot to ask from you so please respect it and go live your lives. We worked hard and made many sacrifices in our earlier years so you and our grandchildren will never have to worry about money. Now it's about how you use the money and how good, charitable and honestly you can live your lives." "Mom, it sounds like there is something you are not telling us," Joanne says. "Yes, Mom, I agree," says Karen, "What is it you are not telling us?" Lisa replies, "There is nothing to tell, just be kinder to each other." Lisa smiles; on the inside, she is not so happy, but she and Mo decided not to tell the kids that she has developed dementia and it is moving at quite a pace. That's why they decided to do this now and move to a warmer climate.

Andy remained perturbed about the property business and was particularly irate about the car collection, but he realised he had no choice but to accept it. Joanne made a conscious decision not to inform Steven about the matter. She saw it as her personal safeguard in case Steven reverted to gambling, and she had previously warned him that she would file for divorce if he did. Karen was happy as she had enough money from her dad's years to live on, and she would sell sand banks and buy a property in Tel Aviv…

They all left that evening except Karen, who stayed a few more days with her parents before flying back to India. Joanne was working out how she would keep this from Steven, and Andy felt nothing; he had another property, although he also decided not to tell Claire and maybe he would just keep the London apartment a secret and use it when he's on business trips rather than stay in hotels, he definitely had something in mind for this place.

8. She Knows!

Roz is finding the pressure too much; the wedding was getting closer, and entertaining was getting harder, but she was like super woman shopping, preparing, cooking, clearing away, and housekeeping, but the last few months, everything just seemed harder; she found herself sleeping in the afternoons when no one was home and all in all she was just very tired all the time, and she was hiding that along with the pain in her stomach, she didn't want to make a fuss.

She had seen the doctor last week, and he sent her for some tests. She did this during the day when no one was around, and now she was going back to review the scans with him.

"Why can't they just give you the results over the phone?"

"No…they have to call you and tell you the doctor wants to see you. Normally, it's the office girl that calls. She wrote up the notes, so she knows what's wrong with you and calls you with a voice on."

"I don't understand why they can't just call you, tell you what's wrong and then let's get on with it." Roz was more worried than she told anyone.

She arrives at her specialist, "Mr Davison, please, I have an appointment." "Your name?" "Rosalind Cohen."

"OK, Mrs Cohen, please take a seat; he won't keep you too long." She's already looking and smiling at me like I'm on a timer and going to die very soon. "What's wrong with these people? Do they think I'm stupid?"

"AAAAAH, it must be serious; the doctors come out of the surgery to get me. You see, nothing gets past me."

"Come in, Roz." He puts his arm around her shoulder and guides her into his office. Now, she is worried.

"Doctor, can we please get to the point? I just want to hear it plain, simple and direct."

"OK, sure, Roz…" Roz rolls her eyes, "Mr Davison says something is showing up on the scan. The thing is, it could be something. It could be nothing. I'm afraid I need to send you to have some other tests and some biopsies a little more invasive." "How much more invasive can it be than me lying on a table with a stranger while my knickers are around my knees and my chest and stomach are on full display?" The doctor responded, "Well, this procedure will require a closer look inside with a small camera. The good news is you can be in and out of the hospital in just one day. However, you'll need to be brought to the hospital and taken home since you'll have to be under anaesthesia."

Roz asks, "Doctor, I'm not good with waiting and tests and waiting and waiting; in your professional opinion, what do you think is wrong?" "Honestly, Roz, I have no idea. Let's wait and see when we have the tests back." "So, I have to wait?" "Yes." "I'm not good at waiting. Let's get it done quickly; what day would you be free so I can book everything for you." "Eeeerrm let's see, I've got a crazy time coming up. This is important, Roz. We need to get this done as soon as possible." "OK, how about next Monday?" "That's fine; my secretary will send you a letter and call you to run through the procedure." "OK, sure, that's fine, but please use my mobile as I am rarely at home and don't answer it as everyone has our mobiles."

Roz knew something was wrong, and she knew it was serious. She seemed to have a feeling about these things, and this one was bad. She left and drove around for a while, then arrived at a cafe on a small parade about two miles from her house; they have tables outside. Roz ordered a black coffee and a tuna and mayonnaise sandwich, but she barely touched her meal. She sat there alone, and as she did, a car pulled up outside. A woman leaned out of the window and shouted at the top of her voice, "Carol, Carol, is my order ready? Be a darling and bring it out to me." The woman smiled at Roz and added, "I'm in a crazy rush, got a lot to do today, and I'm out this evening." Roz smiled back in response but didn't say a word. Shortly after, Carol came out with a box, which she handed to Claire. Claire carefully took it, promising to settle the bill tomorrow, and then drove off. Carol returned to the shop, wearing a smile and shaking her head.

9. Friday Night Dinner

It was Friday, Roz was out shopping for dinner tonight, David was still working, and Andrew was meeting a family who owned a funeral business on the other side of London where they lived. He was trying to buy the business as he always wanted to open in this area but never wanted to start from scratch.

Claire was having hair/nails/spray tan and a reading and getting herself ready for the evening. Becky took the day off to help her mum whilst Michael and Stephen were also at work.

"Mum, let's get these, they look nice."

"What do you mean?"

"It's Friday night."

"I want to stick to tradition. I think it's a bit heavy for tonight. I want it to be a light dinner party, not a heavy Shabbat dinner."

"Darling, we have been doing it for years. I want the Andersons to see us as we are, and I bet they have never experienced a Friday night Shabbat dinner with prayers; I'm sorry, tradition it is." In total, today they have been to seven different shops to get various things for tonight, including one shop just for the potatoes as Roz likes the shape of these and they were still covered in dirt like they have just been picked. It also meant she had to clean them like she cleaned everything else.

They go home and get started on her heavy Friday night dinner. Becky laid the table, and Roz came in, checked everything and moved it all around. "Sorry, darling, but you know I have my ways, and I want it perfect tonight."

It was 4 p.m., and the table was impeccably set. The chopped liver was prepared, the soup had been simmering since yesterday, the chicken was roasting in the oven, and the potatoes and rice were poised to join it. The broccoli and peas awaited their turn as well. Roz was just adding the finishing touches to the apple cake before sliding it into the oven. The fruits salad had been meticulously cut and was chilling in the fridge. Just in case, she had also prepared a cheesecake.

Roz went to have a bath, leaving Becky in charge to ensure no disasters happen and David was bringing the wine home.

At 6.30, Roz has done this so many times she goes on auto pilot and knows exactly how to perfect the timing to prepare and serve each course.

The first to arrive was Stephen without Abraham, as Roz explicitly said just the immediate family for tonight, I don't think Stephen was very happy, but he was on time, came in with flowers for his mum and said to Roz, "What if they are complete arseholes?"

"Stephen, watch the language, please they won't be. If they're not nice, we will be incredibly nice."

"Becky is nervous enough as it is. Let's remember tonight is about her, not you,"

"OK, Mum, get off your high horse. I was only asking, and behave tonight."

"No rows with your father."

Then the key went in the door; there was David late, but not too late as he walked in, Roz said, "Where's the wine?"

"Oh shit, I forgot."

"David, one thing I asked you to do, we must have some here."

"We don't, and if we did, don't you think I would know? I suppose you want me to go out again?"

"Yes, go now and don't be a shnora (miser). Buy good wine, three red and three white, OK?"

"I'm going, I'm going."

Michael arrived a few minutes later. He was really shaky as he knocked on the door. Becky answered the door, kissed him, and he came in with flowers for Roz.

David got home just in time with two red and two white wines. Roz just looked at him with her rolling eyes as he walked in and said, "Get washed up, please, and don't be long."

Anthony and Claire were in their car. They decided to drive themselves as Claire felt uncomfortable turning up in the big Bentley with a driver, so they took her two-door Bentley, which also meant she would not drink as she was driving…a big result otherwise, God knows what she could have said.

As they parked, Andy remarked, "How can they afford this wedding? It's like they won the lottery! The cost must be half of what houses around here cost." His partner, Claire, replied, "Andy, please, not tonight. This isn't about you. Let's see how the evening goes. The wedding may not even come up in conversation. We're here to celebrate our kids' engagement and the meeting of our two families. Be kind, and don't come across as arrogant. Remember, not everyone grew up with everything handed to them." Andy chuckled and countered, "You always make me feel like the poor one." Claire sighed and said, "Oh, that old chestnut! You're just worried about what I'll do when I have even more money. Well, you'll have to wait and see."

Claire had a big box, and Andy had a bottle of champagne. As they knocked on the door, Becky said, "I will go." She opened the door and hugged them both in the hall way as they came in, which was about the size of their seventh guest bathroom. Becky made the introductions, a hug from Roz to both of them.

David shook hands with Andy and uncomfortably hugged Claire; Stephen was next, "This is my son, Stephen," said David, "He doesn't live here. He has an amazing flat in the dock lands and works in the city."

"Great," says Andy as he shakes his hand.

Stephen says, "Haven't we met before? You look so familiar."

"I don't think so," says Andy. "I'm in the funeral business, so hopefully we won't meet for a long time."

Roz says, "David, let them in the front door before you start telling them our life stories."

Everyone laughs politely. Claire gives Roz the box and says, "I never know what to bring for these occasions, so I thought I would bring you a cake. I made it," she says, making sure no one else hears her and Roz opens it and sees an amazing lemon drizzle cake, Roz thinks there's no way she baked that it's too perfect, "Thank you, Claire, that's really kind of you what a lovely gesture," then she remembers the loud lady in her car collecting the same box from the bakers as she had her coffee.

"OK, David, fix the drinks. What will you have, Claire?"

"Do you have any gin? I would love a gin and tonic."

"Eerrrm, I'm afraid not. I have some vodka. I can fix you a vodka and coke."

"Oh no, that's fine; a glass of white wine would be great."

"Sure, no problem, Andy, how about you?"

"Do you have scotch?"

"Sure, do give me a minute, ice?"

"No, thanks. I hate ice in my scotch; it kills the real taste."

"I agree," as David pours his away with ice without Andy seeing.

They are sitting in the front room that has two two-seater sofas, a coffee table separating them and a single-seater at the head, making a cosy square around a mock fire place. They all sat, of course, David at the head in the single sofa, the Rubin's together and Michael squeezing in. Becky sat with her mum and said, "So it's so nice to meet you. What do you think of our exciting news?" says Roz.

"It's wonderful," replies Claire. "Your Becky is so beautiful. We're absolutely delighted."

Andy replied with a smile, "That makes two of us. We loved Michael the first time we met him. He's almost part of the family already."

Claire nodded in agreement and added, "That's nice."

Then Andy continued, "We hope to feel the same about Becky. We just haven't spent much time with her yet…" The mention of Becky led to a moment of awkward silence. Claire gave Andy a look that spoke volumes.

"Where's Tami?" asked Michael.

"Oh, you know your sister is always running late and she does have the furthest to go."

"Yes, but she doesn't have a proper job," says Andy. "So, there's no reason for her to be…"

The doorbell goes, "Ah, that must be her."

Becky goes and welcomes Tami; they have met a few minutes before. She walks in looking so sweet in a short, above-the-knee flowing dress. Her long golden red hair tied up in a bun like she didn't have time to do it but still stunningly beautiful, she says, "Hi to everyone, and Roz announces, "Why don't we all sit down." The dining room table, when extended, sat ten, so they had plenty of room. Roz told everyone where to sit, so we had David at one end, at the head, to his right was Roz, then Tami and then Claire at the other head was Andy then, Becky and Michael and then Stephen, Andy and Claire were told by Michael about the prays format so no one starts digging into the challah bread.

Roz had such a proud look as she smiled from the second she picked up the matches to light the candles as her hands gently coupled the candles three times, she said the prayer and then wished everyone good Shabbas and said, "We want to welcome you all and I hope this will be the first of many times we break bread together in the future, as our two lovely children start their life together," and everyone very loudly replied, "Good Shabbas."

David was next, "Who would like some wine?" and started serving the wine.

The conversation was very polite to start with David being his normal inquisitive self, started with Tami, "What do you do darling."

She replied, "I'm an artist."

"What type of artist?"

"I didn't think there were types. As someone who's ignorant about art, I have no idea," replies David.

"Mainly painting, although I have tried my hands on sculpture."

"Very nice," David said. "Have you ever sold anything?"

"Dad," said Becky, "that's not nice."

"Sorry, never meant anything by it, that's OK?"

"Yes, I seem to be selling well at the moment. I have a new show coming along any time now."

"That's great," says Roz.

"She's the creative one of the family," says Claire.

"I wish I had her talent. What about you, Stephen?" claimed Andy, "So what's your story?"

Claire kicked him under the table, "What do you do for a living? He meant," said Claire as she smiled.

"I am an analyst for a bank and I work in docklands and live there as well."

"That sounds complicated."

"Not really. I studied for three years and it's easy really. I just work with figures and predict the economy growth or decline based on politics/the weather, etc."

"It's over my head." says David.

"But you would be shocked at what they get paid."

"We don't need to discuss salaries," says Roz.

"Right, I will just get the soup. Becky, come and help serve."

"Can I do anything?" Claire asks."

"No, that's fine, you just stay there," says Roz.

The conversation was OK, you know when you have a dinner party and only one person speaks at a time and everyone listens to the answer? That's how it was going, no small chats yet happening around the table, the wedding so far has not come up, in fact, it has not really come up at all since the announcement.

"You have a beautiful home," says Claire.

"Thank you, it's not big, but we love it here and I'm close to all my friends and family, so it's very convenient, yes we thought about moving to a bigger house, but Roz loves it here."

"What do you do?" asks Andy.

"Oh me, I'm a black cab driver and have been for over 20 years. I know London like the back of my hand, and you, Andy?"

"We own the stone masons/funeral home Anderson's."

"Yes, of course," David says, "it's a good business, I bet; we all got to die, right?" as Andy smiles, thinking. *I've only heard that a thousand times.*

"Where do you live, David? We live two miles away. What about you?" says David.

Claire replies, "It's the house opposite the church on the corner,"

"On the corner," says David, looking puzzled, "There's no house on the corner, just a set of double gates."

Guilty, Andy says, "We live through those gates."

"How many houses are in that development?"

"Just one," says Andy…silence.

"OK, I will get desserts," Roz disappears and looks up to the sky from her sink, thinking next thing you know, he will be going through his bank account like the father of the bride, *Give me strength…*

Deserts go down well and then Tami says, "Do you mind if I smoke?"

Stephen says, "Oh, I would love one. I will join you; let's go outside." Becky and Michael join them whilst the parents go back to the lounge and have coffee, "You made an amazing meal. I wish I could cook like that. I've never been very domesticated."

"That's alright, we all have our thing, mine is football," says David, "And golf."

"Me too," says Andy.

"Yes, I hear you're a Gooner. Are you a Spurs fan?"

David replied with a smile, "Yes, although it's a shame about the result the other week."

Andy smiled politely and responded, "You'll have to come and be my guest in our box one week, Anthony."

Anthony graciously accepted, "I'd love to, as long as it's the Spurs game."

Andy added, "And bring your son along."

Roz chimed in, "That's very kind of you."

"I know," says Stephen, "You were at the hotel we were in, in Greece, a few weeks ago; remember the mojito?" "I don't think so," says Andy, as he laughs, "I could certainly do with a holiday in Greece." "No, I'm certain," Claire butts in and changes the subject, "So what do you think about our kids?" "It's wonderful news; when are they planning to get married." "I don't know," says Roz, "We haven't discussed it with them." "Well, maybe we can ask them. It would be good to know how much time I have," says David. Andy was just about to answer when Tami came in and apologised, "Apparently, I've had a flood in my studio my flatmate called. I need to go." "Of course," says Roz. "You go; I hope it's not too bad," Claire says. "Bye darling, call you later," Tami replies. Claire kisses her and says, "Goodbye."

This was just too much for Tami, having spent four weeks in the clinic surrounded by support staff and very understanding patients. This dinner was a lot for her to handle, so she made an excuse and left. Claire knew something was wrong but was happy she decided to go, things have been very difficult as Tami has an incredibly tough time dealing with her anxiety and depression, but she's seeing her doctor twice a week and goes to the clinic as a day patient three days a week, she suspended her exhibition, her gallery was very angry with her as they had spent a lot of money preparing and promoting the show, she could not care less, and Andy got involved and sent a strong letter from his lawyers and dared them to sue an artist who was suffering with mental illness, they were now being quiet and patient.

Not long after Tami left, Stephen came in and said, "Mum, I need to go. I've got a birthday party. I should really show up to it. It's one of Abraham's sisters."

"Oh, of course," says Roz, "You go speak later," and he exits the house.

Becky and Michael join them in the house and then it happens Claire very quietly has now had four glasses of wine, not good as she says, "Right, you two, what's happening with the wedding. It's so exciting; I can't wait to get going."

Becky says, "Well, we haven't decided yet, but we are thinking the end of August next year."

"That's only 11 months; everything gets booked up so quickly, we need to get a move on. I know of an amazing hotel in London. We held our gala charity dinner there last year. It's amazing; they have three rooms: one for the ceremony, one for the reception and a huge ballroom with a band stand it's gorgeous and we can get special rates to stay there."

Becky says, "We haven't decided where we want to get married yet."

"What? You aren't thinking of getting married abroad?" says Claire, who seems to be the question master.

"You are more than welcome to have it in our place on Lake Como. It's really gorgeous, and we have the grounds," says Andy.

"I thought you wanted a more traditional wedding," says Roz.

"We're not sure yet." David is keeping quiet, and Roz prays he does.

"I hear you play golf?" says David.

"Yes, I play at Stockton Manor."

"Oooh, a bit pricey for me; I play at Hibbs farm."

"Nice, I've played there as well. Maybe you can come and play with us at the club."

David appreciated the gesture, "That's two things you've offered me to join you for, and I haven't returned the favour yet."

Andy replied, "Let's not keep score."

David agreed a little sternly, "I agree. You're more than welcome to come with me to White Hart Lane when we play you again. Just be aware that you'd need to be quiet because it's right in the parking lane with all the passionate Spurs fans."

Andy nodded, "For sure."

Roz asks Claire. "Tell us about your charity work. I'm really interested in it; it's my passion. We raise money for children with learning disabilities. It's an amazing charity." "I love it in fact, we are having our annual gala dinner on the 25th at the Regents Hotel. Why don't you all come as my guests." David coughed and spit his coffee all over the table, "David," Roz said. "I'm sorry, it went down the wrong hole. Thanks for the invite, but we have a surprise birthday party for a friend that night." Roz, looking confused, says, "Thank you and I will for sure talk to David about this later."

"Well," says Claire, bringing the conversation back to the wedding, "We need to get going, or we will miss out on the best venues/ bands/ caterers/ florists. I'm sure you agree. Roz."

"Well, I haven't thought about it yet, have we, David?"

"Not so much, but we need to be careful. I don't want a too big wedding, I want something intimate, I was thinking."

"If it's about the money," says Andy, "I'm sure we are happy to help with whatever you need…"

"Thanks," interrupts David, "It's my daughter and my responsibility to make the wedding all I'm saying is we need to not go too crazy."

The evening is getting a little dangerous. Roz offers more coffee and Claire goes to help along with Becky and Michael.

"Listen," Andy says, "I'm happy to pay for it. We could be looking at 70,000–80,000, easy for a wedding nowadays."

David says, "really, do people actually pay that much?"

"They sure do. It's easily done. Well, I'm happy to pay it all if you want or whatever."

"Thank you, that won't be necessary. I can manage. It will be smaller than that, but it will be great, well the offers there, we will be family soon, so happy to help."

The evening comes to an end, and David and Roz say goodbye to Claire and Andy, and Michael says to Becky, "Call me when you are ready for bed, young love." Claire says, "It's so lovely." Off they go. David shuts the door, and then he's off, "Who the f—k does he think he is with his double gates, villa on the lakes telling me it's going to cost 80 grand, and he will pay for it, that much," says Roz. "That sounds madness." Becky starts to get tearful, and Roz cuddles her and says, "Don't worry, we will work it all out." "I hope so," says Becky as I overheard Claire talking to Andy and saying with friends, family business associates, people from the tennis club and the charity, their guest list alone will be over 200 people. David laughs and says, "They've got to be joking. I was thinking half that for the wedding." Becky runs upstairs crying, and Roz follows her up. David goes to the garage to get a cigarette, comes back and thinks, "Shit, my 31,500 policy is not going to work." Then everyone goes to bed, David on his own, Roz in the double bed with Becky, "Thank God, that's over. It could have been worse, I suppose," thinks Roz. David couldn't help but feel a growing sense of unease. He knew he hadn't gotten away with the lie about the surprise birthday. Soon enough, Roz would question him about it, and he found himself in a difficult predicament. He had already signed a contract for the singing gig, and the thought of showing up to sing in front of his mishpokhe (new family) was causing quite a mess of anxiety. David realised he needed to make a decision—either come clean or find a way out of this tangled web of deception.

Andy and Claire get home, they haven't said a word, and as they walk in, Andy says, "All I've got to say is if he thinks my son is getting married in a dingy hall with an up and coming band and flowers from Tesco's, he needs to get his head tested we are going to have a lavished affair if I have to make it myself." Claire walks up to the bed and quietly says, "Let's see what happens, it's not about you. It's about two young people in love, maybe they want different things for this wedding, let's sleep on it. I need to get to bed. I drank too much; God knows what else I said."

Becky never did phone Michael; she was too upset, and he sent her a message saying, "I hope you are OK. Everything will be fine; let them all calm down, and we will have a magical day even if we have ten people in Lake Como. I don't care; I just want to make sure I marry you xxx love you always, Michael." Becky replied with xx, then went to sleep.

10. It's a Small World

It was very close to the fundraiser, and the day after the Friday night dinner, there were definitely some ramifications from the evening. Stephen called his mum to thank her for last night, but Roz said, "OK, say what you want to say. In all the years I've made this dinner, you have never phoned to thank me once." "OK, OK, Mum, I wanted to tell you that Andy is lying. I and Abraham definitely saw him in Greece. He was staying at our hotel, and he kicked up such a fuss over a mojito. I could never forget that voice, and when I saw him, I knew straight away I'd met him before, and Mum, he was with a lady much younger than him, oy veh (omg)." "Stephen, it's none of our business. We can't get involved in their family business, but Mum…" "No, buts, just leave it alone." "OK, OK, one more thing, I need to see you. Can you and Dad come over for Sunday lunch next week?" "That would be lovely, see you then, bye darling." Roz shakes her head as she puts down the phone. "It's such a small world," she thinks, "Who would have believed Stephen would see Andy in Greece."

Claire was up drinking coffee, no breakfast on a Saturday, she was waiting for Andy to come down, she was on the war path, she sat there getting more and more angry, and when he came down, she hit him with it straight away, "What is wrong with you?" "Oh my God, woman, really?" as he descended the stairs. Roz didn't hold back, retorting, "Yes, you arrogant jerk." Andy, attempting to mediate, chimed in, "If it's about the money, David…" Roz interrupted, "What's wrong with you? How could you embarrass him like that? He knew exactly what I meant." Andy responded firmly, "No, the only thing clear about that comment is that you have loads of money, and, quite frankly, who cares? You come across as arrogant and rude. Don't forget the life you lead." Andy made it clear, "And don't you forget I'm not reliant on your money." "I have plenty of my own for this lifestyle, and I'm not sure you want to start with me right now." "I'm really ready for a fight. I haven't forgotten about Greece, but to be honest, I can't take any more. I've got more important things to worry about. Your daughter left the party and was very unwell. I thought she had a flood?" "You are so wrapped up in your own life. You don't see the pain your daughter is in?" With that, he heads back upstairs, and she says, "I haven't finished with you yet, so be ready for our next conversation," he slams the bedroom door, and Claire sits there and starts to cry.

David is up as he was working days on any Saturday when Spurs play away, and Roz was already up, "What an arrogant arse hole that Andy was if it's about the money! Fuck him."

"I understand." Roz says very calmly, "But is it about the money? Maybe, but hearing it from that moron was embarrassing, I've got over 39 grand saved up for this wedding, and if I have 11 months, I can definitely get it to 50 grand, but that's it."

"Why don't we sit and chat with the kids and see what they are thinking? You might be surprised.

"We should, doesn't change what a moron he is."

"I agree," says Roz. "But as we are just talking, can we please discuss this surprise birthday party we have on the same night as the gala charity event? Prey tell me my husband, whose birthday is it?"

"OK, OK, since when have you become Mrs Jackie Mason…"

"No, I'm not joking, what's going on?" "I just have no interest in going to a gala event with all their rich friends when they clearly will be there spending thousands to appear charitable. I don't need to do that to be charitable. I collect food from Tesco for the synagogue and distribute the parcels every week. I never miss a week, do I? I do my bit, so I don't need to feel stupid in front of all her friends whilst they are throwing their money around, and I can't bear to see that arsehole."

"OK…"

"I just don't want to see him."

"OK," she says, "I will tell her we can't go, and that will be that. Maybe you can take me out for an expensive meal that night."

"I would love to, but I've swapped with Maurice, and I'm taking his night shift."

"Typical," she kisses David on the head, and he heads off to work.

As he gets in his cab, he says to himself, "Now, what the fuck am I going to do? I've managed to convince my wife not to go. I'm working nights that night. So, I can sing at the gala dinner, but now I know my muchatainister (new son-in-law's parents) will be there in fact, technically, she hired me. What a mess!"

Claire called Tami to see how she was; there was no answer, so she headed over there. When she arrived, Tami was literally walking out. She was surprised to see her mum and said, "Mum, what are you doing here? I called and called, but you never answered."

"I'm sorry, I was in the shower and had the music on."

"I'm fine. I'm having breakfast with some friends, but last night, yea, I'm sorry it was all a bit too much.

Claire shared her concerns, "There were too many questions being asked when we went outside for a cigarette, and you know I can't talk about it yet. I'm still feeling very fragile, and I'm trying really hard to not give in and go back to the clinic."

Tami expressed her understanding, "I know, darling. I'm just worried about you."

Claire reassured her, "I'll be okay."

Tami suggested, "Why don't you come with me and join my friends and me for breakfast?"

Claire hesitated but then agreed, "Are you sure?"

Tami smiled, "Yes, come on, let's have some fun for a couple of hours." And so, a very happy Claire went for breakfast with her daughter.

Michael was not seeing Becky today as they had arranged to see their respective uni friends for lunch, but Michael thought he would pop over to see Becky late in the morning. It was the right thing to do. As she opened the door, she started to cry, and he gave her a big cuddle, "what the fuck happened last night?" she said. "Your dad was a complete dick, and so was my brother. This dinner could have caused a break in our two families before we actually became family. How sick is that?" "It won't, don't worry, they will all calm down, and I'm sure my dad will be told by Mum how he needs to repair what he said and what your brother said." "I've no idea, it wouldn't surprise me if he was right. My dad is an arse, and my mother lets him do exactly what he wants to do, which he does, any way I'm sure it will all be fine." "Go and have a few drinks and enjoy your lunch with your uni friends. I will call you later unless you go on to a club and make it an out evening," she laughed and kissed him, and he left feeling good if he could high five himself, he would, and Becky was feeling better, phew that could all have gone tits up had the evening gone on a minute later.

11. Old Blue Eyes

So, at Friday night dinner, there was just Roz, David, and the two kids, no Michael or Abraham. They were still talking about the other night. "Roz, you are going to upset Becky." "She is marrying into that family, and we all need to act civil about it, talking about them." "Tami called me," Stephen said and invited me to sit at her table for the event. "You don't want to go to it, it's just full of rich Jews throwing their money around." "Dad, that's not fair. Claire works really hard for this event, and she raises a fortune." "OK, you're right, anyway, I thought you had a surprise birthday." Becky says, "No, it's been cancelled. The birthday boy found out and didn't want a surprise. They are just having a family dinner. Sorry, Dad." "I'm definitely going with Michael. I'm sitting at their parents' table." "Well, then, I'm going," says Stephen. Roz says, "Well, it's rude for us not to go, so I'm deciding for us." "You are overruled. We are going," There's a shock, "Overruled, should be my middle name."

"Roz, we can't go. I want this family dinner that night, and I want you all to follow my lead." David, with a touch of humour, replied, "Obey me, Roz? What is this, the 1800s?" Roz chuckled, "My lord, you know what I mean. Why can't you all, for once, do what I ask?" David sighed and attempted to explain, "We will, Roz, just not this time." David lowered his head into his hands, then reluctantly admitted, "Okay, okay, okay. I can't win. You can't go because I'll be singing there. They booked me…" There was a silence, "Did I just hear right? you are singing at the gala dinner, and they booked you?" "Yes…" "Would you mind explaining how this singing came about as? I have been with you for over 25 years, and I've never heard you sing in the bath or in the synagogue, so how is it you can sing at a gala dinner in front of 400 people, including our future muchatainister (new son-in-law's parents)." "Oh, my God, these two families won't make it past this, so you know how embarrassing it will be for us, Dad." "Yes," agrees Stephen. David bangs his hand on the table and says, "Right, I don't want to hear another word from anyone. Do you understand me?" Not a Single word, "I've been singing all my life when I first got a guitar. I taught myself to play from about the age of eight. I kept it hidden away, and none of my friends knew. They would have taken the piss, especially as my music was all around Sinatra and in that era, I was always old for my age. I also knew none of you would understand, so I never told you. I've been doing gigs in the evenings for 20 years. I don't do many, but the ones I do, I do when I'm out on the cabs. All I've ever wanted to do was play the guitar and sing and write my own music as well, everyone is entitled to have a dream. Well, that's mine."

Roz semi-smiled and said, "OK, let's all come down. I think you underestimated your family's ability to love and support you, so I think we all have a gala to go to, and your father is going to sing, and we will be there to support him." No questions asked, she looks at him and smiles and says, "You better be good!"

12. Please Excuse Me

I suppose Claire was so crazy busy with the gala event she never had time to put two and two together and work out David was the singer. Claire and Andy arrived about four, five hours early as she had Andy running around checking things for her as she was involved in every detail possible; it was like making a wedding.

Stephen was getting dressed, and Abraham was a bit pissed he could not come, but Stephen explained and explained, "This would all be over Sunday when my parents come over, and we tell them. Just chill; it's only a posh gala dinner, and the venue is dressed in pink with pretty cocktails and flowers. Oh my God, everywhere, bright flowers." "Stop taking the piss. I'm not listening to you. I hope you have a shit time," Stephen looks once more in the mirror and off he goes.

Michael can get ready in peace in his place and is picking up Becky and her parents in half an hour. Tami called Mum to say she was not coming, and in between everything, Claire got in her car, went to see her daughter and got her dressed, made up and said, "I need you there. Can you do that for me?" Tami said, "Yes, but why?" "Because you are the only member in this family who understands me, I had to pick the (crazy) one to understand me." They both laughed, and Tami left with Claire a little more composed but trembling.

The guests arrived to a grand spectacle. A long red carpet stretched out, with pretend paparazzi snapping photos as they walked in. The scene resembled Alice in Wonderland, with people dressed in clever teapot outfits serving guests. There were numerous tea parties set up, each surrounded by incredible toadstools. Men were offered remarkable high hats in gold, while women were presented with Alice's aprons to put on.

Laughter and merriment filled the air as everyone enjoyed this fantastic sight, and all of this was just the prelude to the main event in the dining room.

Claire was in great demand to say hello and introduce and be introduced to everyone. She saw us out of the corner of her eye and ran over to us, and said, "Well, what do you think?"

"It's amazing," They all said, "we are so proud to support you."

Then David realised he never told Claire. He can't do it now in case she has a fit and assumes I'm shit and cancels me. It looks like it will have to be a surprise. Fingers crossed, Claire also saw that Simon, her friend, had come, and she wanted to embarrass her husband, Simon.

She shouted, "Claire, how are you? You made it, thank you so much, and this must be your beautiful wife, Alex."

"Yes, it is. It's so nice to meet you, and thank you so much for the invite."

"Oh, don't be silly, let me grab Andy, Andy, come and meet some friends of mine. This is Simon and his wife Alex."

Silly me, "You must know each other because you both play at the same golf club."

Simon said to me the other day that he never saw you there very often anymore, and I said, "That's not possible as you are there at least four days a week and sometimes five days."

"Right darling, yes, darling, very much, so maybe we have just been missing each other on the course."

"Maybe," says Simon, "but do you stay for lunch?"

"Erm, yes, sometimes, very strange. I'm there four days a week, always ending with lunch, but I suppose it's possible we just keep missing each other. I'm sure that's it."

"Please excuse me," as Andy makes his exit. Claire stayed talking about their family, and then she left. When she felt she had stood there for long enough to repay their kindness in attending (even if it was for a reason, it was worth the £400 just to see him squirm).

Claire invited everyone to their tables to sit down and made the welcome speech, "Please enjoy our dinner. I will get up a little later to draw the raffle, and my husband Andy will do the auction. Then I hope you will stay for an incredible voice later with the band he is the fabulous David Frank, OK, OK, that's all I could think of in short notice," they all laughed for about five minutes. Everyone in the room was trying to work out what's funny…David Frank.

The dinner was incredible; there were some stunning women in amazing gowns, and Roz's table looked like they all needed a holiday, whether real or fake. Everyone had a tan; they looked like the table of the poor white can't sit out in the sun brigade.

After all the toasts were done, it was time for Claire's appeal. The guests were shown incredible films depicting the work the charity does and the remarkable children living in the charity's warden flats. The stories and images were truly inspirational. The charity even organises international bike rides, covering distances of 100 to 150 kilometres per day. They take a tandem bike for one of the kids with Down's syndrome, who participates every year. He's remarkable but hard work, especially when tackling hills. The money raised from these events is truly remarkable and goes towards supporting the charity's important work.

So, Claire makes her appeal, and then beautiful women come around with like a donation form. It has a small metal tube attached to a piece of string with £1000/£5000/£10,000/£25,000/£50,000 holes for your pin along with your details, name, address and credit card numbers if you have them, or they can send you the invoice. Roz looks at David, and David fills out the £5,000 one. "Roz says to him are you mad? You don't need to do this." "Oh, yes, I do. It's not as much as many of them, but I tell you something, the £ 5,000 means more to me than their donation means to them, that's for sure." Roz agrees, and nothing more is said. Just when you thought everything was done, Claire gets up next and says, "Now for our special guest, he has appeared all over the world, and we have him for one night and one night only, David Frank." And she points over to the stage, and then she hears a few noises from the audience. The clapping starts small and all from their own table, and then more people start clapping, and as David gets close to Claire, he whispers in her ear, "I'm getting up to sing. I haven't decided if I want to embarrass you the way your husband embarrassed me in front of my family," he kisses her on the cheek, Claire walks back to her table stunned and now very nervous then David starts with Mac the knife and his voice is silky, and he hits every note perfectly he invites people to the dance floor, and he wooed them for two hours with dancing and singing and everyone had a great night, he even forced his wife to dance with him as they danced to the song they danced to on their wedding day. "I've got you under my skin" Roz felt very proud that night and never wanted to utter her under-the-breath comment. She told her husband he looked gorgeous in his tux singing up there, and she loved him very much, but if he ever keeps another secret from her again, he better pack his bags.

As the evening was finishing, Andy wanted to talk to David. They went with two large scotch's and two cigars and sat on the terrace. "I'm really sorry, David, I acted like a complete prick, an arrogant one. The truth is I really never meant any harm. My offer was genuine; I just sometimes speak before engaging my brain, and I did that night. I really am sorry, and I hope you forgive me."

"Thanks, Andy. it takes a man to admit he's a prick, and I accept your apology."

They both laughed and drank their scotch had their cigar, and Andy said as they were leaving, "I'm here if there is anything I can do."

He whispered in his ear, "Fucking money, I can't spend it all if you need it, just come over and take it we won't mention it I promise."

"I will think about it, thanks. Andy."

13. Never Assume You Know Someone

Stephen called his mum and invited her and Dad over for Sunday lunch, which he had never done before. Obviously, his mum was delighted to be invited. I think deep down, she knew what was coming and was fully prepared. It was hard to judge David and how he would react. We would have to wait and see.

Sunday came around very slowly for Roz. Every day was an effort as she was so tired all the time. They were getting dressed and ready to go, as Roz was chatting with Becky, who was having to work at the museum as she had a delegation from Russia that she was showing around.

Two miles up the road, Andy was out playing golf, and Claire was going shopping with her three friends. Michael was still in bed, and he was playing 5-a-side football with his mates in the afternoon.

Tami was supposed to have come out with her mum and her friends but woke up feeling pretty bad and cancelled. It left Claire so conflicted about what to do, but she thought she would leave her be today.

Roz and David arrived for lunch, and Stephen answered the door. Abraham was getting ready, "Dad, can I ask a favour? For the Spurs game next week, can I have your ticket?" "I have a big client in town, and he is a mad Manchester United fan. Are you serious about such a big game?" "I was really looking forward to it." "Nothing like making your son feel guilty. Don't be so selfish, your son is asking for a favour. You should have just said yes." "OK, OK, mind your own business," he replied. "And when have you ever known me to mind my own business?" Roz quipped, lightening the mood, which drew laughter from the group. David approved, saying, "Yes, that's fine, Stephen." "Thanks, Dad," Stephen replied. He then turned to Abraham and asked, "Hi, Abraham, how are you?" "I'm great, thank you," Abraham replied. "Okay, shall we sit down?" David suggested. The flat they were in was amazing. It was the penthouse and offered incredible views of London. The dining room had glass on three sides and was connected to the kitchen with a huge central island, giving it the appearance of something you might find in a James Bond film.

When they went into the kitchen, there was a man in the kitchen dressed like a chef, so he must have been a chef. "Sorry, Mum, too much pressure cooking for you." Roz laughed and said, "That's fine, so what do we have for lunch?" The chef said, "My name is Romero. I normally work full-time for Mr. and Mrs. Anderson, and they allow me to do private work when they don't need me. When I told them where I was going, they laughed and said, 'enjoy,' they are lovely people, and send them our love."

"For lunch, you have asparagus wrapped with Parma ham and Parmesan shavings with sliced burrata; for the main course, you have roast beef and honey glaze with roasted potatoes, a mixture of green vegetables, and a Yorkshire pudding, and for dessert, you have apple crumble with home-made custard and a fresh fruit salad with cream."

"I hope you have a lovely meal. I have instructed Abraham what to do. I wish you a lovely lunch, guys; thanks a million," said Stephen and Romero left.

"Let's open a bottle of really good red," said Stephen. "How about a bottle of Barolo?" "Perfect," said Abraham. "I agree," said David. Roz laughed, which was a bit naughty as he knows as much about wine as she does about football, thinks Roz.

The lunch was amazing, and then they were having coffee after putting the world to right, and David then said, "OK, darling, we have to go now." Stephen looked at Abraham, and David said, "I'm only kidding. I know you have something to tell us; otherwise, why would we be here?" David continued and said, "Before you start, can I say two things? Firstly, Stephen, you are my son. I am so very proud of everything you have achieved, and I may dig you out often, but I love you more than you can possibly know. I reached a certain age, and instead of concentrating on my dreams whatever they may be, I decided it was about supporting the dreams of my children, you have almost reached all your dreams, but it seems you have now ticked the last box by finding love with Abraham; so, I know you are gay and I am no less proud of you now than I was a few moments ago…" "Any more coffee?" There was a pause Stephen was speechless, Abraham cried, and for the first time in a long time, Roz looked at David with love in her eyes and thought, "Wow where did that come from, I never thought my husband had it in him to surprise me." They all laughed, there was a lot of hugging and then Roz walked over to David, kissed him and said, "I really love you at this moment more than I ever thought possible."

David shouted, "At last, I've done something right." Roz laughed, and David was still hugging Stephen as he cried like a baby and said, "You know, Dad, I will never forget this moment for the rest of my life." David just smiled, and then Abraham came over, ready for the big hug as well David said, "Wow, hold on, let's be like men," and he shook his hand. Roz never needed to say anything to Stephen as he knew how much he was loved, and for her, this would not be an issue. For her, this was the perfect day and also took her mind off the tests she needed to have done.

14. Ding, Ding, Round One

She managed to find the time to have the tests without anyone knowing, the fact no one even had a clue upset her, as she was able to do this without any of her family knowing, made her think that they all took her a little bit for granted, but Roz being Roz she just put it to the back of her mind and smiled, she had the uncomfortable tests, but she knew it had to be done and arrived home with her shopping to make sure no one suspected anything, she asked the radiologist if he could see anything and he said, "Everything will be sent to your specialist. He will discuss it with you," the appointment was booked, and again she used her shopping time to go and see the specialist. For some reason she was extra nervous and started to prepare herself for bad news this time when she went to see him, instead of being shown into the office by his secretary he came out to collect her and very gently put his arm around her as they went into the office they sat down.

She was now feeling incredibly anxious, with a swarm of terrible butterflies fluttering in her stomach. She knew she was about to receive bad news. The oncologist's smile had vanished, and he was now scrutinising the test results through his glasses. Roz sat in silence, a deafening quiet that stretched for about 20 seconds but felt like an excruciatingly long 20 minutes. Finally, the oncologist removed his glasses and gently began, "Okay, Roz, I have the results here, and it appears that we have some work ahead. I want you to focus not on the words I'm about to use to describe what we found but on the steps we will take next. Unfortunately, the sample we took from that area in your stomach indicates the presence of stomach cancer, and it's malignant." Roz just breathes out heavily. "Now we can treat it, and it is still early days so we have a really really strong chance of getting it all, but it will require chemotherapy followed by an operation," he explained, Roz did something she hasn't done in front of anyone for many years she broke down in tears and just felt this sick feeling in her stomach as it dawned on her what she'd been told, I think it's hearing the word cancer that made her feel this way it's something you never ever think is going to happen to you, and she has so much going on. He gets up, walks around his desk, pulls up a chair, grabs her hand and says, "Roz, let's take it one day at a time and tackle it. I'm good at what I do," she holds his hand tight and noticed his hands were cold but strong, and she said, "I'm not ready to die," He immediately came back at her and said, "It's not going to happen you've just hit a bump in the road that's too big to go over or too wide to go around so we are going through it, a bit messy, lots of noise in your head but we will get through this." She knows he can't give her guarantees, so she never asked the question.

Is this something she could keep to herself? The specialist told her, "It will be impossible, as you will need three months of chemotherapy followed by an operation. I will be with you every single step of the way, and if you would like me to explain it to your family, I'm happy to arrange a meeting with whoever you would like there." At this point Roz was furiously wiping the tears away as she didn't want anybody to suspect anything when she went home, she said, "I would like a couple of days to take in what I've heard and come back to you about the meeting, how soon do I need to start the chemo?" She asked. He replied, "The quicker the better every day that goes by is a day lost so I would say it's Monday, today let's aim for Friday and we will take it from there, my secretary will message you with exactly what time you need to arrive for the first session." She was tempted to ask him a question that she sees on every television programme that involves the word cancer, "How long do I have" but she decided not to ask the question partly because she doesn't want to know the answer and partly because she doesn't know how she would take it if he wasn't offering this information, as he sounded positive and she felt she was in the right hands, Roz got up to leave, the specialist stopped her put his arms around her and said, "I'm here for you; Sarah and my team, we will get you through this." She felt reassured as she took advantage of his strong arms around her shoulders by leaning in and resting her head on his chest; the tears started again, but she said, "Thank you," and left. She sat in her car for a few minutes and thought how on earth am I going to face the family without falling apart.

She decided to park the car and get some fresh air. She bought herself a cappuccino and a muffin which is something she never does, sod it, she thought to herself, "I'm going to eat what I want now." and went to sit in the park by the lake to gather her thoughts this was one day she will never ever forget, she felt very alone and scared, and she just wanted to curl up in a ball and be looked after for a change.

Whenever Roz invited the family over, they rarely declined the invitation. This time, she made sure they were all available for a mid-week gathering. As they each inquired about the occasion, she simply told them it was a casual get-together with her children. She was feeling too tired to cook, so she decided to include Abraham and Michael and order fish and chips for the meal.

I don't think Roz has ever been so nervous about anything and had no idea exactly what she would say. She just decided to see what came out of her mouth.

Slowly but surely, they all arrived, and David was running a little bit late as he had a last-minute airport run in the cab. When he arrived home, they all sat down just as the fish and chips arrived, with Stephen, Abraham, Becky and Michael; they all wondered why they were there. I don't think they believed her reason and yet no one asked the question, they just turned up when Roz booked a dinner.

Stephen was the first to ask, "Mum, why are we here? Don't get me wrong, it's nice to see you, but Mid-Week, fish and chips, what's going on…?"

Roz took a deep breath and said, "You're right, Stephen; you are all here for a reason. I have something to say, and I want you all to listen to me carefully and try not to stop me, or I may not get through this," Becky's eyes started to well up. Stephen grabbed Abraham's hand and nearly squeezed the life out of him. David almost stopped breathing as he waited for what Roz was about to say.

She closed her eyes as there was no way she could look at her kids whilst she spoke, and she faced down at her shoes in fear that something might force her eyes to open.

"Here I go," thought Roz, "I have not been feeling well for a little while now, some of you may have noticed, so I went to the doctor a couple of months ago. I went and had some tests," "Why did you not tell me?" says David. "Please." says Roz, "Let me get through this. The test results came back, and I was referred to a gastroenterologist (stomach man). He is a really amazing guy and one of the best in the UK with whole team behind him, I went to see him and went on my own as I didn't want to bother anyone in case it was nothing," as she put her hand on David's leg but still with closed eyes, facing towards at her feet, her hand was shaking, and she could feel her heart beating fast, "It turns out, I have stomach cancer, and it's malignant." Becky starts to cry, as does Stephen, David squeezes her hand, and there is a really terrifying feeling that just swept into the room and seems to send crazy butterflies and sick feelings to everyone's stomachs, she tries hard to continue not to give them too long to digest what they heard until she finished… "Now my specialist says he thinks we have it early, I will need an operation that I will be having in three months following my first round of chemotherapy which starts in three days." "Three days?" screams Becky. "Yes, three days then hopefully, if the chemo works and then after the operation, some more chemo to finish its job, I will be in remission, "A lot of ifs," says a very stunned Stephen. "My doctor really sounded very hopeful and thinks although there is a long road for the next year, I should make a full recovery (lie…he never said that), and I trust him very much.

The revelation left everyone stunned. Becky rushed out of the room, and the sounds of her retching could be heard as she threw up in the toilet. David, on the other hand, sat in silence, tears streaming down his face as if these were the most painful tears he had ever shed. Stephen went over to his mother, embracing her from behind and resting his head on her shoulder. She tenderly cupped his head with her hand and reassured him, "It will all be fine, I promise." Abraham was behind Stephen with his hand on his shoulder, just to let him know he was there....Michael was holding Becky's hair back as she was still wrenching in the toilet, and Roz went to the toilet and said, "Michael, leave her to me," as he left the bathroom, she sat on the floor, and they hugged longer and closer than they had ever done before and Roz managed to calm her down and she said, "Mum, no," said Roz, "How do you know what I'm going to say?" replied Roz, "Because I do, this will not beat me and remember I have a wedding to play hostess for," Becky said, "You're mad, we will cancel the wedding." Roz snapped at her, "No, no, no, firstly I'm still here secondly I need something positive to look forward to, and thirdly, we carry on with our lives," fifteen minutes passed, and Roz and Becky came into the room, "Where's your father?" "He's gone to the garden shed, probably for a cigarette." "I want you all to go home now; I need to spend some time with your father, and I don't want anyone else knowing until after all my treatments. Michael, tell your parents, but please ask them to respect my privacy on this," "Of course, Roz," as he gets up, hugs her hard and tears are rolling down his face, Roz rubs her eyes hard kisses Stephen and asks Becky to go home with Michael this evening, they all agree and leave together in silence all stunned and horrified at what they just heard. Stephen kisses his sister, and they cry a little together, and they all go home.

Roz catches her breath and walks out to the shed and finds David crying/shaking/smoking. When he sees Roz, he says, "I'm so so sorry. I didn't want you to see me like this," she sits next to him and says, "it's me who should be apologising to you for not telling you or having you by my side when I had the tests and saw the specialist," "It's not important," David says as he dries his eyes, "What's important now is that I will be by your side every step of the way from now on and I will be there for you like you have been for all of us for years and years, it's your turn to let me take care of you I love you with all my heart and we will get through this."

She kisses him and says, "OK," as she manages a very slight smile and they walk back towards the house as he puts his arm around her and she nestles into his chest.

Friday came around very quickly, and it was a good day in one way because she had the weekend to really rest from the chemo. It was bad as there was no way she could make the family dinner, and that seemed to upset her the most.

She arrived at the hospital early and was directed to a private department where only patients and one family member were allowed. In the waiting area, a few people were moving about with gowns attached to some sort of drip on wheels, and others were sitting patiently. As she walked through the area, she passed a room with a large TV on the wall, displaying a board listing the films that would be shown. Another room was set up with board games, and there was a small café nearby, it was like a small community, and it dawned on her that everyone she saw had one thing in common with her. They all had cancer and were undergoing treatment, which upset her the most as for that moment, she forgot she was one of them and got upset about what they were going through. Then she realised she was one of them, and she took a huge breath in and out to stop her from crying again.

David never really took in where we were. He just held my hand as we sat, waiting for me to be called into my first treatment. She heard her name called, and a nurse came over and said, "Rosalind, please," "It's Roz," "OK, Roz, my name's June, and I will be looking after you for all your sessions with us, we will get to know each other very well, so you better get used to seeing me," as she smiled and held out her hand to Roz, who grabbed it tight and said, "OK, then let's do this," and off she went, David waited for her to return and sat there feeling powerless to do anything.

The chemotherapy was brutal for Roz, someone who was on her feet running around after her family, cooking, cleaning, and basically running her family. This all came crashing down on her as she just could not do it as much as she tried. After every cycle of chemo, she really suffered, and it took her body a week to recover. Then she had one week of relative calm before the next session. She had lost a lot of weight and looked very thin, her eyes had sunken into her face, and she was almost a yellow colour, and her worst nightmare came true, losing her hair, she never looked good in hats and decided on silk scarves fitted tight around her head and tied at the back, she looked like the mother in fiddler on the roof. David worked nights as she knew Becky was there, and he looked after Roz during the day. She knew how to give lists to David, and he completed every task without question. He also was exhausted, and at the weekends, Stephen and Abraham came around to take over, so he got some sleep. Roz hated it and was a bad patient, often David would come home at 5 a.m. from his night shift to find Roz up and polishing the windows. He never shouted at her as I suppose it was better, she was fighting than lying in bed giving up. Roz was going to fight this as much as she could. She also had a wedding to plan and look forward to.

It was hard to say how Stephen had taken the news as he was not a good communicator; he kept everything inside and decided to just throw himself into his job, and Abraham gave him lots of space. Becky, I think he took it the hardest; she was really struggling. She just could not help herself but think about her wedding. What would happen if her mum was not there? It filled her with dread, and she often thought of telling Michael that they should cancel everything and forget the wedding and getting married ever existed so they could all focus on her mum, but deep down, she knew it would not change anything. She needed to be strong and support Roz.

Nothing tears through a family quite like cancer. It's a spectre that we often believe won't touch our own lives or the lives of our loved ones until it does. For someone like Roz, who was always vibrant and took immense joy in cooking for and spending time with her family, this was an incredibly challenging trial. But when you have a strong and supportive family, you find the strength you need to face adversity. One of the most challenging aspects for her was the loss of her hair. It felt like a visible symbol of her battle. The headscarf, the sunken eyes, the slightly yellowed skin tone – they all shouted "Cancer," and everyone could see it. But this was something she couldn't control, and she was still in the process of coming to terms with having cancer. The stage of anger and frustration would come later, but for now, she was adjusting to her new reality.

15. Swallow Your Pride

Andrew had left a few messages for David to join him for golf, but David kept saying, "No, thank you." Roz was a few weeks into the chemo. The first one was bad; she really struggled and was very sick. The second week, she was better very slightly, and she was fighting, she drove David mad, "Stop saying no to Andrew go and play golf you know you want to…" it was the morning, and David was waiting for Andrew to arrive he asked for the fifth time if Roz was sure, she said, "Go, I'm fine. I'm having lunch with Becky and Stephen. Go have fun."

Andrew arrived with the range rover and his driver. David loaded his clubs in the back, and off they went. Andrew said, "It's only 9 a.m." David said, "No, thank you."

They arrive at the club. David had never been there before. It was the top private members club in this part of the world. The doorman arrives, "Good morning, Mr Anderson; welcome, sir," he says to David, "We are almost family," says Andrew, "Then you are especially welcome." "I will park the car, sir, go to your usual table, and bring the clubs to the buggy area when you have had breakfast."

"Well, this is the golf club's way, isn't it? Smoke and mirrors, smoke and mirrors. Everyone here seems to have their own set of issues, and you really don't want to become a part of this club. I promise you that." Curiosity got the best of him as he turned to Andrew and asked, "What about you, Andrew? What's your story? What secrets are you hiding?" Andrew said, "Oh, David, my story is quite a complex one, and I doubt you'd ever truly understand it. I've just become rather skilled at putting everything in its own little box and storing it away. Thankfully, I can afford plenty of storage space! But how about you?" "Me? I'm a simple guy who really had big dreams once, but nothing really came of it, and now, with Roz, I just want to take care of her." "Of course, I understand… anyway, David, can we have an honest conversation?" "Of course." "I am a wealthy guy, you know that?" "I sort of assumed." "Well, I am. I'm making money all the time, my business never knows recession, and I only invested in my business and property, so without sounding arrogant, paying for a wedding at almost any cost is no issue for me, but for you it's different, and I understand, you want to make your daughter a wedding blah blah blah, for fucks sake David I have more money than I can spend, you don't. We are going to be family. I can give you the money no one ever needs to know it came from me, and happy days are had by everyone…what do you say…? "Wow that was a very convincing speech. Let me discuss it with Roz, Roz, Shmoz." "Can't you make this decision without Roz?" "You mean, don't tell her?" "I mean, don't you think she has enough to think about how nice it would be if you had enough money in the bank to say yes to everything your daughter wanted? Maybe even have a little extra to take Roz on a proper holiday somewhere really special, she only knows you've been putting money to a policy for over 25 years, well it turned out to be a real winning policy…you get me?" "I get you," says David. "I never expected this conversation with you. Well as the godfather says, someday I may call on you to return that favour," they both laughed, David less, but then they hugged it out, and Andrew said, "the money will be in your account tomorrow, "now let's play golf, you have a fabulous wedding to make and a holiday to book."

As David contemplated Andrew's offer, he weighed the pros and cons. "Why not?" he thought to himself. "I do have some savings, and it would be wonderful to take Roz on a proper holiday. Can I trust Andy, though? He does seem genuine, but there's always that underlying uncertainty." David noted that Andrew appeared both nervous and excited about being able to let go and not worry about the cost of the wedding. It was a tempting offer, and David knew that accepting it could alleviate a significant financial burden.

The next day, David checked his account a few times and £100,000 was put into his account. He got a message from Andy saying, "David's money should have arrived. Let me know if you need more, now go make a great wedding and remember the godfather, best wishes Andy."

David was very troubled by this money but kept it for now. Roz booked a Friday night dinner, her first since the chemo started. Everyone was there as usual, plus Andrew, Claire and Tami. Roz looked exhausted like she had aged 20 years, and the silk scarf was making her look worse, but she almost had no hair at the moment, so it was a must to keep wearing it.

16. Friday Night Dinner

They all arrived on time, and it was the first time they had got together since that awful Friday night when everything went so badly. Everyone was on their best behaviour, and I suppose looking at Roz made them all feel so lucky for what they had. Everything else seemed irrelevant.

David made a toast to the future, "Mr and Mrs Anderson, I think it's time we start planning this wedding and getting things rolling. I want this to be a day to remember, and I want to make the exact wedding you have dreamed of." Roz looks at him and frowns, thinking how can he say that we have a certain amount of money, that's one to bring up with him later. Andy says, "We can't wait to celebrate it with you, to which Claire smiles and agrees."

Claire's says, "I would like to talk about Xmas this year. I would like it to be at our house, and I would like you all to come," she stated. Roz, ever the traditionalist, quickly responded, "Thank you, but we always do it at home." David, on the other hand, chimed in with a different perspective. "Well, maybe this year we should do it differently," he proposed. Roz seemed troubled by his idea, but deep down, she knew she wasn't feeling strong enough to host the traditional holiday feast, considering her ongoing health battle. With a sense of relief, she turned to Claire and said, "We would love to come over; thank you."

Tami was very quiet this evening, and you hardly noticed she was there. Claire recognised the signs and kept an eye on her as she sat without really speaking the entire evening until the coffee was served and Tami said, "I've got a sort of announcement to make, most of you know I have been suffering from terrible anxiety and depression, and lately, it's getting really bad, so I have decided to check myself back into the clinic for a month, during this month I won't be allowed visitors or my telephone, I will be out just in time for Xmas, in fact, I come out on the 23rd," Everyone wishes her well and tells her how brave she is being, Claire said, "OK, we will talk about it tomorrow, Mum, I'm going straight there from here," Claire looks angry but keeps it under control as she can't say or do anything without causing a fuss.

The subject changed, and Stephen also had an announcement that he and Abraham were having a baby, which caused a bit of a silence while everyone was thinking… "How on earth do they do that?" Abraham stepped in and said, "Obviously, we can't have a baby the biological way so we are adopting and should have a baby January next year. So not long, we have been pregnant five months already so to speak," everyone laughed and congratulated them, there was so much going on and many announcements that no one realised that Roz had slipped out and gone into the kitchen, where she was standing over the sink with tears running down her cheeks thinking, "I don't want to miss one Friday night again and I want this to last forever," then David walked in and put his arms around her stomach from behind and cuddled her hard to make her feel protected she pulled him in closer and he said, "I know, don't worry you will be here to see everything for many years to come," they both went back inside to a loud laughter as Becky and Michael were talking about hen nights and a stag night that is happening in Sitges in Spain which happens to be the gay resort of Europe whilst Becky is going to a spar hotel for three days and they were laughing as Michael was quite nervous and Andy was taking the Mickey out of him and realised he had two gay guys in the room and over stepped the mark but they all laughed.

As the family got ready to leave, the first said their goodbyes to Tami. She said, "There is absolutely no way you are driving there on your own. I will come with you." This was what Tami had secretly hoped for, and she also wished that her father would join them. However, that didn't seem likely. Andy kissed his daughter and offered his support, saying, "Let me know if you need anything," but in his mind, he knew that the one thing he could readily provide was financial assistance. They left, and it was sad to see the pain in Tami's eyes as she sat in the car with her nose against the window again, something she had experienced before. Nobody should have to go through such mental torture, but I suppose unless you have been through it yourself, you can't understand how powerful it is and what it can do if it gets a grip on you.

After she left, there was a sombre mood to the evening now. Andy left quickly afterwards. Stephen and Abraham also left, apologising for being insensitive and announcing their news after Tami announced hers. Roz kissed them both and said, "You are both good people. The fact you recognised it was proof enough for me, and I love you both." Becky and Michael helped clear up, as Roz had no energy left and reluctantly went to bed.

The evening sort of brought both families much closer without them knowing it. They just shared sadness and joy together without any jealousy or anger…it never went unnoticed by Roz.

17. Roz Had Lunch with Her Mum

Roz's mum lived close by, in a warden-assisted apartment. She was a very sweet lady and very much like Roz, she knew nothing about Roz's cancer as it would probably kill her, so she decided not to tell her. The apartment building she lived in was like a country all on its own, it had its own rules, everyone new everything about everyone and their families as well, the common room was ruled by a couple called Sonny and Ruth Curtis, they organised all the activities; sent out messages by dropping notes through all the doors and you had to drop a note through Ruth's door if you were coming, you could not just turn up unless your name was on the list. The men got together every Wednesday in a group called chaps that chat. They had tea and cake together and moaned about everything for a few hours. Thank goodness the men did not need to write notes and post them to attend. It was hilarious as there were always people wandering about dropping notes off. They probably walked a mile every day doing this (not a bad thing).

Whenever any family friends visited, there were a few ladies who made a point of approaching them and either consoling or congratulating them on their news, just to show that they had heard about it from their parents.

Then there were the bakers, a few women who baked and always brought the cakes to the common room, and there were always a couple of men who liked a drink and always brought a bottle. The TV in the common room was quite a problem as agreeing on what to watch was harder than the Israelis agreeing with a peace agreement with the Palestinians.

The parking situation seemed to be tightly controlled by a couple known as the parking police, Johnathon and Marion Newman. They each had a car, and since there was only one parking space per apartment, one of the Newmans was always on hand to question visitors about their parking habits and the duration of their stay.

Then, there were a few religious couples who tried hard to make everything kosher in the common room and wanted to take over this room for Jewish services on festivals. This caused a problem and always ended up in an argument as it would clash with football being on or some quiz programme like the chase. Everyone seemed to forget that if they didn't like something, they had their own flat to go back to with their own TV, but the truth is all of this kept them busy, active and gave them something to do.

The other thing is that nearly every apartment had widowed women or couples. Come to think about it, there were no widowed men. You know the joke? Why is it always that Jewish husbands die before their wives do…because they decide to…

Unfortunately, the only thing that happened often was death; there was always someone moving in, and there were many welcoming committees explaining the rules.

Roz's mum, Ethel, made lunch, which drove Roz mad, but that was her thing now, cooking and however hard it was. She always managed to cook a fresh lunch for them. She made something called matzahbry, which was matzah crackers broken up, dipped in egg, and fried either with sugar or salt, depending on your preference. This was a weekly occurrence for Roz; she always wanted her mother at her house for Friday night, but that was cards night, and Ethel preferred not to miss it.

Ethel and Claire had a lengthy conversation lasting around three hours. Ethel inquired about any updates regarding her grandchildren. She expressed her disappointment that they didn't visit her more often, although she never openly conveyed this sentiment. Ethel was the kind of person who didn't want to be a burden but secretly wished her family would visit her daily. She wasn't much into the social scene and had an ongoing feud with another woman, stemming from a long-forgotten disagreement. They both knew they were not on speaking terms, but the cause of their dispute had faded from memory.

Roz left her mum having had lunch, left her shopping and some chicken soup for her to freeze and made sure all her mum's hospital appointments were on her fridge door, and Roz, as always, took her to all of them.

Ethel asked her several times about her health, and it was getting harder and harder to hide it, especially because of the silk scarf…but Roz kept hiding it no matter what. She had decided to have a wig made only for when she went to see her mum to prove she had hair; her mum's eyesight was not great, and she got away with it.

18. Xmas Together

Roz agreed after a big fight that this Xmas, she would take it easy and let someone else do the cooking. Although it might sound hypocritical for a Jewish family, she always celebrated Xmas. They never had a Xmas tree or decorations, but for her, it was family time and reason to treat the kids, she looked pretty drained, and her hair was still hidden behind a silk head scarf, and her eyes were sunken into her head, the chemo had taken its toll, and it was tough, but she was fighting it, hiding a lot of the pain and, ready in January to throw herself into the wedding as much as she could, but nervous for the operation.

It was Xmas morning, and lunch was at the Anderson's with the Cohens as their guests with two or three additions; family uncles who had nowhere else to go.

Roz was up early as it took her a lot longer to get ready, especially with the make up to give her face some colour, her lips were always dry, and her eyes were sore, but she never moaned, and she was ready. David had loaded the gifts in the car. Roz loved Xmas time and had this insane way of doing things. Becky and Michael would have submitted their list to Roz a while ago. Roz started buying there presents. They had to have the same amount of gifts; the wrapping paper was different to each other but the same, if you know what I mean. Anyway, they were ready to leave. This tradition never ended when they became adults, and as you can imagine, David is ecstatic that his grown-up children put Xmas list of gifts into us and about September.

Stephen and Abraham were en route, and Abraham's parents, along with his little sister, were also invited. They had been regular guests at Roz's house every year. Claire had no objections to their presence, as she wasn't the one responsible for the preparations. The chef and his wife handled everything, and they typically celebrated Xmas on Boxing Day, which suited them well as they didn't have children of their own.

Becky was making her own way there as she was meeting friends with Michael in the evening.

Tami was at home and decided this year she would not enjoy Xmas and new year as she was on her own and the only one of the family with no partner…it sucked, and she was still coming down to earth after a month in the hospital, and her safe place was no longer there, but I suppose having people around helped her as she was used to that.

Andrew was making sure the wine was ready. Romero's wife, Claudine, had made the most amazing table. It looked beautiful, and Romero had been busy for the last few days preparing the food; it all smelt incredible.

His wife would serve drinks and canopies, and for dinner, they had a young girl, Natalie, who worked for Andrew there to do all the washing up. He paid her treble time and gave her an extra five days holiday for helping out. She was OK with it as she lived on her own, and Andrew invited her for dinner as well as Romero and Claudine to join them.

It was a mad day ahead but a lovely one, they hoped. Picture the seating plan: Andrew at the end to his left, Claire then, Michael and Becky then, Claudine and Romero then, Stephen then Abraham. David was at the far end with Roz next to him and Abraham's parents and sister, then Tami and Natalie.

As the guests began to arrive, punctuality was a priority for them. They were all excited about exchanging presents. They gathered in the spacious main living room, laying out their gifts. The next hour and a half was filled with the joy of unwrapping presents, even if they were items they didn't necessarily need. Wine flowed, and they revelled in the moment, finding a touch of escapism from the various news and events, both good and bad, that occupied their lives.

Champagne with amazing hand-made canopies was served. Every taste was like an explosion on the tongue, and they all laughed, trying to guess what was in them. Most of them got it wrong, but they all enjoyed being together. There was a bond forming between them, yet they knew so little about each other. Would it break that bond or make it stronger? Only time will tell.

When they sat for dinner, they had hot handmade bread straight from the oven with butter that was so tasty. This was devoured as everyone drank their fourth or fifth glass of wine, and then for the main meal, he had made an amazing turkey, roast beef with amazing roast potatoes in goose fat. Brussels in honey and butter with broccoli cauliflower handmade stuffing and gravy, and for a starter, a real treat, he made a large handmade ravioli stuffed with a shredded taster of everything he had cooked for the main meal, which was cooked just before serving. It was incredible. Everyone laughed as they all had one each, and they all tasted something different and shouted out what they could taste; it was warming up the lunch for everyone.

This was followed by a rest. Before his desserts, everyone agreed to help Claudine clear up, and with an organised group clearing, washing up, drying and putting away, it was all done just in time for them to get hungry for his unbelievable desserts that included Xmas pudding, a chocolate fudge cake with a hot sauce that melted the cake as you poured it, a fruit salad with ice cream and special handmade dessert canopies each one different for everyone which they had with coffee again. All experiencing a different taste, they each had something inside them that should not be there, and they had to guess what it was. David's had a hint of beetroot, Claire's had a touch of blue cheese, and Roz's had a tiny touch of chopped liver. It sounded awful, but it tasted amazing. They all laughed as they played this game and just enjoyed being together as one family.

Wow, what a day! They all moved to the lounge and sat together, chatting about what was going on in the world; everyone was a bit merry, and then it all started. Andy said, "well, family, it seems we are going to have an no expensive spared, wedding courtesy of the man himself, David Cohen," everyone said, "That's amazing," and David replied, "Thank you, but of course, it will be amazing but not extravagance!" Andy jumped back in and said, "Come on, David, let's go crazy." David was getting angry and said under his breath, "We will see." Tami jumped in and said, "Who cares? Why does everything have to be about money? There are more important things. I mean, look at Roz and what she's going through, and me, I don't even want to be alive, but let's spend a fortune on a wedding." Wow, that was a real moment that sucked the positive energy straight out of the room.

Michael said, "Sis, that's unfair on Becky and me. We want a wedding to remember, do we?" Becky said, "I'm not sure I want my dad spending all his money to make this and be paying for it for the rest of his life…" "That won't happen," said Andy. Claire then got involved and said, "Let's remember, it's Xmas day, a time for family to be together; stop all this stupid bickering. I'm sure David will have a fantastic wedding; let's move on."

Stephen said, "I've got good news. Abraham and I are going to have a girl. It's what we wanted. We know for sure." Andy said, "Wow, that's clever; not only can you get pregnant as a man, but you can decide the sex, although it must be very, very painful giving birth out of a different place." Abraham looked shocked and replied, "No, it's easy. We just drive to Reading and pick her up." Andy laughs and says something under his breath which, although Stephen never quite heard all of it, he heard enough to get up and say, "OK, we are leaving," everyone said, "Sit down, don't be silly." "I'm not sitting here with him, the homophobic pig" and they both got up and left, taking both parents and his sister with them.

Tami stayed in her room upstairs, and Michael took on the task of making coffee, leaving the four adults, along with a rather uncomfortable Romero, Claudine, and Natalie, sitting around the table. Claire broke the silence, addressing Andy, "I hope you're happy." Andy responded with a grin, "Leave me alone; I had a good night." David interjected sternly, directing his words at Andy: "This all started over the wedding. Why don't you keep your comments to yourself, especially if it involves my son? Anyway, I'm handling this wedding; I don't need your input." Andy retorted, "Really, David? What about the 100 grand I put in your account?" Everyone looked at David, and Roz said, "David, is this true?" Claire looked at Andy and said, "I told you not to do that, you arrogant pig," David looked at Roz and said, "Yes, it is true. I wanted to make her a dream wedding, so I thought, why not, but it bugged me as Andy kept saying that he may call on me for a favour soon, it really stuck with me so I decided to send the money back. If you look in your account, it was sent over a week ago." "Come on, David," says Andy, "Don't be such a moron, you need my money." Roz stood up slowly and said, "We don't need your money. We had survived very well before you came along, and we will survive just fine now and make a great wedding. Take me home, please David. I'm really tired." Claire just looked at Andy and then helped Roz up; they all said goodbye, and as they left the room for the front door, Claire told Andy to just stay where he was.

Claire apologised to Andy, which he heard from the lounge, and shouted, "No need to apologise on my behalf. I'm fine, thank you." They all left, and Tami was in her room, and Becky was with Michael in his room. Claire decided not to have it out with Andy now. So, she headed upstairs to bed, and when Andy realised, she was upstairs, he just laid on the couch and fell quickly to sleep. In fact, it saw him through until the morning.

This was Xmas at the Rubin's. It could have been worse, maybe! But it seems someone keeps breaking these families up and putting them back together again like Humpty Dumpty.

19. Who Knew a Wedding Had So Many Parts

Becky and Michael Had been looking on the internet and shortlisted three venues: one was a monastery, one was a beautiful hotel, and the other was a castle. She booked the viewings across one weekend. She thought it would be better to do them together so they all stayed in their minds. At the first viewing, she wanted to go with Roz and David and then, if it was necessary, could take Michael's parents, but probably not. Becky and Michael came around to Roz, and they were ready to go at about ten o'clock. Roz had been busy putting on her make-up to give herself some colour. Her hair had almost gone now, so the scarf was a real necessity as she never wanted anybody to see her without hair. They left for the Monastery, which was about a 25-minute drive from the house. They arrived at two very imposing gates had a long, long drive and at the very end was this really beautiful sixteenth-century monastery, they met the event organiser who introduced herself as Janet, and they began the tour firstly of the grounds which were magnificent and then as you came in the main entrance to your left was the reception room. Straight ahead of you was the ceremony room, and to the right, two huge double doors leading into a ballroom. It had the capacity for about 250 people. As they went through into the ceremony room, Roz pulled Becky aside and said, "The place is really beautiful, but can we really have a Jewish wedding in a building that looks very much like a church? It just feels inappropriate, but of course, I will go with what you think," "To be honest, Mum, I agree it's very quirky but not for us," David stated, and Michael and Stephen nodded in agreement. They expressed their sentiments to Janet, "Thank you, but this is not the venue for us," and promptly left, making their way to the castle. However, when they reached the castle in the afternoon, their initial impression was not very favourable. As they entered the premises, they were greeted by a farm on the right-hand side, complete with a large building and a strong smell of manure that was quite overwhelming. This unpleasant experience led them to turn around immediately and head for the hotel.

When they arrived at the hotel, the drive in from the main road was beautiful. You crossed three beautiful little bridges with running water underneath; to the left was a golf course and to the right, as you came up to the hotel, was what looked like a walled garden. Two huge walls seemingly made of very old brick with beautiful flowers climbing the walls and two really lovely double wrought iron gates giving you a peak to what was inside, and the front of the hotel was really beautiful. They drove under a canopy with pillars. As they pulled up outside. They were met by gentlemen and welcomed to the hotel, he asked what was the purpose of their visit, and they told him that they were coming to see the venue. He said, "Oh, that's fantastic. Let me go and get Sarah. If you leave your car here, I will park it for you. Please take a seat in the reception area, and Sarah will be along shortly." The reception was really beautiful. It was a very modern hotel with the most amazing art and sculptures in the entrance hall with a big sweeping modern staircase that led up to a small selection of rooms that were in the main part of the hotel. They were immediately offered a drink and sat and had coffee, waiting for Sarah as they were 15 minutes early. There seemed to be a lot of activity in the hotel, and everybody was very well dressed, and it looked beautiful. You could see that Becky was very comfortable here, although David was looking a little pale in the face. Roz noticed the handmade little biscuits that came with the coffee and the fact they were warm. She smiled at Becky, and Michael decided to say very little and wait for Becky's reaction.

Sarah arrived, introduced herself, and sat for a few minutes just getting to know everyone. She explained that should they decide to go forward with the wedding. She would be their wedding co-ordinator for the entire duration of the planning and the day of the wedding.

She said, "What I would like to do is take you around exactly as your guests would see it, and then we can look at the hotel itself." So, they walked out of the front of the hotel and walked along the path about 200 feet to two pillars and an entrance that had the same door as the main hotel, in fact, the same doors were everywhere; they were beautiful, with handles looking like twigs from a tree but in silver, there was a car park reserved for the guests right opposite the entrance to the venue.

As you entered the venue, on the left was a coat room, and then you stepped into a vast and brightly lit reception area. Mirrors lined one side of the room, leading to three sets of double doors that opened onto a circular fountain with plenty of seating on the spacious patio. Three steps down led to tables and chairs shaded by umbrellas, all overlooking meticulously maintained gardens. Sarah explained the setup: "Your guests will enter through this area. Their bags and coats will be taken care of, and they'll be offered a choice of non-alcoholic cocktails or various juices. This will be around 2-3 p.m., and guests can enjoy mingling both inside and outside as your reception area extends to the patio and the lower garden, where we've set up additional tables and chairs."

You could see the look on Becky's face already. Then, at the back of the room, on the right-hand side were two floor-to-ceiling mirrors. She called a guy on her small radio and asked him to open the reception/ceremony doors, and then the two glass doors slid open to reveal a very large high-ceiling room and Sarah said, "This is where you will get married. You can have the ceremony centrally or at the far end." The room was gorgeous, with doors to the left as you walked in, all overlooking the gardens and a beautiful white lace wall as the back drop for the ceremony.

Becky was quiet but very happy. Sarah said, "We like to reveal each room individually as you would do at the wedding. These doors would be shut; then we open them when it's time for guests to take their seats for the ceremony. After the ceremony, we would ask you, the guests to go back and continue the reception where we will serve a mixture of alcoholic and non-alcoholic drinks that's up to you along with a pre-selected and pre-tasted group of canopies, then at the appropriate time we will call everyone for dinner." Sarah used her radio again, and all of a sudden, what I thought was a large wall on the right-hand side was two enormous doors that started to slide open and there in front of me was a fabulous ball room with a dance floor stage and four pillars with a glass wall at the end, it was breathtaking, and they all walked around with their mouths open.

Sarah said, "That's exactly the reaction we want from your guests as we reveal the venue, room by room, during the evening."

"This ball room can seat comfortably up to 290 guests without impeding onto the dance floor, and of course, we have a stage at the far end for your chosen band."

It was the first time David had experienced silence from his wife and daughter. It was very pleasing.

"Then let me take you somewhere else if you wish. We have an area you can also hire should you decide to have guests stay the night before, and something you can do is take over our walled garden." They walked across the path, she unlocked the gates, and they went inside a huge garden with walls all around a big conservatory at the far end, a swimming pool and a seating area. "Here we can do a Saturday evening private barbecue with inside and outside space depending on the weather," they had all said very little to each other up to know.

Becky was not looking so happy as she felt she was seeing the perfect venue they could not afford. Roz was thinking, "David must be having hot sweats," Michael was thinking, "Yea, let's do it," and David was having hot sweats.

Sarah said, "Let's go and look at the main hotel, the bedrooms, and then we can have afternoon tea." They saw the rooms, which, as you can imagine, were beautiful. They were led into a room through some arches at the back of the restaurant, and there laid up was a gorgeous table with fresh flowers and all around an afternoon tea with China cups and a very dainty cake stood full to the brim with sandwiches, cakes and a separate one with hot scones and hot crumpets.

Sarah served them, and then Roz asked, "Do you do this for everyone who comes to look at your venue?" "Yes," she replied, "We want you to have a taste of the experience, and hopefully, you'll choose us." David jokingly added, "We might need to come back several times just for the tea," which elicited a laugh from Sarah.

So, David said, "OK, there is no doubt the venue is amazing. Can we talk prices?" "Of course. Well, the main venue hire is £15,500, the walled garden hire is £4,500 based on 200 for dinner, our menu varies from £150 per person upwards, and the barbecue is £65 per head that includes half a bottle of wine per person. I will give you all the menus to look through. Oh, the reception, including soft drinks on arrival canopies and two glasses of champagne, is £35 per person. This would bring the total to £250 per person and totalling £70,000 plus vat, so £84,000. We have a brochure that recommends florists/bands/dance floors/lighting companies." David jumps in and says, "What for that money? We don't get lights," Sarah smiles and says, "I'm referring to mood lighting you may wish to bring in," she continues, "This is a Jewish wedding, am I correct?" "Yes," says Roz. "We can also recommend a chuppah (canopy) hire company, even a rabbi," they all smiled, "We can also recommend a wedding coordinator," David said, "Again? I thought you were co-ordinating the wedding." Sarah again smiles politely and says, "Of course, we are from our side, but you may well need someone from your side to work with us as well. We also have a list of entertainment that you may wish to have as a surprise to your guests and maybe even the bride and groom. We also have very top hairdressers and makeup teams to recommend, wedding dress and groom suit companies, and last but not least, wedding cake companies." David feels himself shrinking every time Sarah mentions another company. She finishes by saying, "Do you have any questions?" Everyone was frightened to speak and looked at David, and Michael was just about to respond when Becky said, "No, I don't think so." "Dad, do you have any questions?" She had to repeat the question as he sort of zoned out, and eventually he answered, "No, I'm fine, thank you, we have some other venues to see, and we will be in touch, thank you for showing us around and for the amazing tea." David was still overwhelmed by the hot crumpets and scones.

One the drive home, David was just thinking, "84,000 is the base price without all the other things we need, plus guests staying overnight, maybe two nights, this is 120–150,000. Maybe I should talk to Andy again and take his money."

When they got back home, Michael left. Becky went to her room. She was a little quiet, and then Roz made tea for her and David, and they sat down in the extension, not really saying much. Then Roz said, "What did you think?" He replied, "I think it's perfect for Andy if he was paying, but for me, it's out of reach unless we borrow against the house." Roz smiled and said, "You're not such a bad dad, are you?" "I hope not," David replied. "Well, I think we can make this happen." "How can we do that?" said David. "Well, when I started working as an accountant, I got put on the company pension scheme, and when I left work, I continued paying into it, and when we got married, I hived off money every month from the money you gave me and kept up the pension, you would never have known as I do the accounting for us." David looks surprised, "Well, he said how much is it worth?" "Well, I can draw out of it up to 120,00 now, and it will still leave 360,000 that I can take out when I'm 60…" David is entirely gobsmacked and says, "I don't know what to say." "You don't have to say anything, and fuck Andy, we are more than capable of making this a day we will all remember."

David responds with, "It's still a lot of money for one day/not even one day. It's ten hours, that's 12–15 thousand pounds per hour. It's crazy."

"Whatever, stop overanalysing it," Roz responded. "It is what it is, and let's be honest, with everything we have going on in our lives right now, what difference does it make? We have the money, we don't want for anything, we owe no money to anybody, our house will be paid for in five years' time, and I have so much to deal with. I want us to get excited about something and not make everything about my chemo. Now go and talk to your daughter and make her dream come true, with that he gets up, goes over and kisses Roz and says, "You don't know how much I love you and how this family is so lucky to have you," she smiles and David walks away. She takes a deep breath and tries to keep those thoughts out of her head about her pending operation.

He went upstairs and could hear Becky on the phone to Michael explaining why this venue was out regarding the cost and how they would just tell her parents that they wanted a more traditional venue. "This is very chic, but not us." David knocked and waited to be invited in. He came in and sat on the bed, "Well, what did you think about the venue? "Erm, it was OK, a bit chic. We want something more traditional than this, it's too grand, and I don't like the high ceiling. I think it's very impersonal, and as for the walled garden, the swimming pool kills the entire space."

"I also don't like the handles on all the doors. It's like something out of the lion, the witch and the wardrobe."

"Ah," said her dad. "OK, Becky, if that's how you feel, we will keep looking." Becky said, "no problem, Dad, I'm going to lie down. I'm a bit tired." OK, David said, "I will leave you in peace, but can I ask you to do something for me?" "Of course, what is it?" "Tell me the truth about what we saw today, as I'm not sure I believe you," Becky looks away and again says, "I am telling you the truth," "Now say that and look at me," as she turns around, he sees a single tear running down her face and she looks at David and says, "Dad, it's perfect everything she showed us is perfect, I wouldn't change a thing but the cost is ridiculous." "I agree it's crazy, but I never asked you about the cost. I asked you about the venue, didn't I?" "Yes, Dad." she replies, "OK, then, so we agree it's perfect, we do…?"

"Can you do me one more small favour, write down this telephone number?" David asked. Becky, puzzled, questioned, "Why?" "Just write," David urged. "Okay, now what?" Becky inquired. "Can you call Sarah and tell her that unfortunately we will not be pursuing your hotel for our wedding as I wanted something more traditional. It's a shame as my parents loved it, it was within budget, and they wanted to book it," David explained. Becky couldn't contain her shock, "Dad, really? What do you mean it's within budget, how?" David, somewhat amused, replied, "What's the difference? You don't like it…" Becky interrupted, "Are you mad? I love it. It's everything I ever dreamed of…" David, realizing his mistake, smiled and said, "Oh, really? Then what are you waiting for? Call Sarah and book your wedding venue."

David goes downstairs as Becky is already calling Michael and screaming uncontrollably. Roz says, "I guess you told her?" "I did." "Good, I'm tired; I might have a lay down now.…" "Mum, Mum, Mum, did Dad tell you?" Becky screams as she runs down the stairs. "I think I knew, Becky." "You need to know this is only possible because of a pension your mum has been paying into for over 30 years, your dad's policy and some hardwork on the cab."

"I love you both. I don't know what to say." "Have you called Sarah?" "Omg, not yet; I'm going to do it right now…"

That was a memorable night for everyone, especially Roz, as she was not sure how she was feeling, happy, scared out of her mind, or at times, excepting that she may not be at her daughter's wedding…time will tell.

20. Family Updates

Becky…

Ever since the venue was booked, Becky has been really busy with work and also looking into all the other aspects of the wedding so she can present it to Mum and Dad.

Michael…

He has been very busy at work, especially since his dad is never there now, and Michael wants to leave the business officially and is waiting for the right time to speak to his dad. Michael is yet to be told about what his grandfather has left him.

David…

Has had his head down working as he still needs to add that extra 10,000 pounds to his part of the money. He feels a bit of a failure, as it's really Roz paying for the wedding, not that Roz thinks that way, but inside, he feels a little ashamed.

Roz…

Super woman, as she is called, is still having the treatment, and it's really tough. Some days, she just cannot get out of bed. She's eating very little and doesn't go out that much. Friday nights have gone back to her cooking, and everyone is getting on with their lives, and Roz is really struggling.

Stephen…

He is very busy at work; he has just been promoted, and he and Abraham are still going through all the final interviews for their adoption. Abraham is getting more stressed than Stephen. I think Stephen is only doing this for Abraham anyway, so he's not in a rush to have a baby. Abraham has agreed to give up work and is ready for January.

Abraham…

He went to see his parents (on his own) to see if he could explain what was going on in his life. This would not be an easy conversation; his parents live in North London, and they lived in an apartment that was at the back of the church where his dad was the reverend for.

He arrived, and his mum had made lunch. His father was out with one of his community members that needed help, so they never waited for him. They started; Abraham's mum was a really lovely, positive lady and ran the church choir. She was a bit like Roz in many ways, a real family lady who cooked amazingly.

"Mum, I need to talk to you. This is a very difficult conversation to have with you." "Please, tell me you are not ill," "No, Mum, I promise." "Then, unless you have committed a crime, whatever you tell me will be OK." "You might not feel the same when I tell you what I've come here to say." "OK, I'm listening…" "Mum, I only know one way to say this, so I'm just going to say it: I'm gay, Mum. I've been living with a man, my partner, for a while now, and that's not all. He's white and Jewish, and we are planning to adopt a child and get married; Michael is his name. He wants us to get married by a rabbi." There was a silence. Abraham had said the entire thing with his eyes closed. They were still shut, his mum cleared her throat, and she started to cry. That's not what Abraham was expecting, "Mum, why are you crying?" "Because I just realised, I don't know my own son. I know nothing about his life. He's like a stranger to me." Abraham reached across the table to hold her hand. She pulled it way, and this really shocked Abraham. His mum got up and said, "How do you expect me to react when you drop this bomb on me, I don't know what to say…gay/living with a man/in love/he's white/Jewish. You are adopting a baby, I suppose that will make me a grandmother, and you want a rabbi to marry you; that's about it." "Mum, I'm sorry, but I had to tell you it's been killing me. And Dad…" "Oh my god, your father, you can't tell him he will not react well to this, and he will be here in 20 minutes." "Mum, I have to tell Dad, no you don't; you can't. I don't know how he will react. I will need some time to process this and decide what we should tell your father. I think you should go. I will tell him you had to cancel the visit." "Mum, are you kicking me out?" I'm just saying, I won't be able to hide it from your father. He knows me too well, and you can't stay here. I won't lie to him," Abraham expressed his concerns. Becky responded firmly, "But, Mom, we're already lying to him by not telling him." Becky's mother considered this and said, "Only if he asks, which he probably won't. Please go, and I need some time." "Alright, Mom," Abraham said as he leaned in to kiss her. As he closed the door behind him, he could hear her starting to cry, and it deeply saddened him. However, he was also relieved that he had shared the truth with his mom.

Andrew…

Has been away a lot and playing golf. He has tried to expand the business by adding other companies to his, but so far, no luck. He and Claire have been on very shaky ground, but Claire is focusing on Tami. Andrew is still mad about the meeting with his father and feels he is being punished. He hasn't told his dad that he wants to see Michael and Tami to explain what he's doing, which is very unfair, especially as he knows how unhappy Michael is working in the family business.

Tami…

Getting ready for her big exhibition that has been delayed for two years since her anxiety attack and two stays in hospital, she's doing OK, but you feel she could go downhill very quickly. She and Claire have got close, and she is very reliant on her mum now, but things are calm, although Tami is walking on her own egg shells at the moment, trying to stay calm.

Claire...

She is doing what she normally does, burying her head in the sand about Andrew and worrying about Tami, but none of it interferes with her weekly pampering and shopping trips. This is the first year she's unsure of what's happening in the summer as she has the wedding at the end of August to plan.

21. The Operation

Roz woke early as she had to be in the hospital by 6 a.m. David was up and dressed before she woke as he knew that Roz would like some space and time to shower and prepare her own bag as she would be staying in for seven to ten days. She still managed while David was at work to prepare and freeze at least ten dinners for him to defrost and put in the oven, she left post-it notes everywhere, and Becky took all her holiday owing to her to be around for whatever was needed at home, Stephen did the same, this was a time for the family to be there for Roz and make sure she never worried about stupid things like the house and food, it all seemed so irrelevant, but they never made it feel irrelevant otherwise it made the life Roz led seem a joke which it definitely was not as she was more than the glue that held it all together.

She was very quiet this morning and looked frightened and almost helpless for the first time. It was time for David to step up, and it looked like he was going to be there for her to lean on.

She arrived at the hospital on time. The specialist came in and met David for the first time. He explained the operation to them both, and in his very reassuring way and confident smile, he told Roz, "Let's go with it. I will be ready in an hour or so. We are going to get the bastard out of you," Roz looked very frightened but mustered up a smile.

The anaesthetist came in to see Roz and David and explained what he would be doing he also seemed very nice and professional. The room was a typical hospital room, small/simple and cold.

Stephen and Becky arrived, making their way to the room where Roz was resting. Roz welcomed them with a warm smile, and, for once, she didn't utter her usual words, "Why are you here? Don't worry about me." The truth was, she cherished having her family by her side.

There was a huge bunch of amazing flowers with a message that just read to Roz: we are thinking of you and always here the Rubins' xx.

The nurse came to collect her, and she waved at the kids, and off she went. David joined her on the walk to the theatre, holding her hand until the door to the theatre hit the trolley. He gave her a kiss, and she said, "It will be fine; we have so much still to do," and he let go of her hand and watched her disappear through the doors.

David took both Becky and Stephen for lunch, as there was no point waiting. She would be in for at least four hours. Lunch was pretty quiet; they just talked about what they would do after the operation to support Roz and make life easier for her, which she would hate but may have no choice.

They came back to the hospital. The time went slowly, but the operation was now five hours into it, and everyone imagined the worst. They were getting very fidgety trying to enquire as to how long she would be, but the staff were so well trained to say nothing yet make you feel everything is going well, then six, hours and 28 minutes later the surgeon came in and said alright guys, "We've finished it went OK." Sorry it took so long, but there was a little more than I thought. We haven't managed to get rid of all of it, but we certainly did a lot of good. The next stage is four to five days to recuperate from the operation as we had to go in open her up a little more, and unfortunately, key hole was not going to work, so let's arrange on Monday to meet by then, Roz will feel stronger, and I would have had the scan results back, and we can talk about the plan, but I'm happy where we are right now, she is in recovery and should be back shortly, she won't be up for a few hours yet, and then she will be very drowsy, I suggest you see her give her a kiss then go home and get some rest, come back tomorrow late morning by then she would have eaten a little, and we might even have her up as we don't want her getting used to the bed." David thanked him, and he left…Roz came back; she was asleep.

They all gave her a kiss, and she briefly opened her eyes but then closed them and went back to sleep.

Everyone was chipping in. David was in charge of shopping, and Becky and Stephen cleaning the house. That was the majority of the weekend done; Stephen said at the end of it, "How often does Mom tidy the house? And when do the cleaners come in? She doesn't trust cleaners, always cleaning some part of the house every day, vacuuming daily. Oh my God, I never realised how demanding that was. And we didn't have laundry to wash and iron, no cooking dinner every night, and let's not forget every Friday night as well… I feel terrible about some of the things I said to her, and I'm filled with self-loathing." David comforted him, saying, "Come on, don't be so hard on yourself. She'll be alright, and she'll get back on her feet and resume her routine. She wouldn't have it any other way."

The Monday came around, and Roz was up and sitting in the chair. She looked very frail and not like the wife and mother. They all new, but they kept reminding themselves that this was just temporary.

David arrived and brought croissants and hot coffee from Starbucks. They sat and had breakfast together, and Roz ate the entire croissant. As she finished, in walked her specialist, "Good morning, Roz, David, so how are you feeling? Tired?" "I think he means me, oh of course, sorry," Roz smiles and nearly laughs, "I'm OK, a little sore but better than I thought I would be." "Well, that's good news, so let me tell you where we are, the scan is back, and as I mentioned, we never managed to get all of it, but we did manage to get at least 80%, "that's good, right?" says David. "Yes, it's good, but we are not there yet. We have the chemotherapy part two to hopefully do its work over the next three months."

Roz says, "That takes me to the end of April. My daughter gets married end of August. I need you to promise me I won't be in the middle of more chemo when she gets married." "I promise, Roz, but it's known about your mental attitude, focusing on the wedding, and you know what to expect with the chemo, so let's take it one week at a time, OK, any other questions?" So many to ask, but they both don't want to ask them now,

"No we are fine," says David, "Good, I will see you Wednesday; hopefully, Thursday, you can go home and take two weeks to completely rest even getting away would not be a bad idea." Roz laughs and says, "It would be very nice to get some sun!"

They thank him, and he leaves. David updated the kids, and Roz just took it easy whilst in the hospital. David thinks she rests well in the hospital. It's when she comes home that's the problem. David kisses Roz and leaves. On his way home, he makes an impromptu stop at the Rubin's; Claire answers the door and is surprised to see David. What's wrong? She says, "Is it Roz? "No, no, no, nothing like that, I just wanted to ask you a favour." "Of course, come on in." "Andy, can you come into the kitchen? We have a visitor." "Oh, hi, David, how are you? Is everything OK? How's Roz?" "She's OK, just recovering, that's why I'm here. We have three weeks until Roz starts her chemo again, and the specialist says she needs complete rest to build up her strength for the next cycle, and I was wondering…" "Of course," interrupts Andy, "How much do you need…?" Claire screams, "There you go again, shut up and let the man finish," "No, I don't want money from you, but in a way, I do. I was wondering if I could take Claire away for three weeks and stay at your villa in Italy. I can't afford a holiday with the wedding, but I thought this would be perfect," Claire sheds a tear and says, "David, of course, we would be delighted you can have it for as long as you need, three weeks is perfect." David says.

Andrew looks at Claire. "We haven't been there for a while. We can just relax for a few weeks. Andrew, do I really need to say it?" "What! They want to go on their own, just the two of them, not with you and me…" "Oooooh OK, sorry, yes, of course I understand."

"Thank you so much. I'm going to book the flights and give Roz no chance to back out during that week," Claire organised everything and provided David with all the necessary details, allowing him to simply arrive and feel at home. What Andy didn't reveal to them was his arrangement for Romero and his wife to arrive one day ahead of David and Roz. They would act as their personal chef and housemaid, attending to their every need. This meant that David and Roz wouldn't have to worry about preparing meals, brewing coffee, or even tidying up during their stay. Claire tells Andy, "Why is it? You can be so thoughtful. There is a good man inside you trying to get out." Andy just takes it as a compliment and leaves it at that.

Roz was swept off her feet when she came home. David gave her two hours to pack. They were being collected to go to the airport by Andrew's driver. David booked first-class seats for the short trip to Italy. Andy arranged for them to be met at the airport and taken to the villa, and to their surprise, Romero and his wife were there to greet them and told them exactly what they were here for and that they needed to do nothing but enjoy the sun and relax.

This turned out to be an amazing tonic for both of them, especially Roz, who by the last week had eaten well every day. The food was incredible; she had a lovely colour to her face, and she looked so different. By week three, she got used to it and was not overly happy to come home as she knew what she had to face, but she was ready for it and in a good place mentally as well. When they arrived home, there was a letter pinned to the fridge, and it read:

"Dear David and Roz,

Please find enclosed a voucher that entitles you to use our villa in Italy for as many weeks as you want from today until we are all too old to travel. This will always include our chef and house maid, and as it's our private villa for family only, there are many months it is unused. Please feel free to confirm it is empty, and it will always be yours.

P.S. I also enclose a voucher for air-miles to be used via my net jets account to fly you there privately.

We hope you enjoyed your three weeks there at our villa at your disposal.

Lots of love, the Andersons."

Roz was overwhelmed by this gesture, and David was too. They unpacked and ordered some food and sat quietly, both thinking about what the next few months would bring. They were both lost in their own thoughts…

22. Who Knew a Wedding Could Cost This Much

So, the wedding is getting closer. Becky and Michael have been busy getting quotes for things, and to be honest, I felt a bit sorry for them as there was so much going on in the family. The excitement towards their big day was not really gathering momentum as it should. Becky was trying her best.

They came over to sit with David and Roz to run through some things. Roz told David to put his wedding face on, and we must start to get into the spirit of these amazing celebrations coming up. It's hard to hide how Roz looks and feels, but she really goes to the effort and gets dressed, make up on a bright scarf and lays a cold lunch so she doesn't have to get up for anything.

Becky and Michael arrive. They all sit down and have a really nice lunch. David clears up, and then Becky pulls out a huge folder and says, "Okay, Mum and Dad, I have broken everything down." David replies, "Stop selling, this is not a presentation at work. Let's just go through what you have chosen. We are both interested and excited." "Okay, then firstly let's talk food." Roz gets interested, and Becky begins explaining.

XO Calamari Burger

A scarlet red burger brimming with squid, mackerel and XO sauce.

Lobster Burger, Panino Nero

A panino nero bun is home to a chunk of meaty lobster on a cocktail stick, then topped with half a gherkin.

Durstone Rock

English goat's cheese with parsley chlorophyll and cep mushroom coating. Don't be put off by the secret ingredient chlorophyll – what one would traditionally associate with photosynthesis – in this case, it operates as a super-super food.

Smokehouse Sea Trout

Instant smoked sea trout presented in the most unlikely way – sat atop a stick, ready to be plucked and enjoyed with wasabi.

"I think we get the picture, OK? Please don't tell me how much each one costs, as I'd rather hear what you want and then hit me with the total afterwards." "OK, says Becky." Then David says, "OK, OK, I'm a sucker, but how much is one of the lobster burgers." "Dad, I thought you said you didn't want to know?" "Go on, hit me with it, it's £4.50…" David lets the number sink in and says, "Calmly, so if everyone has one of these, I assume they are as big as a fingernail that comes to £900." "Yes," David says, "Roz, your maths is perfect. I suggest you eat before you come, that will save £4.50. OK, OK. I'm only kidding. Please carry on, my darling, but we get the canapés." Becky laughs and says, "OK, next is for the main dinner, what we like."

Starters

A fan of sushi, pizza slices of lobster marinated in cognac and caviar, giant lemon prawns and champagne vol-au-vents.

Soup

Gaspachio, pea.

Main course

Roast venison with all the trimmings, Dover sole, grilled deboned in a lemon and garlic sauce with fresh small potatoes, broccoli and spinach.

Desert

A trio of champagne-soaked strawberries with a handmade ice cream.

"There is one menu we really wanted to have but were not sure if you would agree," Stephen began. "OK," says Roz, "Let's hear it." "Alright, Mum," Stephen continued, "Chopped liver or egg and onion followed by chicken soup and then roast chicken with roast potatoes and baked rice with broccoli and runner beans, accompanied by a homemade stuffing. For dessert, there will be apple crumble with custard, cheesecake, or fruit salad with cream. And on the menu, it will say at the top 'inspired by Roz'." "Are you serious?" Roz asked in surprise. "Deadly serious," says Becky, "It's our wedding, and that's what we want," Roz looks at Becky and starts to cry, Becky holds her tight, and they have a moment together. I think David gets it, and he looks at Michael and mouths to him, "Thank you, what a lovely idea. To be honest, I hated the other menu. At least everyone knows what they are eating and won't go hungry," "You're right, Mum, but remember you are not cooking or supervising the food, you get one meeting with the chef at home, and he watches you cook a Friday night dinner, then it's up to him and his team to recreate the whole meal," "It's a deal," Roz says.

Then Becky says, "OK, that's the food; we think we have found the right band; they do everything." "Jewish music and modern music for our friends, there is one problem, they don't do swing, so I was wondering Dad, if you would sing a few songs for us." David looks confused, "You mean you want me to actually get up and sing?" Becky nods. "Oh my god, of course, it will be an honour. I won't let you down," "I know, Dad, I've heard you sing." David gets a bit emotional now. It's getting a bit silly; everyone's crying except Michael, who never cries. He did once recently when Roz told them all her news, but otherwise, no.

"Florist, we are using a friend of ours, and the photographer and videographer is a uni friend who got a degree in photography, and he's agreed to do it. Rabbi is coming from our synagogue, you know him. Well,

Rabbi Levy, he's bringing the chuppah, and the band will sing at the service."

"Dad, I want to walk down the aisle to sunrise and sunset. I know it's what you danced with your mum at your bar mitzvah, too, and it's a way for me to have her at the wedding, dresses and all that jazz, Mum, we will do together, and I think that's about it."

"Wow," David remarked, "That's quite a lot to digest. You've planned this meticulously. I'm at a loss for words, except to say that I'm immensely proud of both of you. Becky, your decisions reflect your kindness and thoughtfulness, which are qualities that define you and more." As David spoke, Roz simply smiled at Becky, and that smile conveyed a thousand words of appreciation for both of them.

Becky so badly wants her mum at her wedding, but she's not naive. She's sort of preparing herself for what happens if she's not there by doing things that have her mark on them.

They all live in the hope that it will be a joyous occasion with everyone who can come right now will be there on the day.

The really crazy thing is that it became such a lovely day going through and hearing about all the amazing surprises David forgot to ask the price. He told Roz, "See, I'm not all about how much. I can also get caught up in the moment," "I know you are amazing," says Roz, "Let me ask you one question. David, when they left, you went to the toilet, did you phone Becky to get the price?…truth please" "OK, OK, so I did…, and we may have enough left over for me to eat a canopy or two," Roz smiles and says, "I'm sorry but today really knocked me out I'm going to bed." David watches her go up the stairs and has his own moment as it dawns on him: how could he possibly live without her?

23. Fred Delivers

It was a dark morning, and normally, Claire was up hours before Andy. Still, this morning, Claire had a migraine and slept it off, she finally rose at 11, and Andy was still there. However, dressed and ready to go out, but when Claire saw him, he said he didn't feel right leaving her in bed, so he thought he would wait until she was awake, that's was kind of him, and Claire began to make herself some tea and dry toast, and Andy said yes to the coffee.

Andy seemed on jitters this particular morning; he kept looking out the window, and Claire noticed it. Andy said, "It's just I'm waiting for some important post about a new business I'm waiting to buy, and we should expect the letter from his lawyers today. Why don't you call him old fashioned fart wanted to do everything by letter writing, can you believe it, go," she said. "I'm up. If it comes, I can open the letter," "No," says Andy, "I need to sign for it personally to prove I received it, some stupid law," Claire is now smelling something. Still, eventually, Andy leaves, thinking there's no post to look at.

He is off to see his seventh, or eighth new business that he has tried to buy and bought a total of none so far, and they are all re-hire him to be away for three days at a time. Claire continues her day, although somewhat slowly, and then Fred the postman arrives. He's very happy. He's been their postman for years when they go away, he keeps all their post and delivers it back when they get home, he picks up all the parcels left outside when they are away in case people realise, they are away and the house is empty.

Fred was preparing to give a talk on his experiences as a postman and his personal philosophy. One of his neighbours happened to be a motivational speaker and often cited Fred as the embodiment of exceptional work ethic and going above and beyond in one's job. Some companies even instituted 'Fred awards' in recognition of outstanding dedication and performance. He was gradually becoming a bit of a superstar in his own right, yet he remained deeply passionate about his work. The thought of giving it up never crossed his mind.

"I picked up this and got told it must be signed for by the Mr in the family," says Fred. "I suppose he's not in," "Correct," says Claire. "Mmm, well, OK, Claire, it's not like I don't know you. It's almost ten years since we met."

He hands over the post and leaves. Claire sits at the kitchen table and goes through every piece, some trash and flyers, then there's a letter from the company he went to see last month in Leeds. She opens it and sees the news is good. It seems he's finally been successful at buying one of these companies, and then a strange letter to Mr Andrew Anderson and Miss Adriana Salvino. She stares at it for a while and keeps thinking she knows that name, but she's not sure where from anyway she decides to open the letter it says:

"Dear Mr Anderson and Miss Salvino

We are delighted to inform you that Poppy and Summer have both passed the examination for the American School of Performing Arts in Rome. However, we require a meeting with you both to secure their position. As you must appreciate, we have many students wishing to attend this school, and your family interview will be very important for the acceptance process.

I look forward to hearing from you in order to confirm the date in August for us to meet.
Regards

Headteacher
Mrs Montoya."

Claire read the letter several times and just sat there quietly she poured herself a glass of wine and then the phone rang it was Andy… "Well, did the letter come…?" "Errrm, yes, yes, it did, and it seems you were successful." "Oh, that's great news. What's wrong? You sound terrible" "Oh, nothing, I will be fine, just having one of those days," "OK, take it easy. I will see you later," "OK, bye." She placed the phone down and, feeling overwhelmed, she read the letter repeatedly. However, her mind soon became a jumble of thoughts, leaving her in a state of confusion. This mental chaos was part of the issue she was grappling with. In her distress, she reached out to her mindfulness coach, and fortunately, he was available. They engaged in a 30-minute mindfulness session, which helped to calm her down and regain clarity.

She hung up and decided to take the letter, put it away, and return to it soon. Claire had always had the ability to let things go or park them, but as the saying goes, 'These things don't go to your boots', and one day they will be released from her box. They will come out eventually, for now, this letter was hidden in an actual box as well as one in her mind, and she decided to go and see Tami who was days away from her exhibition, and Claire knew she would be panicking so she just left the house and went to see Tami. She left everything on and even left the front door wide open as if she was so troubled, she just needed to leave at that moment, the thoughts running through her mind about the letter sounded so crazy and impossible she just blanked it out of her mind.

This could not possibly end well. It was just a question of when she really understood what was going on, and a light bulb came on. That would be a very sad and painful day for her, painful for Andy for sure.

24. The Napkin Rings

"I want to tell you about a thing that took place a while ago. It's all hopefully sorted now, but I wanted you to hear about it."

So, David has been getting hot sweats. He was at home having breakfast. Roz was still in bed. He's eating his favourite, toast well done, crispy bacon sausage and mushrooms. Just as he takes a bite, his phone pings, and he thinks, oh shit, it must be Becky it was the message read, *"Hi Dad, all OK 😀 I'm just finalising a few things, and the caterer wanted confirmation regarding the napkin rings I chose, which works out at 2,000 plus vat to rent the 200 we need for the wedding I'm assuming that's OK, but wanted to let you know ♡ lots of love your little girl xxx."*

David writes back, *"Sure darling, no problem 😊 love you lots, Dad x."*

He carries on eating his breakfast and thinks about the message from Becky, which is a dangerous thing and has a weird thought. He messages Becky back and says, *"Hi darling, just a thought, please hold off ordering the napkin rings, will discuss later xx."*

"OK Dad, but I need to give an answer this week, or we won't get them in time."

Roz comes down the stairs and shuffles into the kitchen. She actually smelt the bacon and felt hungry. David jumped up and said, sit here; I will make you breakfast she smiled and sat down. Roz is very weak but seems to have some colour in her cheeks, and they both sit and have breakfast together, talking about the wedding. David doesn't bother Roz over napkin rings.

It was a peaceful Sunday morning, with Becky busy preparing breakfast for Michael's upcoming visit. David, unable to sleep after his night shift as a cab driver, joined them for breakfast. To their delight, Roz was also up, and they all gathered around the table. As they began to eat, David suddenly said, "I've been pondering those napkin rings." Roz turned her attention to him, curious, and said, "What?"

"I've been contemplating the napkin rings." "I thought that's what you said," Roz said. "Let me tell you my thinking, Becky, you want to order napkin rings that are ten pounds per person, which comes to 2000 plus VAT 2,400 for napkin rings," and says Roz, "Well what happens when everyone comes into the ballroom and sits down what's the first thing that happens," "The bride and groom comes in," "What else?" "The wine is served; the host makes his speech (nu)" "What else?" "Nothing." "OK, the first thing that happens when everyone comes in and sits down, the waiters come around to take the napkins out of the napkin rings. They give you your napkin and take away the napkin rings, these 200 napkin rings that I'm paying 2000 plus vat for make the shortest appearance from all the thousands of elements in this wedding."

"I'm not paying 2000 pounds for them to be there for one minute, then that's it, and I don't even own them. That's just to rent them; they don't come out again, and when have you ever heard someone say, 'Oooh, the wedding was amazing and those napkin rings!' So, you get my point?" Roz says, "Are you OK, David?" Becky sits quietly, and Michael is a bit lost in the whole conversation as he's not good at picking up on this stuff. David says, "Leave it to me, and I will sort them out," Becky says, "But, Daddy, I really like these ones they are beautiful." "Becky, I'm sure they are. I will buy you a set of 6 for your home. You can use them there, BUT I AM NOT PAYING 2,400 POUNDS FOR NAPKIN RINGS THAT I ONLY RENT. I WILL SORT THIS ONE OUT," "OK…OK," Becky says.

The following week, David starts to think about where he can get napkin rings from, and he remembers whilst being in the cab, he passes Shoreditch, a trade catering supplies business, so he stops on the way to town and speaks to the guy behind the counter, "Hi, can you help me, I'm looking for napkin rings," "OK, how many, sir?" "I need 200, say 210, just in case," "We probably don't have that many, but maybe we can order them," "Can I see them?" "Of course, give me a minute," David is feeling really good about this. The guy comes back and says, "Here you go, sir, we have three, one in silver plated, one in gold plated, and this elaborate design with carving," "OK, great, how much are they?"

"They range from 12–25 each plus vat." "Mmm, what discount do I get for 210?" "We can give you our trade price of a 10% discount," "That's still too much can you do better?" "I'm sorry, company rules," "OK, thanks," and David leaves. A few days later, David is having lunch with the boys on the cabs, and he explains his napkin rings dilemma to see if anyone knows anyone, no luck. David was now under pressure to deliver the napkin rings and a lot cheaper than the ten pounds per piece for hiring them.

A few days later, David was on a cab run to Gatwick Airport. As he often did, he struck up a conversation with his customer. "So, where are you headed?" he inquired. The passenger replied, "I'm off to Spain for business, I'm afraid." Curious, David asked, "Mind if I ask what line of work, you're in?" The man answered, "I own an events company, and it's an annual conference where all our suppliers and new event ideas come together." David couldn't resist: "I know this might be a long shot, but do you happen to work with catering companies?" "Yes, of course, it's vital for us, but we also own a huge warehouse with equipment as it's too expensive to keep hiring the equipment." Then David launches into his story, and the guy thinks it's hysterical. Such a typical man thing to do, says the guy, "We have to win on something even if it ends up costing us more; we need to show we make the decisions." They laugh about it, and as the guy leaves, he gives David his card and the name of his warehouse manager. "I will email him to help you out and see if we have what you need." "That's really kind of you," says David, "Have this trip on me." The guy refuses but thanks him for his offer…

David gives it a few days and calls the guy. He is expecting David to call, so the guy kept his word and did email him. David explains his problem, and again, he thinks it's hilarious. David says, "Why does everyone think it's so funny? It's serious stuff I need to deliver here," says David. The guy laughs with him and says, "OK, so give me a minute I will check," he comes back and says, "Yes, you are in luck. We have boxes of them in storage," "Great," says David, "So how much would it cost to hire or buy them?" "You can't buy them as we need them. Still, you could rent them, not that I have a clue how much to charge you. Still, it's irrelevant. My boss told me not to charge you as long as you collect them and deliver them back to us." David says, "That's amazing, thank you, can I have the address?" He says, "Sure we are about 40 miles outside Dublin on a small industrial estate," David thinks shit I thought he was in London, "OK," says David, "Leave it with me, and I will come back to you."

"This now is not about how much it costs. It's about saving face with my family." David looks into flights to Dublin and starts to plan his trip in secret. He can get in and out in one day and pay for an extra weight allowance so he can take one big suitcase and two cabin bags, which he plans to take out empty and bring back full of napkin rings. David cannot really believe what he is doing, but once he starts and puts his foot down, he could not go back. It sort of gathered momentum, and now he must deliver.

Meanwhile, David was on the hunt for a local supplier but wasn't having much luck. He thought to himself, "I know, let me give Steve a call; he knows a ton of people." So, he dialled Steve's number, and like everyone else, Steve found the situation quite amusing. He said, "I might have an idea, although it's a long shot. I'm currently supplying kitchen equipment to a Chinese gentleman who's opening a new restaurant. I'll inquire if he uses catering companies." "Great," David replied, and while awaiting Steve's response, he continued his search. A few days later, Steve called back with some promising news, saying, "I think we're in luck." "This guy is having a grand opening of his restaurant, and he will be inviting over 250 people. He will be using napkin rings, and, well, I told him about your problem. He thought it was really funny, and he said of course you can borrow them as long as you put some leaflets in your cab and bring clients looking for food to his place." David said, "Deal, how and when do I get them? well he's opening the week before the end of August bank holiday. You can have them after that." "Fine," says David, "The wedding is a few days after that. Still, I will get one of my cabbie mates to collect them and take them straight to the hall. What are they like?" "Hold on, he sent me a picture, got it?" "Yes," says David, "They look OK, silver with a little motif that's perfect, Steve, you are my hero, no problem any time."

Phew, David can rest; he saved over 2000 pounds on bloody napkin rings. He starts to think, "I wonder how much more I could have saved if I really get involved in everything," then thinks of Roz and decides to leave well alone, he's delivered, and that's all he cares about.

25. Claire Takes Her Parents Out

Claire wonders why her relationship with her own kids is not great; her own relationship with her parents is fantastic, so why can't she get it right with her own…? Today she's having supper with her parents at a local Italian restaurant, her parents go there every Thursday at 6.30, at the same table. They know the owner and the staff, and the food is great, so what's to complain about?

Her parents are very successful. They started a small bakery over 40 years ago in Stamford Hill, and they went on to open another ten within the same area and then brought a city type in to help them expand. They ended up with over 250 small high street bakers that got sold to a hedge fund for an enormous amount of money. We are talking many hundreds of millions, and they still live in the same house about three-minutes' walk from Claire's house. It's a magnificent eight-bedroom, 30 acres of land, swimming pool, gym, hair salon, cinema room and many other things that they never use.

They live half the year in Spain, in Marbella, and they cruise for at least six weeks and the rest of the time they spend in their home in the UK. They are very humble people and never lose the value of money. They worked very hard to get to where they are now and still feel young enough to travel. Claire arrived first at the restaurant and met with the owner for a quick drink before her parents arrived. They hated seeing her drink alcohol, which she never did anymore in front of her parents. The parents arrived shortly after, and they all sat down together to enjoy a good Italian meal. Claire's parents had never held much affection or trust for Andy, and they had long held the belief that Claire should have left him years ago. Claire found herself in a state of anxiety, particularly after receiving that letter, as its contents began to unravel in her mind. She had yet to decide whether she should share this with her parents, as she feared it might not be the best idea. She knew they would react strongly, and she didn't want to agitate them further.

They talked a little about her brother, Stuart, as he was not doing very well with his job, and this will be the third business he has started and failed. If it wasn't for his parents, he would've had to go bankrupt. Claire's father was explaining that a friend of his owns a really successful delicatessen he was retiring, and he thought it would be a great business to buy and give to Stuart. There is no way he could make this fail, especially as they know all the staff will stay, and all he needs to do is manage it. Claire agrees it's a great idea. She gives them an update on Tammy and on Michael. They avoid the subject of Andy. It is probably better that it's not discussed, as Claire is on the verge of telling her parents but manages to hold it back. They were looking forward to the wedding and told Claire what they were hoping to give as a wedding gift to Becky and Michael. It was incredibly extravagant, but they could afford it, and they would rather give them money while they were alive. This is beginning to sound like *Groundhog Day,* as Andy's parents have just done exactly the same thing. One thing is for sure: Becky and Michael will be very wealthy for the rest of their lives, and so will all the great-grandchildren eventually, which I suppose is every grandparent's dream to be able to give help to two or three generations in their family.

Claire decided to be straightforward with them and told them that it's their money, and they can use it however they see fit. She didn't have a strong opinion. I think she has a lot on her mind, and money is not her primary concern.

As they were about to leave the restaurant, Claire's father pulled her to one side and said, "Claire, I know something is wrong. What is it?" "It's nothing, Dad, I promise." "I don't buy it," says her father, "If you don't want to discuss it in front of your mother. Just give me a call, I'm not stupid, and I know you very well. I also know it's like me to have something to do with that husband of yours." "Dad, please stop. I don't want to discuss it at the moment, but I promise I will give you a call in the next few days." "OK, darling," her father replies, "I'm going to hold you to that."

26. The Results

It was the morning Roz was going to see the specialist, she hadn't told anyone, and she made David do the same, it was easy to sneak away as now David would go shopping with Roz as she couldn't really push the trolley or (Shlapp) carry, heavy things around, plus we all know how much David enjoyed going to seven to eight different shops to get exactly what Roz wanted from each shop.

They were meeting him at 9.30, which suited Roz as she would rather not hang around all day. It's bad enough she knew this day would come and was really dreading it, as I think deep down inside, she thought she knew what the outcome would be.

David helped her sort herself out. She was a little frail and took her time doing everything. The kids were getting on with life, and she was very happy about that. Her hair had not grown back, but everyone was used to seeing her in a scarf, of which she now had many. She tried hats for a while, but that did not suit her.

Arriving a few minutes early, they took their seats in the reception area, just in front of the receptionist's desk. The receptionist was engrossed in a phone call when they entered. Roz could overhear her conversation but wondered for a moment if there was anyone on the other end, hesitating to make eye contact. She had a nagging feeling that the news wouldn't be good, and her mind was spiralling into negative thoughts. Sometimes, her mind seemed to wander uncontrollably, as if she had little influence over the anxious thoughts that flooded her.

Mr Davidson came out, smiled at them both, and said, "Come in," they went in, "Would you like a drink?" "No, thank you," said David, "I would love a lemon tea if that's possible." "I'm sure we can get you that." Roz's mouth was really dry, and her throat was also, the secretary came in and put the tea down, not looking at Roz, she started doing it again as she left and seemed to zone out of the conversation. Then she heard him say in a rather load voice, "So tell me Roz, how have you been?" She shrugged her shoulders and said, "Fine" to which David said, "She's not fine" and Roz smiles at him and said, "What do you want me to say? I can't get up in the mornings. I feel very weak, and my stomach cramps are so painful. I can't eat much, and what I do eat doesn't stay down," Mr Davidson was listening to her and said, "OK, so let's discuss what's next for you. Everything you are telling me is not out of the ordinary based on the treatment you are going through."

"We have had the results back, and I'm sorry to say that the cancer has spread." Roz starts to cry. "Roz, it's not by a great deal, but it has spread; all your symptoms are as we expected. I think we have two courses of action; firstly," "Sorry to interrupt, but you once told me to listen to your words about what we are going to do next, and this is the first time you have started with 'I think'." "Well, I want you to come in for a few days, maybe a week, give us a chance to give you lots of fluids and nutrients to help build up your defences. You look very weak, and that is something we can really improve on. Then I would like to try a relatively new treatment called immunotherapy, which we would give you every two to three weeks to see if it helps get things under control, works on boosting your immune system to then battle cancer, it's like arming an army with guns to go and fight the enemy."

Roz is not sure what to say. David looks totally gutted at what he is hearing, and there is a silence as they both look beaten, as if they have just given up any hope. Then he says to Roz, "Now it's your turn, ask me anything. She looks at David and says, "Will I still be alive for my daughter's wedding in six weeks?" The question was aimed at Mr Davidson, but Roz was still looking at David. She closed her eyes as Mr Davidson said, "I honestly don't know at this stage." David said, "Are you telling me there is nothing you can do?" He replies, "Well, we are taking the next steps and I have had patients who have reversed the cancer through this treatment. So, I think this is absolutely the right step." Roz still has her eyes closed but then opens them and says, still looking at David, "Whatever you do, whatever you pump into me, you make sure I can be here for my daughter's wedding, even if I have to come back here the day before to get some more fluids pumped into me." He says, "We will do our best, now I want you to come in right away, like now, I will make all the arrangements but this I will not accept no for an answer." David says, "OK, let me go home gather some things." Roz replies, "Please let me call the kids, I don't want them to know much." David agrees and leaves Roz in the waiting area while Mr Davidson's secretary starts to make calls to get her a bed and the treatment set up.

Roz decided to call both Becky and Stephen to inform them of her upcoming hospital stay. She explained that she would be in for about a week to receive the necessary nutrients and fluids to improve her health. After the calls, she confided, "I'm not entirely certain they believed my explanation, but that's the story I'm going to stick with, no matter what."

Roz is left in the secretary's office with the secretary, who is making calls to arrange things. Roz can see a tear coming down from her eyes, and she can't look at her. Roz gets up and walks around to her side of the desk, puts her hand on her cheek, and gently kisses her forehead. She looks up at Roz and smiles. She goes and sits down again, and nothing was ever said between them. Roz thinks about the things she thought about her and realises how tough her job is and some of the very sad things she must see. Well, Roz is determined she is not going to be one of those cases. She's going to do what she can to beat this and try to enjoy every day, preparing for her daughter's wedding.

This hit Becky hard as the wedding was getting closer, and there was still so much to do. She looked at her list and realised that had she been well, Roz would have taken on many of these things for her, and then it really started to hit her about what if...how would she cope without her mum.

This was a testing time for the Cohens, and the Rubins were not exactly doing OK with all the millions that they had. It certainly does not give them a free pass to avoid problems in their own lives.

27. David Takes His Dad Out

David's father is a very sweet old man. He was a tailor all his life and worked for a guy who had four menswear shops, and Lou was with him for over 60 years. It was his only job. His wife passed away a few years ago, and now, at 92, he's amazing, full of energy and can't sit still for too long. He helps out at a centre for old people, which is a bit ironic. David just convinced him to give up his car and stop driving as for sure he would have had an accident. He travels by bus and taxi and lives in sheltered accommodation, funny enough on the same road as Roz's parents but in a different building.

They meet once a week for coffee. Lou prefers it if they come to him as he doesn't like the three women who question him every time he comes there. He says they are like the Gestapo patrol.

David updated him about the wedding news and how Stephen was doing. He also knows nothing about Roz. It's just unfair to burden a 92-year-old man with such awful things.

Stephen, funny enough, sees more of him than anyone and even convinces him to go and stay with Stephen for a few days when Abraham is away, and they have fun together. It was so nice to see, especially for Roz and David.

Lou never really liked banks and kept all his money at home in jars, vases, cupboards, under the mattress, and God knows where else. Lou was a strong old man with tattoos, which is unusual for an old Jewish person, especially because of the numbers put on the arms of the prisoners in the death camps during the war, but Lou had fought in Burma, which they say was like Vietnam but much worse. They had no training; they were literally picked up, given a uniform, walking boots and a gun and sent to the dense jungle halfway around the world and expected to fight, most of them died of disease as much as anything, but Lou survived and had plenty of stories to tell.

His dad had a fondness for Wimpy, and fortunately, there was one of the few remaining sit-in Wimpy restaurants nearby. That's where they decided to go. His dad ordered a classic Wimpy cheeseburger with a side of chips and a Coke. After the meal, he indulged in some ice cream, savouring every bite as he used a knife and fork to eat it slowly. David, who rarely had burgers when Roz was around, took the opportunity to enjoy a quarter-pounder with cheese and chips. He insisted, "You've got to try their special burger sauce; it's something else." Both David and his father had a special fondness for it. After the meal, David made sure to return Lou in time for his afternoon activities in the common room, followed by a brief rest before dinner.

This is their ritual once a week, and a nice one it is, too.

28. Friday Night Dinner (16 Days to Go)

Roz has been feeling much better since that stay in the hospital. She has got the colour back in her face, her hair is coming back, she has got some energy back, and she went to see the specialist yesterday who told her that the treatment is working, so far so good. She feels hope again.

She decided to make Friday night dinner for the entire family before the wedding. She really wanted to have a fun evening with two families who have their shit going on, but when they come together, they are there for each other…that's her hope anyway.

It was 3 p.m., and David had the day off from work. He embarked on his regular round to gather the ten key ingredients from seven different shops. He knew the routine by heart, and the shopkeepers were familiar with him. Meanwhile, Roz was in her element, meticulously setting the dinner table. She found herself lost in thought, her mind drifting towards the wedding, her return to work, and plans for an upcoming holiday. Today, her thoughts were filled with optimism and positivity.

David arrived with all her shopping. He unloaded the car and then new it was time to leave the kitchen and let Roz unload the shopping and begin the master craft of a full Jewish Friday night dinner.

Everyone was invited for 8 p.m. as Roz wanted a later start as she felt stronger now.

Becky got home at six; she was the only one allowed in the kitchen while Roz was cooking. They chatted about the wedding, and she reminded Roz that the caterer was coming over tomorrow so he could go through all the ingredients he needed for the food. Roz was very excited about that, and Becky was glowing. She was so excited. Next thing they heard was Stephen walking in through the door shouting, "Dad I'm home!" "Very funny, Stephen. Before you leave, I want all keys to this house returned to me." Roz just laughed and said, "Do you want mine as well…" "Not funny." "Oh, lighten up, Mr grumpy." Abraham was very quiet, and Roz asked him what was up. They had a little chat in the kitchen, and it seemed he and Stephen were having a few problems, and he was not sure Stephen wanted to have a baby. Roz said to him, "Don't worry, I know my son. If he wanted out, he would have done it a long time ago, he's just nervous and worried about how it would affect his nearly perfect life. He's yet to learn that having a child makes your life perfect. It will be fine, trust me."

The doorbell rang, and the entire Anderson family arrived together: Andy with the wine, Claire with the flowers, Tami with the chocolates and Michael with a cake that Claire baked (Romero baked). "Come in, come in, throw your coats there, let's get this wine open." There was a lot of hugging and kissing, and they all chatted for a while. Roz was in the kitchen with Claire and Tami, Stephen and Abraham were sitting at the dinner table eating the HaImisha cucumbers, Michael was with Claire in the lounge, and Andy and David were outside. Andy wanted to show David his new car, which was an Aston Martin vanquish. He always wanted to be like James Bond; he fell a little short, so he had to settle with the car.

They all sat down for dinner. Roz stood up, and there was silence as she lit the candles. There was a warmth, a glow in the room as everyone looked at Roz. She smiled so wide and wished everyone good Shabbas. Then the food was flowing, and everyone was chatting in little groups it was so wonderful to see how this family had come through so much and yet now were breaking bread together.

Roz rose from her seat, and a hushed silence fell over the room. She began, "I wanted to share a few words with you all. You know I'm not one to speak often, but when I do, there's usually a good reason." Her words elicited laughter from the family, with Becky chiming in, "You've always had plenty of reasons." Roz continued, "First and foremost, I want to express my heartfelt gratitude to each of you for the incredible support you've shown during this challenging period in my life. Each one of you, in your unique way, has displayed acts of kindness that have truly brought us together as one family." "I hope now I am starting to beat this sucker and will get stronger and stronger," everyone clapped and raised their glass to that, "I want to thank my husband for being amazing and supporting me. I know I can be demanding," David nods in agreement, but Roz continues, "I'm also very lovable," everyone nods and laughs. "I want to raise a glass to Stephen and Abraham; they are expecting the greatest gift you can receive, and it will completely change their life only for the better," everyone shouted, "Mazel Tov." "I want to say to you, Tami, I have never met anyone who has your bravery to go through what you have been through and still complete your art exhibition, which we are all, I mean all, coming to Monday evening, you are an amazing person and definitely have your mum's character and determination, hear, hear!" Everyone raises a glass, and Claire hugs Tami and says in her ear, "I love you, and I'm so proud of you." "To Claire and Andy, just thank you for your kindness and support, and oh my god, the villa is amazing," they all clap, and Claire puts her right hand on her heart and looks at Roz as she smiles at her. "I want to say that I am so so proud of my daughter not only for what she has achieved but for picking a partner who is her Yin to her Yang; together, you will be a strong, loving couple and I want to raise a glass to what will be a spectacular day as we welcome the new Mr and Mrs Rubin." David grabs his wife and hugs her, and they sit down. It doesn't take long for David to stand up and say, "Don't worry, I won't be as long as my wife, but as we are saying thank you, the biggest thank you goes to Roz, she is truly the head of this family; the glue that keeps us together through good times and bad. I nearly felt what it was like to lose that; it was the most terrifying thought I had to live with. Her bravery throughout her chemo, operation and still ongoing treatment is truly inspirational, and this is just as much a celebration of you my amazing wife. We are better for having you in our lives, and we all have many more

Friday night dinners to share. We all love you." They all stand and raise a glass to Roz, "We all love you." They sit down, and Andy gets up and says, "Enough with the speeches. Can we get some crumble now?" everyone laughs and continues eating and drinking. The night was an overwhelming success.

29. Family Update

Roz has been having her new treatment, and since her week in the hospital, she has looked and felt so much better. She noticed her hair was starting to return. She was happy and trying really hard to remain positive and very present for Becky. They had the final dress fitting, and Roz was so happy to be there. Roz had the head chef over for her to show him how she cooked the Friday night dinner so he could try his best to replicate things. Roz did so many things that many chefs would never do, but it goes to show that nothing can beat experience.

David has been writing out lots of cheques and transferring money most days, none of it unexpected, but between that and working as he's still 5,000 pounds short of his target, which is more of a principle victory than a need the money one, and keeping an eye on Roz. He's a very busy man at the moment when he does get a spare hour here. There, he prepares his speech and also his playlist for the wedding so the band have the music.

Becky was fully immersed in the wedding preparations, but it proved to be quite challenging as she juggled her demanding job alongside her wedding planning duties. With only three days left at work before her departure for the honeymoon, she was giving it her all. Her positivity was unwavering, especially with Roz's improving health, which made a significant difference. Having her mom there to assist with all the wedding details was a tremendous help.

Stephen is getting closer to the day he gets the baby. Abraham is busy buying/decorating and generally running around like a crazy person, spending loads of money. He has retired from work and has the time to do it. Stephen is not getting remotely excited about the baby coming, and

Abraham is starting to feel it. There is no excitement that there should be when Stephen gets home from work, normally between 8–9 p.m. Abraham has many things to talk about, but for Stephen, discussing paint for the babies' room, and which buggy to buy, is so not interesting for him. He just zones out, and it really pisses Abraham off. They definitely have some problems to work out.

Abraham

His mother called him, and they met for coffee. She explained that this was a big shock and I needed time to think about it. "I realised that I had two choices: accept it as you are my son and be involved in your life or don't accept it and probably lose any relating with my son."

"So, I decided to accept it. I love you very much and want to be in your life, and I always wanted to be a grandmother. I think I need to meet this Michael very soon." "You will, I promise Mum and thank you, I'm very happy and would not change a thing in my life." She then holds his arm and squeezes it and says, "Your father, it's a different story, if broached the subject and decided to only tell him about the fact you are gay, it would be too much for him otherwise," "And how was he? what did he say?" "Nothing for a day or so then he seemed OK with the idea, he will be here in ten minutes." His father did arrive; they sat, chatted and then hugged it out together, small steps is the way with him.

Andy and Claire's communication has dwindled, with Andy seemingly spending more time away from home than ever before. He senses that something may be amiss with Claire, but he's hesitant to confront the issue, choosing to bide his time, fearing he might be mistaken. He's preoccupied with taking charge of the new business he recently acquired, which keeps him away frequently. Notably, Andy has distanced himself from any involvement in the wedding preparations. He's already devised a unique wedding gift for the couple, firmly believing it's a genuinely cool idea. Interestingly, he hasn't shared this plan with Claire and doesn't have any intention of doing so. We'll have to wait and see how it unfolds.

Claire is still unsure what to do about that letter, so she decides to take it to her family lawyer, and they are looking into it for her. She is pretty calm at the moment as she's all about Tami and, of course, the wedding. Andy can (Plutz) stew for a while, let him think she's angry with him, but he doesn't know what it is, which is actually the truth. Claire has been with Roz a lot the last couple of weeks and has been taking her shopping (food shopping) most days.

Tammy is manic and full of anxiety; that's not a good sign, but her exhibition is about to open, and she is really getting stressed. She has seen her doctor, who upped her medication for two weeks and is keeping a close eye on her. She has finished the art, but the thought of 150 people or more being at an opening and it all being about her is very stressful. Claire is speaking to or seeing her most days at the moment which Tammy likes it gives her a lot of comforts.

Michael is very chilled; he's not involved in the wedding and is not working much at the moment. He's still not had the conversation with his father about leaving the family business, but what would he do? He did get a strange call to go and see his grandfather this weekend, which he is doing. He doesn't know why, but he will find out very soon. Wedding suits have arrived, all tried on with his ushers and best man. His ushers played a joke on him and swapped over the jacket and trousers with one of the other guys who was much, much larger than Michael, so when he tried on his suit, it looked like it was made for a man twice his size, he panicked like a crazy person and literally ran out the house and got in his car with this suit on and headed for the tailors. He was so mad with panic, and he left his mobile at home so there was no way they could reach him, they jumped in their car and headed to the tailor as they arrived Michael had the poor guy around the neck. His trousers were around his ankles, we had to pull him off and calm him down, and we told him what we did, he never saw the funny side, until at least a week later. That was a side of Michael no one had seen, the anger just coming over him like a wave.

30. Tami's Exhibition 13 Days to Go

Tami's exhibition was in a gallery in Soho; she needed a large space as she had over 50 paintings and they were all quite large. The exhibition title was changed and is now called 'me from the outside looking in'. It was a very powerful collection of work, there were many collectors, gallery owners and journalists there along with the entire Anderson and Cohen family with one late arrival, her father! Thank goodness there were so many people wanting to talk to her she never noticed. They all walked around looking at each piece and then the title and trying to make sense of it, but they couldn't. Then the owner of the Gallery spoke and said how proud he was to represent Tami, and he felt this body of work was for sure her most revealing and expressive, showing her vulnerability as a person but communicative skills as a real artist. Everyone applauded, and so did the Jewish contingent.

Tami was holding it together with tape and blue tack. Inside, she was very troubled but needed to get this exhibition away so she could go and hide forever (is how she felt).

For the time being, she wore a warm smile and gracefully participated in interviews, exuding beauty, though her mother couldn't help but notice she appeared thinner. As the evening neared its conclusion, Tami approached a tall, dapper gentleman in his early forties and introduced him, "Mum, I'd like you to meet Paul." Claire extended her hand, her thoughts racing, "Wow, he's quite charming. Is my daughter trying to set me up?" She warmly greeted Paul, "Hello, Paul," and he replied with courtesy, "Hello, Mrs. Anderson, it's a pleasure to meet you." "Please call me Claire." "Claire, you have an amazing daughter; she's very talented and very beautiful." "Oh, thank you, you must know what it's like. Do you have any children yourself?" "No, I don't." "Do you mind me asking what you are doing with my daughter she's half your age." "Mum, I can't believe you," "That's OK, I don't want to cause a problem on this hugely successful night for Tami." "No, we don't it's nice meeting you." "You too," as he slips away. Tami walks with him apologising as he leaves, she comes back and walks over to her mum when her father walked in and said, "where's my Tami? This is great; well done. Did you paint all of these?" "Yes, Dad, I did, and you are late." "Why bother?"

Tami heads off to a bar with her friends and never says good bye to anyone. I think Claire may have said what's on her mind in the wrong place.

The next day, Claire is on Tami's doorstep at ten with coffee and every type of croissant you could imagine. As Tami sees her mum standing there, she smiles and says, "You better come in."

"I'm so sorry, Tami. I should never have said what I said." "It's OK, it's not really serious." "I just like him because he's so different and takes me out of myself. I think your art certainly did that." "Why Mum?" "You are now an art critic." "Not at all, but I am a critic and wait till I see your father; he will quickly understand what a critic I am." Tami laughed, "Mum, why do you stay with him? I'm sorry but he's an arsehole, and he treats us all like we aren't his family." Claire just grins and thinks, "Wow how right you maybe." "Let's not do this, I'm just sorry for what I said and if you want to see Uncle Paul that's fine." Tami laughs and says, "Nah, not for me, I need a good-looking older man who will take care of me but maybe not that old." Claire agrees.

31. Five Days to Go
(Baby Is Ready)

The wedding was rapidly approaching, yet for certain family members, significant life events were also unfolding. Stephen and Abraham were on the verge of picking up their baby from the adoption agency after a lengthy journey of interviews and preparations. This plan had been in motion for a year. They had made the mutual decision that Abraham would step away from his job, primarily due to his lesser career ambition compared to Stephen's higher-paying position. Their financial stability was not a concern, and their apartment had been thoughtfully adapted for a baby's arrival. They felt well-prepared for this new chapter, except for one thing…Stephen was not ready. He woke up the morning they were going and went for a run. He was in a mess and did not know what to do.

He did what most male adults do when they have a problem: call their mother.

"Mum, it's Stephen." "What's the matter?" "Something is wrong, it's 7.30 in the morning, Mum, I'm having a panic attack." "Where are you?" "I'm out running." "From what?" "I'm not running from anything; I went for a run." "Are you sure?" "Of course, I'm sure I went for a run." "No, I mean are you sure you're not running from something?" "Mum, what are you talking about?" "I'm talking about the baby that's what you're running from, isn't it?" There was a silence, "Yes, Mum, I don't know if I can go through with this, I'm not sure I want this baby." "OK, calm down breath, breath, are you calm? "Yes." "OK, you can't run away from this, Abraham must be going out of his mind wondering where you are, you need to go home and face this, I'm sure it's just panic, you have been planning this for over a year." "Abraham has been planning this for over a year, I just went along with it, I didn't want to upset him." "Do you love him?" "Yes, do you want to lose him?" "No." "Then you need to go home now and talk it through with him, you need to face this." "But what if I don't connect with this baby? what if I don't want my life turned upside down? I'm selfish, I like my life, a baby will change everything." "Yes, it will, but in a very special way. When you hold that baby and realise you are responsible for another life; when you realise you have a chance to teach a child right from wrong to bring them up as good people you will realise it's the biggest, best and most important job you can have, are you listening to me?" "Yes, Mum." "OK, then run home and go and talk to Abraham." "OK, thanks Mum, love you, bye."

"What was that about?" David said. "Nothing to worry about. It's Stephen just having a bit of a panic attack about the baby." "OK, I think he got it straight from you; he did."

Stephen arrived home, and as he put the key in the door, Abraham was there and greeted him with, "Where the f—k have you been? We are supposed to be leaving in an hour to collect our new baby and start a new part of our life. I wake up and find you have gone, not answering your phone…who does that? What's wrong with you? "Calm down," Stephen says, "I'm sorry I just went for a run I needed some space to think." "Think about what?" "The baby, I had a bit of a panic attack but I'm back I'm here, and I'm ready." "This cannot be happening if you are having panic attacks. Now how are you going to feel when we have a child here tonight?" "I will be OK; I just need to get used to the idea. "You have had over a year to get used to it and could have stopped this at any point, but you've never said a word, why?" "I don't know. I just saw how happy this made you feel, and I love you, and I don't know." There was a silence. Abraham went onto the balcony to get some air, and Stephen did not know what to do, so he just left Abraham outside to have some space.

A few minutes past, and he came back in and said very calmly, "Stephen, I'm going to get in the shower, get dressed, and I'm going to collect our daughter. I will be back around 6 p.m. tonight if you are here when I get back, I know I have a partner for this child if you're not here, I know I don't, and then we can decide who moves out, but I'm not changing my mind. I'm bringing this baby home, and if you can't deal with it, I will happily bring her up on my own."

He walked into the bedroom and closed the door. Stephen entered the kitchen, and within an hour or so, Abraham exited the bedroom and left. He never spoke to Stephen. He just grabbed his car keys and left.

Stephen got dressed and drove over to his mother, when she opened the door, she knew straight away and said, "Come in, do you want breakfast?" "No thanks." "Have you eaten?" "I'm not hungry." "I'm making you breakfast, so what happened?" Stephen explained everything that happened and Roz said, "I must admit, I can't entirely blame Abraham. Your behaviour hasn't been exemplary," her mother remarked. Claire responded, "I understand, Mum, but I'm really not sure what I want in this situation." Her mother offered some advice: "Listen, I'm not here to persuade you one way or another. However, one thing is clear: you need to make a decision, and whatever you decide, Abraham deserves to know it today. Head home, give it some thought, and make the choice that feels right to you. Just don't delude yourself." "OK, I will," Stephen goes and Roz sits down and starts to cry, she is gutted, she can see the pain in Stephen's eyes and he is a good person this must be killing him. David comes in and they sit together and Roz thinks, "this is all we need with a few days before the wedding. I just hoped we would have no more dramas and we could focus on Becky and the wedding." "We will don't worry, it will all work out," says David.

32. Four Days to Go Tami Struggles

We have four days to go and it seems that there is plenty of activity happening as well as a wedding, thank goodness that both Becky and Michael are so wrapped up in everything they are not aware of the real drama's happening in both families, Claire was on her way to Tami following a call they had and Claire can always tell when Tami wants her without actually asking. She turns up, knocks on the door and the door was open, she walks in and shouts, "Tami it's Mum, did you know the door was open?" She can here crying and walks into the bathroom and sees Tami on the floor in the shower with no clothes on, no water running just all curled up in a ball. Claire swiftly fetched a towel, wrapped it around herself, and scooped up her daughter, carrying her into the bedroom. She settled onto the bed, holding her tightly and gently rocking her as Tami sobbed. These tears seemed to well up from the depths of her being, and Claire could feel the profound pain her daughter was experiencing. Gradually, Tami's sobs subsided, and Claire tenderly placed her in bed, drawing the blinds to create a peaceful ambience. She sat there beside Tami as she drifted into sleep, softly stroking her forehead. Once Tami was soundly asleep, Claire made her way to the kitchen and prepared a cup of tea. Sitting at the kitchen table, she rested her head in her hands, grappling with a sense of helplessness and uncertainty about how to support her daughter through this challenging time.

Claire made some calls and cancelled her hair and nail appointments, so she had a free day to be around for Tami.

When Tami woke up, she entered into the kitchen, and Claire made her some food and sat there while she ate the food. Then she took her into the bathroom and stayed with her whilst she had a hot bath. She then got her dressed, and they went to the lounge and sat and watched a film together; Footloose was their favourite. They never mentioned what happened. Claire just waited for Tami to talk or not, but one thing is for sure. She was not leaving her daughter in this apartment. She was bringing her home with her to keep an eye on her.

When Tami is like this, she agrees to everything. I suppose she just wants someone else to make the decisions. She packs a bag, and Claire takes her home. She goes up to her room, gets into bed and falls asleep. Claire leaves her and at least knows she is safe.

She comes downstairs to an empty house, which she is getting used to. Andy has been gone for three days; he said it was a conference. Claire is convinced he was in Rome for a meeting with Miss Salvino, whoever she is. Still, she has more important things to worry about, and she has the wedding to get ready for.

33. Three Days to Go, Where Are the Napkin Rings

David has not really been too involved in the wedding. Everything was taken care of, Becky and Michael did a great job, and Becky's friend, who is the coordinator along with the coordinator from the hotel, has everything under control. Becky is starting to relax and enjoy the next few days and take it all in.

The only thing that is not sorted yet are the napkin rings, the hotel messaged David today and asked if he could please get them to the hotel for tomorrow as they are beginning to lay out everything and this is the only thing they don't have on the premises, it had completely slipped his mind, he calls his mate Steve, "Steve it's David how are you?" "I'm good, how are you? "Haven't spoken for a while, how did the wedding go?" "It's in three days' time, that's why I'm calling. I completely forgot about the napkin rings and I need to pick them up and get them to the venue for the wedding." "So, what do you need from me? Just go ahead and pick them up."

"I would if I had the address." "Oh, yeah, got a pen? It's Jimmy's Cantonese Kitchen, 124 High Road, Heathmore Village, Birmingham." David was surprised, "Birmingham? Are you serious?" Steve clarified, "No, mate, I'm not joking. What's the problem?" David sighed. "It's Birmingham; I thought it was in London." Steve assured him, "No, I never said London. You better get a move on then." "Alright, thanks, Steve, bye," David replied. He then started making calls to find someone willing to drop everything and drive to Birmingham to pick up the supplies, realising that this wouldn't be an easy task.

David panics, a lot of that going around at the moment. He then has an idea, "it means calling Andy," so he rings him and gets a foreign ringtone; "Andy speaking." "Andy, it's David." "How did you get this number?" "You gave it to me." "Did I? Sorry mate, I only use this for work." "Sorry to call. I need a favour." "Can it wait until I'm back from my business trip." "Not really, I need some help today." "OK, go for it. What do you need?" "Can I borrow your driver for one day tomorrow? I need something collected from Birmingham, and I've been let down." "Err OK, sure I will get a taxi back tomorrow, look, call him on this number. I'm messaging to you now and do what you need, I will message him and tell him that he's working for you tomorrow." "You are a star, thanks, Andy, see you at the wedding for sure, take care."

David makes the call and arranges for the collection and the drop off at the hotel all tomorrow. He calls the hotel coordinator and tells her it will arrive tomorrow. Not sure she expected them to arrive in a chauffeur-driven Bentley, but hey-ho, nothing is a surprise this week.

34. Two Days to Go, Andrew Comes Home

Claire had been postponing a conversation with her solicitor, apprehensive about what she might hear. With only two days left until the wedding, she longed to immerse herself in her son's preparations. However, Andrew was returning from his supposed business trip, and Claire couldn't bring herself to face him. She found herself repeatedly gazing at the solicitor's number, picking up the telephone, but ultimately hesitating. Andy's arrival was expected later in the day, and he had shown no interest or involvement with the children in the lead-up to their wedding. Claire's anger towards him left her unsure of how to react when he returned home.

The house was empty; Tami had gone to stay with a friend for the day, and Michael was running around for Becky today's last-minute wedding stuff. Claire was so gutted she hadn't been allowed to enjoy the wedding yet, but with everything going on, the closer it gets, the more she has to deal with.

She pours herself a glass of mid-morning wine lights a cigarette and calls the solicitor, "Good morning, is Mr Giles in?" "Yes, who's calling?" "Please tell him it's Claire Anderson," "OK, please hold, Claire how are you?" "I'm OK, Tim, how are you?" "I'm OK, thank you, are you all ready for the wedding." "Not really to be honest, I haven't had much chance to think about it and I wasn't sure I was going to call you before the wedding, but then I thought I would only ask you at the wedding and that would be worse (Tim has been her family's lawyer for 30 years and therefore really has her best interests at heart) so let's get it over with, what did you manage to find out?" "Well, firstly, I looked back through all the work we have done for you and Andy to see if I can find anything that relates to that letter and I did find something but it might be a coincidence. The name Silvano, there was an Adriano Silvano who was the local estate agent who you bought the villa in Italy through, I knew I knew that name it has been bugging me for ages." "Yes, you're right, she was a very young and very pretty little thing at the time I remember her well." "Also, I looked into the school and the names poppy and summer and nothing came up; but I then checked the same names in the area where the villa is and there were twins born 14 years ago in the April called summer and poppy. I got in touch with the town hall and managed to get access to their birth certificate," at this point Claire's heart sank," "Yes, what did you find?" "They are registered to an Angelina Salvino with father unknown." "Great, what does that mean?" "Well, I looked at the address and they live in a house in the village Santa Maria which is ten minutes from your villa and I looked into the ownership of this and it's registered to a company called Gunners ltd and that company is registered to an Andrew Anderson, which means he owns the house they live in, so unfortunately there's your connection." "Claire, I'm so so sorry but it's pretty conclusive that he must be the father. Otherwise, why would he own the house and go to so much trouble to hide it, not that he's that clever. I mean gunner is the Arsenal nickname, I don't need to be Colombo to find this," Claire is trying to process this it's all a bit too much, "Tim, so what you're saying is my husband has been screwing that young tart, who sold us a villa, got her pregnant, had twin girls, and bought them a house and god knows how many times and where he has seen her, it answers a lot about his short trips and golf every day during the summer at the villa and I bet these three days he's been away he's been to Rome to carry out the interview to get his other kids into the school in the letter." "I think you are correct, Claire, the question is what do you want to do? "I want to kill him firstly, secondly, I want to kill him as well and anything else seems too good for him." "I understand, Claire, but now is not the time to react. You have your son's wedding in two days, and you need to get into wedding mode for the sake of your son. We can deal with this in a week's time, for sure financially he will be in trouble. We can take him to the cleaners, and it will affect his life dramatically." "OK," says Claire, "I need some time to process this, and the bastard will be home in an hour from his business trip."

Claire thanks Tim and hangs up. She sits down and just thinks, "why me? I'm not such a bad person, a bit selfish at times, but why would he do this to me?" She doesn't know what to do for the first time in her life. She really doesn't know whether to confront him when he gets home, and god knows what he will do or say and what it will do to the wedding.

Claire wrestled with her thoughts, pondering whether she should wait until after these upcoming days to address the situation. Could she look at Andrew and bear it? Was she strong enough to contain all her emotions? As she contemplated her options, the sound of a key turning in the front door sent a shiver down her spine. Her stomach knotted up instantly. Turning around, she was relieved to see Michael returning from his errands. "Hi, Mum," he greeted her, a broad grin on his face. "You, OK?" Claire managed a reassuring smile and replied, "Yes, I'm fine, darling. What about you?" His nervousness was apparent, but excitement sparkled in his eyes. "I'm nervous but very excited." Claire encouraged him, "It will all be fine. I can't wait to see you under the chuppah."

I think that made her mind up for her. She was going to wait. "What have you been up to?" "I've just moved my stuff into our flat." "Oh my god, I forgot my son is moving out. How will I cope?" She laughs, and he says, "At least you have Dad to keep you company." "You're right, I do."

With that, the door opens, and in comes Andy. "I'm home," he calls out. "We are in here," says Michael. He comes through to the kitchen, drops his bags and says, "what a trip, it was so boring. I'm so pleased to be home. Right, let's get this wedding underway. I'm ready, are you more to the point? My son," Michael nods, "Yes, I'm ready," and Claire says, "I'm sorry, I need the loo," she goes into the hallway and the loo. She wants to be sick; she just can't believe how he can do this but then she realises he's been a liar to us all for 15 years he's capable of anything. She composes herself comes out and says, "Right, let's get this wedding underway, I don't want to talk about anything else apart from you, Becky and the wedding." she kisses her son, and they all sit and have tea.

35. Family Updates

Roz has been speaking with her specialist most days over the last two weeks, and she went missing for one day to go and have some fluids and nutrients added to her to give her a bit more strength to see the next few days through. She agreed to have a break from her treatment during the week leading up to the wedding, which the specialist was happy with. She has an important scan coming up to see how things have progressed, but for the moment, she has put it completely out of her mind, she wants to be the hostess and the mother of the bride, her dress has been taken in many times, but it's ready for her, and she is having her hair done, all she needs to do now is worry about herself everything else is ready.

David is just relieved he sorted out the napkin rings. They have arrived. He called and left a message for the hotel to tell them what time they were arriving, and she did call him back, but he missed the call. They must be there by now. David is finishing his welcome speech and has not shown it to anyone. Roz was not happy about that, but he was adamant. He has finished paying for the wedding, just the bar bill to pay at the end, thank God for Roz between them they spent 120,000 on this wedding which was such a lot of money to them but they were not in debt, and life will continue. He has his suit, knows what his duties are on the day and where he needs to be.

Becky was at home, busy packing for the hotel where they would all check in the next morning. Her maid of honour and her friend, who was coordinating the wedding, was with her, going over a few final details. It was remarkable how relaxed Becky was, but that was her nature. In a crisis, you'd want her by your side. She had thought the wedding might not happen due to her mom's illness, so she was overjoyed that her mom was okay. However, deep down, she knew the problem hadn't disappeared. But, for the time being, she was fully focused on her upcoming wedding and having her mom with her.

Stephen, well, he finally came to his senses. He was there when the baby arrived and was overjoyed when they met for the first time. He was so excited to come to the wedding. They were bringing the baby with them. It would be the first time all the family would get to see her and Abraham who has been amazing. He's a natural, and it helps Stephen as he is very nervous around the baby.

Claire was trying to hold it together, but she was like a ticking time bomb. She managed to park it and is with her son and daughter, and everything else can wait; she's at the hairdressers, having a full make over ready for the event to come. She went to collect her outfits as they were all ready for her, she had one last fitting, and all was good, she was waiting for Tami to come home so they could pack for tomorrow.

Andy was home and getting over wherever he was and whatever he was up to. He is oblivious to the tsunami he has created and what is about to happen. He has his new suit, and he has his surprise gift for Becky and Michael that he plans to give to them at the wedding, along with his speech that no one knows he is making, but he is hardly speaking to Claire and Tami is so angry with him for turning up late at her big exhibition. She has not forgiven him yet.

Tami, with the support of her mom, had moved back home and seemed to be holding herself together. Her wedding dress was ready, and Claire had arranged for a beautician to come to the house that evening to do her hair and nails, providing her with a full evening of pampering. Romero, the family cook, had prepared homemade, fresh pizzas for dinner. Tami was visibly looking healthier, and Claire was relieved to have her at home where she could keep a close eye on her. Tami, in turn, was relieved to have her exhibition behind her and no longer felt pressure from anyone.

Michael, Mr happy go lucky is absolutely fine. He doesn't seem to pick up on good or bad vibes from anything happening to his family. Maybe he's the smart one; he's very excited about marrying Becky he has been working on his speech and is very nervous of standing up in front of 300 people, but he's ready. The apartment they are renting is ready, and he has moved his and Becky's stuff in there already for when they come back from their honeymoon, the apartment is incredible it's a rooftop penthouse with three bedrooms, a separate dining room and it even has a gym. Michael did this on his own, and the rent is high, but he can afford it, so he thought what the hell, let's start our marriage off in a cool place.

36. The Arrival at the Hotel and the Barbecue

There were 80 people all converging on the hotel for the wedding. They were carefully selected to stay at the hotel for two nights and join the family for the barbecue tonight and the main event tomorrow. There were another 40 people not staying over but coming tonight for the barbecue and then returning for the wedding the following day, and the balance of 180 just coming to the wedding tomorrow.

The first to arrive were the bride and groom. They wanted to check in and be at the reception to greet all their family and friends, and their two rooms were ready at 9 a.m., so they were there sharp, unpacked and had breakfast at the hotel. They were both really excited. It seems every member of staff was given a picture of them and were told to congratulate them whenever they were seen, that's exactly what did happen, and they felt so special, like celebrities.

People began to arrive slowly. Claire and Andy were the first to check in, accompanied by Tami. Shortly after, Roz and David arrived. Finally, Stephen, Abraham, and their new baby, Rose, made their entrance. The reception area buzzed with excitement, as you could well imagine, but it was all in good spirits. Throughout the day, everyone went about their own activities, but they all eventually converged at the restaurant for lunch. The family effectively took over the restaurant. With a diverse group of Jewish individuals, a buffet was a delightful choice. Jewish people have perfected the art of trying a bit of everything, even if the flavours don't necessarily complement each other, all while balancing everything on one plate. After all, they prefer not to be seen making multiple trips to the buffet.

There was a lot of introducing family members of both sides, and at that moment, the lovely thing was, religion didn't matter. They were just two families beginning to meet and join together.

The good thing was there was a lot of laughter…

Roz and David were having lunch with many of their family and some of Claire's whom they just met.

Stephen and Abraham were busy showing Rose to everyone.

Becky was with her friends in the spar, having some treatments.

Claire and Tami were having a massage.

Andy was nowhere to be seen.

The day flew by, but it was nice walking around the hotel and constantly walking into people you knew were here for the wedding.

The barbecue started at 7.30, and the weather was glorious, so everything could take place outside. The walled garden looked amazing, with lights in all the trees and candles directing you along the path from the hotel to the wrought iron gates, and as you entered, the small candles sent you on this mazy walk amongst the flowers to an open area full of white couches and small coffee tables, the pool was lit up, there were four to five chefs in bright white jackets working on the barbie and four to five waiters and waitresses also dressed in white serving drinks, there was a saxophonist playing jazz music and a small five-piece band with two singers setting up to take the party into the small hours.

Everyone was on time and mingling. Roz was smiling from ear to ear seeing everyone together and finally some peace between everyone, the barby was amazing, fresh steaks chicken on skewers with peppers roasting, sausages handmade burgers with melted cheese if you wished and toasted buns, several amazing salads and everyone was having a great time, David decided it was time for him to welcome everyone, his big toast he was saving until tomorrow, "Ladies and gentleman can I have your attention for one minute, firstly I would like to welcome you to the wedding weekend of Becky and Michael, we invited everyone or you this evening as you all mean so much to us and have played a role in the lives of Becky or Michael or the lives of ours. I won't keep you long as I will bore you again tomorrow but for now, let me just say please help us kick off this weekend of surprises with good food, good wine, good friends and the sound of laughter to the future. Mr and Mrs Anderson cheers. "That was so nice," said Roz as he went over to David planting a kiss on him and saying, "Very nice David, very nice."

The evening was going like a dream, both families mingling. There seemed to be a rather large group gathered on the couches as Roz explained to Michael's family the format of the ceremony and the meaning of the bride walking around the groom seven times, why get married under a canopy, and why the groom stamps on a glass. It was so beautiful to see this, the family were really interested and honestly looking forward to the experience. Roz was doing such a great job with this as she explains it with such joy and warmth.

Roz had settled into her seat and hadn't stirred for some time. She appeared quite weary, and David approached her, suggesting, "Why don't you take a rest? We have a busy day ahead." She gazed at him and replied, "Thank you, but not a chance. I'll be one of the last to leave. I intend to savour every moment of this wedding." David kissed her, and a tear welled up in his eye as he contemplated life without Roz. She returned the kiss with intensity, clutching his hand, and declared, "Alright, could you fetch me some dessert? I'd like to sample everything."

Becky was beaming; she had spoken to everyone and made everyone feel they were really important. Watching her mingle around the beautiful setting as the sun set was an art. Now it was 9 p.m., and the walled garden looked beautiful. The group had broken into many areas and were all enjoying their company and mixing, which was a delight to see.

The dancing started, and everyone was on their feet. Roz was trying but really was getting exhausted. She never wavered at all, and even when Becky came over and grabbed her hand to dance with her daughter, they hugged through four minutes of Adele. Both knew what each other was thinking, but neither dared say it as they didn't know how they would react, Roz let out a big sigh and just said to Becky, "Do me one favour, do everything today and tomorrow slowly, enjoy every second you can't get time back, I love you so much, and I'm so proud of you. You have made all my dreams come true," she kissed Becky. She said, "Right now go be with your friends, your mum is going to sit and have tea and more desserts. Have you tried the tarte tatin it's unbelievable."

Then completely unexpectedly, Andy got up and everyone could here that sharp tapping on the glass as he stood up, he did it whilst standing with his back to Claire as they were talking to different people. Claire turned, grabbed his arm and said Andy, "What are you doing?" He said, "It's fine, Claire, let go of me," everyone went quiet, and Andy stood, took the microphone and started to speak.

"I want to say a few words as the father of the groom. I hope you don't mind, David," and as he looked over, David just nodded and waved a hand as if to say the floor is yours.

"Firstly, I want to thank Roz and David for this great evening and his generous hospitality everything is perfect and we are all looking forward to a fabulous no expense spared weekend," he laughed but not really anyone else, "Anyway, I wanted to tell you that Michael and I have not always been very close but he is my son and I love him very much and when he met Becky, I could not be more pleased and surprised how well they got along and also how well suited they were for each other. I always tried to bring Michael up to be honest," at this point Claire does not know whether she wants to throw up or stab her husband. He continues, "hardworking and invest his money wisely," Claire was dreading where this was going, "I wanted to use this small gathering to give Becky and Michael their wedding gift from Claire and myself," David was getting angrier and angrier, Roz just smiled at everyone as Claire could not look up, with that one of waiters walked in with a trolley, on this trolley was a large object under a big white cloth. Andy continued, "I wanted them to have the start in life together that we never had; what a joke," Claire thought as she considered that Andy was given a business without having to work for it. Andy invited Becky and Michael to come and stand next to him. Claire was inadvertently left out of the spotlight, but she didn't mind. Andy continued, "So, I thought, what could I do for them to give them that start?" He then dramatically unveiled a model of a beautiful development with six new apartments, the top of which was illuminated to stand out as the penthouse. Andy revealed, "This is a development I own that is just finished being built in Hoxton, and the penthouse is my gift to you both." Becky was speechless, Michael shook his dad's hand and there was a lot of chatter in the room, everyone applauded Andy for his speech and generosity but there was no love for him in the room. Why couldn't he have done this privately? Why in front of everyone? Why today? Why make what Roz and David who have worked their lives to save for and put on this amazing wedding seem so insignificant and try to trump them with a penthouse apartment? But I think it backfired on Andy as he didn't get the response, he expected at all. He sat down and Claire leant over to him and whispered in his ear, "I could not hate you any more at this moment for what you have just done and for where you have been the last few days." She turned her head away and Andy seemed to watch the colour drain out of his head as he sat there smiling at everyone.

Everyone was crowding around the penthouse model, and Roz was feeling gutted for David. He has worked so hard to make this weekend magnificent, and Andy does something like that in front of all their friends and family.

Becky and Michael, naturally, were taken aback by the generous gift and extended their heartfelt thanks to both Andy and Claire. They didn't grasp any of the atmospheres Andy had created by presenting this gift in public, which, in retrospect, was a blessing. They were elated, basking in the joy of the moment, and for tonight and tomorrow, in that room, they were the most important people.

They carried on late into the night the food was great and the venue could not have been more perfect, when it all finished and everyone had either left or gone to bed, Roz was sitting on the couch whilst David rubbed her feet. Claire was sitting talking and laughing with Michael and Becky was just kissing Stephen and Abraham as they went to bed. She walked over and slumped down on the couch and just said, "Wow, that was the best night of my life." "Wait until tomorrow." Michael said. Becky just smiled and closed her eyes, the waiters brought the, fresh tea and a few cakes to nosh, but what David really wanted was a bacon sandwich on white thick bread with ketchup. Everyone got in on the act and they sat there with tea and bacon sandwiches talking about the evening until they noticed the staff wanting to clear up, so they all went to bed. Becky walking arm in arm with her mum, Michael with his mum, David was walking and laughing with Tami and everyone was thinking where is Andy as his absence was noticed for a change.

37. Day of the Wedding

On the morning of the wedding, the day was dawning. It was 7 a.m., and Roz and David were already up, sipping their morning coffee on the lawn after a brief morning walk. Claire occupied the balcony of their room, a courtesy upgrade provided by Andy, where she enjoyed a cup of tea and a cigarette. Andy, on the other hand, was sound asleep, and in Stephen and Abraham's room, the new parents were tending to their baby after a somewhat restless night. Tami remained fast asleep while Becky was in her room, organising breakfast with her maid of honour and bridesmaids. She had some time before the flurry of activities, including hair and nails, was set to begin at 10 a.m. Michael was just beginning to stir, and his best man had arrived with a Bloody Mary, a remedy for a night of overindulgence. As a man, he had a bit more time to spare, a quick shower, dressing up, and a bit of grooming with gel, and he'd be ready to go.

The hotel was all action stations and the coordinators were very busy but determined not to bother Becky. Everything was going to plan: the florist was there, the lighting specialists were setting up, and the band were just arriving as they had to sing and play in three different parts of the wedding, so they wanted to get everything set up and tested early, the chuppah was being dressed, and the tables were being laid, the photographer and videographer were busy filming the set up for the film they would make and soon would, appear at the doors on both bride and groom to get early morning films of them both preparing. So, all in all it was all stations go only the rabbi to come but he was being picked up by one of David's cabbie friends and was not due yet, whilst upstairs in the bedrooms it was starting to get busy.

Andy woke up and jumped straight in the shower. He wasn't ready to face Claire. By the time he came out, she was gone to have her hair done in Tami's room, who was now up and having breakfast, anyway, so Andy never had a clue what to do or how to deal with it. He was panicking although he's convinced himself she has no real idea what is going on or has for the last 15 years. Claire was keeping out of his way as today was about their son. Andy can squirm, she thought.

It was now approaching 1 p.m., and everything was really coming together. The bride was having her hair and makeup nearly done. She had two and a half hours before she walked down the aisle. Michael was still watching a film and would jump in the shower as he did not want to hang around after the shower. He wanted to get dressed and go.

Roz and David were both getting ready. Roz was hogging the bathroom, and the makeup lady had just arrived to help her as she needed some special work done to cover up a few lesions and also to give some colour to her face.

Tami was in the shower and seemed OK. She was just enjoying the fact there was no focus on her, and she could be invisible; it suited her mood.

Stephen and Abraham were a bit stressed getting ready, feeding the baby and trying to time it so he would be asleep and full of food during the ceremony. Fat chance of that happening.

So, all the immediate family members and people participating in the wedding were doing OK. Roz and, David, and Claire had been checking on their parents. They all seemed OK. They were in their rooms, taking it easy.

As you drove through the entrance to the hotel, you were met by small candles (not real ones electric ones) but they lead you all the way across the bridges right up to the main hotel entrance where planted in the grass was a heart with the initials R and M inside, with a small light in the ground making it shine. you followed at least five to six more of these as it led you up to the parking area for guests. Outside the main entrance to the wedding venue, two floral hearts adorned the two pillars, each with the initials of the couple inside. As guests approached the entrance, they were met with double doors featuring a stylish twig design in silver for handles. Upon opening these doors, they entered a stunning, high-ceilinged, and exceptionally long reception area. The space was aglow with the warm flicker of candles placed throughout, creating a truly enchanting atmosphere. The lighting was quite low inside as you looked through to the doors at the rear end of the reception which were fully open with waiters all in white serving non-alcoholic cocktails and small snacks just to get everyone in the mood. They were Parmesan crisps and tiny sugared doughnuts the size of a finger nail, guests were arriving everyone was dressed beautifully and the reception inside and out was stunning and everyone was wondering where the wedding was going to happen as you had no idea from the reception area. There was a saxophonist and a female singer singing jazz in the background. She had a beautiful voice and was dressed amazingly.

Time was marching on, and David was ready and waiting for the call to see his daughter in her dress for the first time, ready to escort her downstairs.

Michael had come downstairs with his dad and ushers, talking to a few people and downing a scotch as he seemed very nervous.

Everyone was asked to take their seats for the wedding as proceedings would start in ten minutes. From the reception room, these two huge doors slid open. Everyone looked stunned. As you walked in, the huge windows to the left that looked over the gardens had been blacked out. No wonder you could not see in from outside. Tiny candles were lighting the gangways and the chuppah was dressed in green and white simple foliage down the four small wooden pillars, with tiny lights wrapped around them. There was one amazing floral display that was in the middle of the blacked-out windows, and on either side, projected on the blacked-out curtains, were black and white photos of both Becky and Michael as children, which was incredibly subtle. Everyone walked through this before taking their seat. The chuppah was in the middle, behind where the rabbi would stand, was a huge wall from floor to ceiling with a piece of lace with lights from above lighting it. The chairs were plain wooden chairs with a simple lace covering.

The whole room looked incredible and so different from the feeling of the reception. There was no natural light, all candles. The band had one female singer and now a pianist just playing and singing some back ground songs as everyone came in to take their seats; everyone had a seat number, so it was not a free for all, it was all pre-planned.

Michael was chatting to the rabbi. Michael had a black three-piece dinner suit, very slick single-breasted with curved collars and a handkerchief just coming out of the pocket in white but completely flat. He stood now under the chuppah with his best man, waiting for the arrival of his bride. Everyone was ready.

David was making his way to see Becky he knocked on the door and Roz opened the door and she said, "I think you had better prepare yourself as you won't be ready for this," he kissed Roz and walked into the lounge, it was chaos it looked like they had been burgled, all the bridesmaids were all just leaving with the maid of honour to get ready to walk down the aisle, then David closed the door and there was a silence. Roz was sitting on the sofa she looked beautiful her dress fitted perfectly. She went for a wig and a hat and David was so proud of her at this moment, then he went into the bedroom as the sun was shining brightly through the windows and there standing in front of the window was Becky, "Hi, Dad," she said, "What do you think...?" "He took a deep breath and started to speak but no words came out, his voice went up a pitch as he just cried through the words he was trying to get out, he walked over to her, held out his hand which she grabbed tightly and he kissed her gently on the forehead and said, "Never in my dreams, did I ever imagine I could be so proud and so lucky all at the same time. You look completely breathtaking and I love you so much" and the tears were running down his face and she was crying; too lucky the makeup lady was waiting in the bathroom for any touch ups. Becky called her in and she worked on Becky as David contained himself and went out and said, "Roz I..." "I know she said, you don't have to say it, we got there, the truth is, I never thought we would, let's just enjoy it," and she squeezed his hand tightly like she did when she told everyone her news. Becky wore a very tight figure-hugging dress that I could not do justice to by trying to describe it, except to say she looked like a modern-day princess full of class and beauty.

As everyone departed to make their way downstairs for the procession, David and Becky descended the grand staircase leading to the entrance. They could hear the music and the joyful conversations in the room beyond, but they remained hidden from view as the doors had been closed. A brief hush fell over the gathering as the singers paused. All eyes were fixed on the back of the room at the two expansive windows.

"Ladies and gentlemen, please welcome the wedding party." Then the pianist started playing, and in came the three young nephews and nieces of Michael, followed by Claire and Andy, then by Roz and Stephen; they all took their places. They had not noticed the doors had shut again, then an announcement, "Ladies and gentlemen, please be upstanding for the bride and groom." as they stood, the song sunrise sunset started to play, with those opening lines…

Is this the little girl I carried
Is this the little boy at play?
I don't remember growing older
When did they?
When did she get to be a beauty?
When did he grow to be so tall?

Then the doors slid open, and there was Becky and David. Everyone smiled and very slowly tried to make eye contact with everyone. They walked down the aisle; David looked so proud, and Becky just looked breathtaking. Becky whispered to her dad, slowly, I want to savour this moment with you. A tear started to come down David's face, and everyone noticed it as he let it make its way down his cheek.

As they reached the chuppah, he reluctantly gave her hand to Michael, and everyone laughed. He then went and stood by his wife, who looked incredible. Everyone sat down, and the service began.

The rabbi welcomed everyone and promised to explain everything he did so everyone could participate in this service.

It began, and very slowly, Becky walked around Michael seven times to the sound of an Israeli song called Jerusalem of gold. The service was very special, and David was looking at everyone as if they were enjoying the service and the rabbi's words.

Becky and Michael decided to say their own words to each other which was very nice then came that moment where Michael had to stamp on the glass covered in a white cloth before he did the rabbi said, "Now, Michael, you need to understand this will probably be the last time you will stamp your feet and your wife will listen," everyone laughed and then came that moment the stamp, and as he did everyone jumped to their feet, shouting, "Mazel Tov." and then the music stared and the rabbi grabbed the groom, bride, best man, bride parents and they started dancing around the chuppah whilst everyone clapped and shouted.

For a few minutes, the room was filled with a shared sense of joy and congratulations. People began to mingle and make their way outside to the stunning garden area, where refreshing drinks and delightful canapés were being served. As they strolled out, they were serenaded by a singer and pianist performing beautiful, soft music. The bride and groom were gently guided to a designated area at the bottom of the gardens for their photos. The unique arrangement allowed everyone to have a clear view of them, even though they were positioned three gardens away by the river, while the reception continued in the top garden.

The reception was in full flow as different members of the family and friends were called for photos with the new Mr and Mrs Anderson.

An hour and a half passed, and then the toast master walked and stood in front of two huge glass panels, and then he said ladies and gentlemen, would you please be seated as dinner would be served. Both glass panels slid open and revealed the ballroom. The band were already playing as everyone started to make their way into the ballroom looking around.

There were soft lights wrapped around the four main pillars in the ballroom each table had an incredible vase. In the centre of each table the vase had a stem that was no thicker than a pencil and it rose up in the air so everyone could see each other across their own table and the vase ballooned into a heart shape with green and white flowers and some small lights entwined in between the flowers. There were 29 tables, so you can imagine how it looked. The dance floor was black with lights running through it and the stage with the band was at the back of the room with a ten-piece set of musicians and three singers. It took a while before everyone was seated and then the toastmaster requested for quiet as he said, "Ladies and gentleman please welcome the very new Mr and Mrs Anderson," and as they came in holding hands everyone stood and clapped to the sound of "*All I need Is Love*" by the Beatles. Once everyone was seated, it was time, David was shaking and rustling around with some papers and the toastmaster announced, "Ladies and gentleman praise silence for your welcome speech by your host, David…" Everyone cheered as he made his way to the stage and stood. In front of the microphone on a stand and a musical stand was placed his papers he was about to read.

"My amazing daughter Becky, my new son-in-law, Michael," everyone cheered Claire and Andy, family and friends, well, we did it. "We got here," another cheer; "My wife always tells me to speak up and say what's on my mind, and I always respond by telling her I don't need to; being married to you as you seem to speak for me," everyone laughed, "Well, tonight my wife will have to sit down as I say a few words and words she has not read," everyone, "oooohhhs."

"Before we start, I owe everyone an apology, I decided to not get involved in any choices made for the wedding and with two strong women, three of you including Claire, I had no chance, but there was one thing I could not let go and that was the price to hire napkin rings," everyone starts to laugh, "So, I took it upon myself to sort this one thing out, to my daughter's horror, this took me many places and many phone calls, eventually I found them after a lot of hard work believe me, the only thing was, I was so pleased to find them, I forgot to look at them more closer," laughter, "I did however achieve something that I think is a first, I managed to choose napkin rings that everyone picked up and studied for a long time, normally they are the first thing removed as you sit down but not my napkin rings." more real laughter, "My apology is because I hope I never offended anyone as I never knew my napkin rings would be engraved all around with sex positions from the Kamasutra," everyone was now hysterical and then clapped for him.

The build-up to this wedding has been marked by numerous challenges and even some heartache. Yet, I soon realised that it's quite typical for a wedding, so I entrusted the organisation of this day to the incredible women in my life. What a remarkable job they have done, and I can assure you, there's much more to come. As for me, I had envisioned this day since the moment Becky was born. Still, no one could prepare me for what I witnessed just a few hours ago. Roz had cautioned me, but believe me, a father can never truly prepare himself for the moment he sees his daughter in her wedding dress for the first time. He took a deep breath and needed a minute as he started to cry, someone bought him a glass of water, as he took a sip and controlled himself.

"When I walked into that room and saw my little girl standing there saying, 'well, Dad, what do you think?' I could not speak; all I could see was my little girl showing me a picture she had painted when she was five, or showing me when she put her first school uniform on or when she wore a dress for her first party or the exam results she got from school/ university or her masters or when she got the job at the museum or when she started going out with Michael or when we sat in her room and she asked me what I think of her getting engaged to Michael. Then when she had her wedding dress on, it was like a quick flash through her young life, where does the time go, I cried no words would come out all I could do was kiss her. She looks breathtaking and for sure will always be the little girl who painted the picture, I am so proud of her what she has achieved, and most importantly she has grown up to be a good caring, honest respectful and loving daughter who could ask for more."

"Now, my son-in-law," everyone laughed; David responded and said, "the first time we met him, I never liked him. That's no slight on him. It's just a slight on all boys worldwide that Becky would have brought home. My daughter, but seriously, Michael, I could not be happier to have you as a new member of our family. You have always been respectful to us and caring to my daughter. You are hardworking, sometimes…" more laughter, "And I know you will take care of my little girl and give her a good life for that I am deeply thankful."

"Claire and Andy, welcome to our family. I want to personally thank you for respecting our religious beliefs and being on board with a Jewish wedding and for you and all your family for taking so much interest in what is a very important symbol for us.

We look forward to having and sharing celebrations with you in the future, and, along with your gorgeous daughter Tami, welcome again to our family.

Oh, I just have one thing: I can't believe the Anderson family are Arsenal fans. That's not good." There was some cheering and a lot of booing.

"We are lucky to have here with us the grandparents, and I would like you all to raise your glasses to them, and how proud we are to share this day with them. I also would like you to raise a glass to my son and his partner, Abraham, and of course the new smallest member of the family, baby Rose.

Last but not least, my amazing wife, Roz, is looking down at this point as she hates fuss. Roz, what can I say? You are the rock, the glue that holds this family together. You have taught us all what is important in life. Our Friday night dinner has become famous. It doesn't matter where we are; you made us understand that nothing gets in the way of family time, which has been respected for nearly 30 years. You look incredible this evening and I love you with all my heart."

"I eagerly anticipate spending the rest of my life with you," David begins, but he struggles to say the words without tears welling up. He sobs and takes a deep breath, then continues, "I'm sorry." The room fills with applause, and David regains his composure. "Spending the rest of my life with you has been an absolute delight, and I know that every future day with you will be a precious gift from God. Ladies and gentlemen, please stand and raise your glasses to Roz, my wife and my dearest friend." The entire room rises, toasts to Roz, and takes a sip.

"I have taken up enough of your time, so to end, please promise me you will make this day memorable for the new couple. You will eat our food, food that has been inspired by Roz," and everyone laughs, "and dance the night away and make this a night to remember."

"Ladies and gentlemen, please stand and raise your glasses. The new Mr and Mrs Anderson," everyone joins in, and David gets a loud applause as he goes to his seat via Becky and Michael. He hugs Becky, and she just whispers, "I love you, Dad," he kisses Michael and makes his way to his seat, where Roz stands and hugs him and tells him how proud she is of him. He sits and downs a scotch, thinking I'm glad that's over.

The meal was served, and everyone was shocked to see chopped liver or egg and onion to start with fresh hot bread, followed by chicken soup with kreplach, remember this from before. Kosher chicken breast with roast potatoes, baked rice and butter beans with broccoli and peas, homemade gravy and stuffing, this is followed by apple crumble and fresh cream. Cheese cake, apple cake and a fresh fruit salad, this would be followed later on in the evening by a cheese board and crackers with tea and coffee, there was not one more morsel of food left on anyone's plate it was a success as Roz knew it would be.

The best man's speech, to put it generously, was rather ordinary. He shared stories that elicited laughter, mainly from the groom and his close friends. Michael's speech, while sincere and touching, was somewhat forgettable. Thankfully, Andy chose to remain in the background, perhaps realising that after last night's events, it was best to keep a low profile.

The dancing started and was in full swing, the dance floor was packed and then it was halted for everyone to have the cheese and biscuits as this was getting towards the end. It was around 10 p.m. and then Becky got up and grabbed the microphone to a huge cheer, "I won't be long, I want to thank you all for coming and for your amazing gifts. I also want to say that a little while ago. I found something out about my dad that none of us new for most of our lives, it was quite a shock," you can tell everyone looked puzzled, "So without further ado, I give you my dad, David Cohen," everyone applauded as he made his way up to the stage, grabbed the microphone, he sent a kiss to Becky and said, "I would like to start with the song I danced to at my wedding," he began singing "*I've Got You Under My Skin*," everyone was shocked and clapped and cheered as he sang it beautifully with his very silky voice, he carried on for an hour, singing one song after the other from an amazing era back in the day with old blue eyes. He left to cheers as he handed back to the band to play us out until 1 a.m. when the last dance, noticeably and sadly missing Claire and Andy as Claire danced with Tami.

Wow, what a day! What an amazing experience. Claire and Andy's family had never experienced a Jewish wedding before. They thanked everyone as it was customary for all the immediate family to be in line by the exit door to literally thank every guest as they left.

It was now 2 a.m., and David, Roz, Claire, Andy, Tami, Stephen, Abraham, Rose, Becky and Michael were slumped around a table as the waiters brought in bacon and sausage sandwiches with hot tea. They laughed and shared some amazing moments together, looking back on a magical day.

Roz was the first to give in; she stood and said, "I'm sorry, I need my bed," she smiled at everyone and turned to leave. She told David to stay, which meant she wanted to be on her own, and as she walked slowly towards the exit, everyone had their own individual moment. As she reached the exit, Becky ran over to her, hugged her tight and whispered something private between the two of them in her ear. She held her hand until Roz walked away and their fingertips were no longer touching.

Becky returned to everyone and hugged her dad and said, "Thank you," and then they carried on, eating and drinking for another half an hour, Claire was thinking, "Omg if Roz does not make it, I will need to step up and keep this family together, how on earth does anyone step into Roz's shoes and worse, how will this family cope if life is without Roz."

38. The Day After the Wedding

Breakfast in the hotel was until 10 a.m. David had arranged a private room at 11 a.m. for the entire group who stayed overnight, which was about 80 people. I think David will be pleased when his hospitality is over as I'm sure it will take him several months to come to terms with the cost, but on the other hand, compared to what Roz is going through, it's fairly irrelevant.

Gradually, one by one, like the steady drip of a tap, everyone started to gather for breakfast. Becky's radiant smile upon her arrival was simply unmatched. She seemed to float around, embracing and thanking everyone. When she pulled up a chair next to her father, David's heart swelled with happiness. Meanwhile, Roz had yet to make her appearance downstairs, as she always took her time getting ready and preferred solitude during the process. David was well aware of this routine. Claire and Tami were also missing.

Andy was there sitting with Michael, having breakfast. Michael was explaining to his dad that they have a couple of days before they go on honey moon and he is going to see Grandpa. He wanted to see him, so he arranged it last night to meet for lunch today. Andy was not happy to hear that, but the truth was he had no control over it he could only delay it. Michael knows he has to think about the rental lease he just signed and how he could get out of it and move into their new home, Andy said, "You have just encountered your first rich people's problem, I'm sure you will work it out," said Andy.

David was settling the final bill with the hotel and the bar bill. Surprisingly, it was less than he had thought; he felt like celebrating and telling the world his news, but he realised only he cared about the saving.

Roz had come down and was having coffee with Becky whilst the bags were being put in the car, and they were getting ready to leave the hotel. Roz's phone was ringing and pinging off the scale with messages of, 'thanks for a truly memorable evening,' all except Uncle Sid who left a message to say how surprised he was to be sitting at the same table as his cousin Phyllis as they hadn't spoken for 23 years. It made the entire evening very awkward…there's always one at every wedding.

Andy was now sitting in reception, seeming a bit lost. The truth is Claire had left first thing with Tammy but not before she spoke with Roz and put her head in to see Michael and Becky. "Everything OK?" David says to Andy, "Yes, sure, all good. I'm just waiting for my luggage, and then I will be off for a great weekend. "David, you pulled it off without my help; that's awesome. I hope you don't owe it to loan sharks." David smiled and said, "nope all good, thank you," and as he walked away. David now had his own under-the-breath comment, "What a complete w—er there is no wonder he's sitting alone the morning after his son just got married."

This is a bit of a recap, as everyone is scattered everywhere today.

Claire left early with Tammy as she was not doing great after really holding it together last night, and they went home to relax.

Andy was heading home alone as, quite frankly, he had nothing else to do today or no one to be with.

Roz and David were on their way home with Becky to spend some time together.

Stephen, Abraham and the baby were en route to the supermarket and then home.

Michael was on his way to see his grandpa for lunch.

It was early evening Michael was heading to pick up Becky from her parents, he arrived a little flustered and when he came in the house he looked all over the place, Becky said come in and sit down have some tea, Michael said I don't want tea I just need to tell you something, "You know I went to see my grandpa. Well, he has decided, listen to this," "I'm still listening, just spit it out," "He's decided to give me his entire portfolio of properties I can't remember but I know it's over 40 and they are all rented out by a company and my job is to manage them, they belong to us now. Becky, I'm in the property business. I'm no longer working for my father; he knows as well my grandpa told him. Oh, and he also gave me his entire vintage car collection. Not that I care about cars, but I know someone who does, your dad. I'm thinking we give him a gift and get him to choose one." "That's amazing," said Becky, "he would love that I'm sure, it's a bit overwhelming in a very short space of time we have been given a penthouse from your mum and dad a property portfolio of over 40 properties from Grandpa Mo and four million from your other grandpa David, this is insane I don't know what to say or do," "Don't say or do anything, let's get packed enjoy our honeymoon and discuss it when we are on the beach," Becky smiles but Michael can tell something's wrong, "Well, come on, Becky, I know you that was not your smile." "I'm sorry, Michael it's just I, I, I don't think I can go away on honeymoon, Mum is looking so ill, I need to be around to help her and sitting on a beach for three weeks feels wrong. I don't think I can enjoy myself, what do you say?" Michael smiles and says, "No problem, I understand, let me get on to the agents and put it on hold," "Thank you, I love you, I knew you would understand."

David and Roz find themselves on their own and decide to have a quiet evening with some matzoh, cheese, strong tea, and an early night.

Tami found herself in her room, having just hung up the phone after hearing the surprising news from her grandpa about inheriting five million now, rather than after their passing. She was in a state of shock and uncertainty, not sure how to react. So, in typical Tami fashion, when faced with confusion, she decided to retreat and clear her thoughts by going to sleep.

Claire is on the wine this evening, and Andy is in his study doing whatever he does.

Stephen and Abraham are having a quiet evening, or Abraham is having a quiet evening. They had a row, and Stephen was in a bar with some workmates, leaving Abraham home with Rose.

Things are actually getting more complicated with everyone at the moment, whether it's because of marital problems, mental health problems, being given way too much money at a young age, or significant life-threatening health issues. That's families for you.

Everyone is deep in their thoughts about where they are in their life at this moment and what is the next part of their own journey for them. Nothing is ever simple unless you are baby Rose, you shit, you sleep, you eat.

39. Roz

Once the adrenaline of the wedding wore off, six weeks have passed, Roz sort of came down with a bang, she continued with her treatment that she had been allowed to stop for a few weeks, that was finished now, she started to recognise some of her previous symptoms returning and was due to see her specialist, anyway, so she held off for a few days, she told David it was just a regular catch up and he said, "OK, if you want me to come, let me know."

She told David that she would go on her own, mentioning a plan to meet an old friend for coffee, and he didn't question it. She visited the specialist, and over time, his office had become an uncomfortable place for her. Roz shared her feelings with him, and he discussed the results of her scan. Unfortunately, he had to be straightforward with Roz, as she had always preferred, and informed her that the cancer had spread to her liver. He said, "It is more aggressive now and we need to plan our next move," "Stop," Roz said, "Whatever you are going to say, just hold on let me think, can I get a glass of water?" "Of course," she sipped the water and really it only just touched her lips, she put the glass down slowly and without it making a sound. "OK," she said, "How long do I have?" He paused and responded shaking his head, "I don't know." "Take an educated guess," she said with a bit of frustration in her voice, "Three to four months and with some treatment I can propose we can possibly make that longer," "But what quality of life will I have with the treatment?" "There are side effects, but it depends on you." "So, what you're saying is, I might live longer up to nine months but the treatment won't make it a fun time?" "Yes," he says. "Thank you for being honest with me, can we leave it there. I don't think I can take any more plans at the moment; I will get back to you." "OK, but it needs to be this week." "I know, it will be, thank you," she gets up, he hugs her and she hugs him back. Tears run down her face slowly and she whispers, "I want to thank you so much for everything you have done for me as she leaves his office." He sits in his chair and thinks, "Sometimes I have the best job in the world, today I have the worst job for sure."

David was back, working quite hard. It seemed the only thing to do now, so he was working nights to be around for Roz during the day as she struggled a little bit. David was not aware of the extent of her meeting with the specialist; his beloved Spurs had reached the final of the cup and was battling for the top spot with Liverpool for the title. It was a good time to be a Spurs fan, and David went as often as he could. Stephen had lost interest in it with the new baby, or that's what he told David. David thinks it's pressure from Abraham that has stopped him.

Becky was enjoying the life. She loved being married, her apartment, work was great, and everything was really good. She was worried about her mum and tried to see her at least twice a week, and Michael was very understanding. He was just starting with his new property portfolio to manage and was so happy not to be working in the family business. He had just rented an office and had employed a secretary to work with him, and he was busy setting everything up.

Stephen. It's challenging to gauge Stephen's happiness. He's deeply engrossed in his demanding job with long hours and frequent trips to New York. Abraham, while aware of this situation before they adopted Rose, is beginning to feel the loneliness that comes with it. Their conversations mostly revolve around baby matters, and Stephen seems somewhat distant during these chats. The question remains: Is Stephen genuinely happy, or is he simply going through the motions? Time will ultimately reveal the answer, as living like this can only go on for so long.

Claire had thrown herself into Tami as she was up and down like a yo-yo. She was still living at home. Claire could not help thinking about her marriage but had not yet brought the subject up, and Andy had not been on any trips at all and seemed to be around all the time. She looked at him at times and thought she would be happy if she had him most of the time. She loved him. In fact, she adored him, and at other times, she wanted to let her lawyer loose and ruin his life, but for now, she did nothing, and life was OK.

Andy was not travelling and did not want to give Claire any reasons to bring up that subject again. He's very naive; if he thinks she will just let it go, there's no chance of that.

He has told Angelina he needed some time at home, and he used Tami as the reason. He could not say anything about Claire as he was supposed to be preparing to leave her, and Angelina was OK with that. For some reason, she was a bit of a free spirit and liked her arrangement. She liked her life, and she had the best of both worlds. Andy was not playing as much golf either and worked and came home, especially as his son was no longer working with him. Claire made her arrangements and was not at home that much in the evenings but Andy just took it all quietly, it was starting to feel like a mountain ready to erupt at any moment.

Tami was living at home; she had given up her studio and agreed with her gallery that she take a year off and sort out her head and decide if she wanted to paint anymore. She has been spending most of her time at home and was also seeing someone whom she met of all places at her therapist's. He was in the waiting room as she arrived, and they got on really well and talked for hours. Both have some real problems but together they seem to calm each other down, Tami was hoping not to ruin this one and was taking it very very slowly, she was also trying to get her head around the five million she had just received from Grandpa Mo and what she wanted to do with her life, she realised now was not the time to make big decisions.

Roz, having faced David with the news of her cancer, she had spoken to the specialist and had refused further treatment to prolong her life, but not being aware of it seemed pointless. She wanted to be as drug-free as possible, so she carried on with a lot of pain relief that her specialist agreed to. Things started to go downhill quickly, and everyone soon realised what was going on. She soon found it difficult to do anything and got breathless quickly. She went into hospital every four weeks or so to get some drugs just to pep her up, but that was it, the family rallied around, and all made significant sacrifices to change their life to be available and to spend time with Roz. Deep down they all knew what was going to happen, but they never spoke about it.

Six months flew by, and Roz's condition had significantly deteriorated. She spent most of her days in slumber, with only three to four hours of wakefulness on lucky occasions. Reluctantly, they had to hire a night nurse, a decision that Roz wasn't thrilled about. However, it allowed the rest of the family to return home and get some much-needed rest. During David's sleep, the nurse attended to Roz, ensuring she had assistance whenever necessary.

It was the weekend of the cup final and David had planned to go then decided he would not leave Roz; it was Friday morning and the match was Saturday. Roz woke quite early and was having breakfast she asked the nurse Jane whom she had become quite fond of if she could help her have a shower and get dressed. Jane said wow, "What's brought this on, you got a date?" "No," she said, "But I want to feel better this weekend, I've got a few things to do." "Oh yes," said Jane, "What's that?" "It's none of your business you will be gone soon," they laughed together as Roz got showered, got dressed, put her make up on and went downstairs just before David got up. When he came into the bedroom where she slept, he got a shock when she wasn't there just like that panic when it happens in a hospital. He came downstairs to see his wife dressed eating breakfast and said, "Oh, my god what's going on?" "Nothing," she said, "Can't I get up and get dressed early if I feel like it. Anyway, the kids are coming over to see me and you've got a football match to go to," "How did you," "It's me, Roz, I know everything, if you don't go to the final today, I will never talk to you again. I will be fine." "OK, OK," he says they have breakfast together or she watches him eat and David didn't want it to end, he ate as slowly as he could to make it last then he went to get himself ready.

She had arranged for Becky and Stephen to come in for lunch. David would only be home around 8 p.m. tonight.

Lunch time came and Becky came in looking so beautiful as she always does and was so happy to see her mum out of bed. Then Stephen turned up looking happy to be on his own with no baby and car full of stuff. They sat and chatted and had lunch together. Roz said to them, "Now listen carefully to me," "OK, Mum, what is it?" "I know you are not stupid and understand what is happening to me," "Mum, don't be stupid what are you saying?" "Becky, please, I may have cancer but I'm not stupid." "OK, Mum, we understand," said Stephen. "I just wanted to see you both and tell you something. Stephen, you have an amazing partner in Abraham, he's strong and loves you very much. Becky, you have an amazing husband who I know adores you and will do anything for you. I'm not worried about either of you. Your dad is a lovely man but he's not a strong man, I don't know how he will survive without me," Becky started to cry. Stephen just sat there as his eyes filled up, "I know this is hard but promise me something; you will take good care of your father and when he says he's fine he's not, when he says leave me alone, he doesn't mean it and when he says he's eaten, make him something." "Mum, Mum, we get it now can we move on and have lunch." "I've said my piece, now I feel better," they joked for the afternoon telling baby stories from Stephen and wedding stories from Becky, the nurse arrived about 6 p.m. and helped Roz to bed as she was exhausted and Becky and Stephen went home. It was a tough day for them all.

David got home, Roz was asleep, but he went up and kissed her on the head, and she whispered to him, "Well, how did they do?" He smiled, "they won 2–0 it was amazing," she smiled and fell back to sleep.

The coming weeks were hard. Roz could not really get up. She slept most of the time and had a day and night nurse now as she needed help with drinking. She got fluids stuck in her throat as she could not swallow, and you could hear this gargling sound as she breathed. There were people at the house every day and most nights it was a sombre place to be. Most nights David would sit with her holding her hand and Becky would come earlier or straight after work. Roz was not aware they were there, and she was getting weaker and weaker, and the noise of her breathing was pretty constant now. Becky and Stephen took Dad out for a quick meal just to get a break, and when they came back, some families were visiting from the other side of London. They were in the kitchen, and the nurse came downstairs to swap shifts and said to David, "I don't think it will be much longer now, maybe today or tomorrow." David took her hand and squeezed it as Jane had become one of the family over the last few months.

Claire and Andy had departed from the house with Tami, leaving David, Becky, Stephen, and Michael to finish a kebab they had ordered. However, their appetites were nearly non-existent. In the living room, a few of Roz's cousins and aunties were sitting. David found their presence irksome. It felt as though they were just waiting for Roz to pass away and constantly demanding tea and cakes. The mounting pressure had led David to lash out at them several times over the past week, and at one point, he had even asked them to leave as he found the situation increasingly unbearable.

The following night they were sitting in the kitchen and it was quiet it was 9 p.m. and Becky and Stephen were saying good night to Roz. David had enough of the family, how much they might mean well, and said, "OK, do you think you could all go now, I want to get some sleep." The family all stood up to leave. Very little was said and what was said was at whispering level. They all got up to leave and David went in to the kitchen to get away from the sound of Roz breathing and when everyone had gone, he went upstairs and said to Jane, "Jane, I'd like to sleep now and I would like to sleep next to my wife tonight." Jane said, "Of course, as long as you don't mind me walking in and out every few minutes to keep clearing Roz's throat." David didn't get undressed he just laid next to Roz and held her hand. Roz opened her eyes, very slightly squeezed David's hand and he looked at her in her eyes and you could really see the terror in her eyes; she knew exactly what was happening to her and there was nothing anyone could do. David kissed her above both eyes and rubbed her forehead as she fell off to sleep and he did as well.

David woke at about 7 a.m. as he could hear the changeover of nurses and got up to have breakfast. Roz was not eating at all, only fluids and mainly through a drip. David felt Roz did not have much time left.

It was Saturday morning at about 11 a.m. Becky arrived with Stephen; Abraham had brought Rose to see Roz, but she never woke up to see her, and Michael came over to see Roz before he went to work. Yes, Michael worked Saturdays; now, he had his own business to manage.

David was too scared to leave Roz and go to football, so he watched it live on television. It was a crucial game, and he may well decide if the Spurs can do the one thing, they have not done for 60 years and win the league.

David had warned all the family not to come over. He wanted a very quiet weekend with no visitors.

Becky and Stephen were having a sandwich in the kitchen, and David was watching the football with the sound down. He needed to hear Roz, however terrible this sound was, and it may well haunt him. At least he knew Roz was still with him.

From nowhere, there was a loud screech from the living room. Becky smiled, "At least Spurs are winning," she said, and Stephen laughed. It was now 4 p.m. halftime in the football game. David came in to make a cup of tea and he normally went out of the kitchen whilst the kettle was boiling because he couldn't hear Roz. This time, he stayed and for a few seconds forgot about the sound. As David described the Harry Kane goal, Stephen listened and Becky zoned out but was happy for her dad.

Jane came down the stairs and put her head over the bannisters, and said, "David, I think you should come upstairs," he rushed up, followed by Stephen and Becky; Roz was very still. The sound was much quieter, and her breathing had lengthened. They used to sit with her and count the gaps. They all knew it was longer between breaths. They all kissed Roz, there were many, many tears, and they sat in the room not speaking. Roz had lost so much weight, and her eyes had sunk back into her head so much she never really looked like Roz anymore, and her headscarf was still tight around her head it was her wish that no one ever saw her without hair. They all went downstairs just to gather their thoughts and pour themselves a cup of tea. At that moment in the kitchen, Becky said, "ssssshhh," as they all waited and prayed for that next gurgling breath. It never came five seconds became six, seven, eight, nine; then the floorboards above them started to creak as Jane was moving around. The three of them seemed to freeze for a second, then Jane came down the stairs, turned sharp left and saw the three of them all looking at Jane knowing what was going to come out of her mouth but stayed transfixed to her with hope she may something else, "I am so sorry, Roz has gone." Becky screamed, "No, no, no, Mummy!" Stephen slumped into the chair, and David turned around and punched the kitchen cabinets very hard before walking out of the back door and down to the shed…it was over. She was at peace now.

Several minutes passed, and one by one, they went upstairs to see their Mum. Becky sobbed as she held her hand, and Stephen was hesitant to go in. His dad insisted that he say goodbye, fearing he would regret not doing so later. Jane was busy on the phone, making arrangements, while David felt uncertain about what to do. Becky called Michael and shared the heartbreaking news, her voice trembling as she sobbed. Michael called his mum and said, "Please come over there with me, they will need someone strong to take control of what happens next and the arrangements." Claire crying as she put the phone down went upstairs and walked into her bedroom to get ready and as she went downstairs, she said to Andy, "It's Roz she's just died." Andy sat down and wiped his eyes as he shed some tears and Claire said, "Listen carefully, I want you to come with me, I want you to take control of all the stuff that needs to happen regarding certificates etc. Michael told me they bury people within a few days in the Jewish religion and David will never be able to cope, that's your job now so are you ready? They left and Andy never spoke a word.

When Claire and Andy arrived, they were both a bit nervous to walk in, you never seem to know what to say in these circumstances but they just went into automatic mode, the door was open as they entered the houses, there were quite a few people there, mainly family that Claire sort of recognised from the wedding, David was sitting in the kitchen at the table with Becky having some tea and not really saying much. He looked up and saw Claire and he looked at her and said, "She's gone Claire, can you believe it? my Roz, my Roz, how can it be? how can she be gone? And he started to really sob as Claire came over and put her arms around him and tried to comfort him. There was nothing to say except what everyone said, "She is no longer in pain she in a better place." I don't believe David believed that for one second, he said to one cousin, "Don't be so stupid," as he screamed. "How can she be in a better place? We're all here how can she be in a better place? Don't be so f—king stupid," then he got up and it looked like he was going to hit his cousin, but Andy managed to calm him down. There was chaos for a few minutes but it all calmed down. Claire called her doctor to come and see David and prescribe something to help with his nerves. He never knew but it also knocked him out, he slept for at least six hours.

It is customary that the body of a deceased person who dies at home cannot be left alone, so David sat with Roz all night. The next day, her body was placed in a basic wooden coffin, and a prayer was said over the open coffin for just the men. Stephen was in a real mess, and again, David compelled Stephen to participate, even though he was hesitant. Whether Stephen would thank his dad or never forgive him for the lasting image he would see, only time will tell. The body left home to be prepared for the funeral. Over the coming days, with some advice from the Jewish family members, Andy took control and prepared everything for a Jewish burial. At least he had some experience in this area.

The funeral was very busy; Roz had impacted so many people's lives. There were many hundreds of people at the cemetery. David was in a complete daze, as were Becky and Stephen. The ceremony is such a cold, simple affair it's something you want over quickly.

David never wanted to turn up in big black cars, so he took the Aston Martin, "Why not Roz would say sod everyone else, you drive it where you want."

He left his house as did everyone else; They all arrived early, and people slowly started to arrive. David never knew half of them; there was the entire staff of her old company, the owners of every single deli and food store she went to every week. The word got around, and all her friends, old and new, came to pay their respects.

About 30 cabbies came, many of the club owners where he used to sing, and the list goes on and on.

Everyone was asked to enter the hall. It was always cold in this place, and as David went in flanked by Becky and Stephen, there it was, that black cloth covering the wooden coffin. Tears started, and David was in a terrible state as he walked over and kissed the coffin and dropped to his knees, he was helped up and calmed himself, the rabbi started the service and said some amazing things as he knew Roz very well.

David was supposed to say something, but he just couldn't control himself, he asked someone to read it, but as they started, he asked them to stop, he composed himself. He spoke about Roz from the heart it was incredibly moving he finished by saying. The rabbi asked me to describe Roz, and I smiled as some of you are doing now. It's not easy, is it? But I would have to say she was a success at everything she tried, not because she got everything right but because everything she did came from a place of only good intention and she believed strongly that no matter where you may be in the world, what you may be doing, make time for family.

Everyone smiled as they followed the coffin to the graveside to say the final prayer. Every Jew will tell you that being the first to throw mud on the coffin makes a noise that is the same the world over. At every Jewish funeral, the sound of the mud hitting the coffin is unmistakable. But it also marked the beginning of a period of mourning, a five-day period with prayers every night. Claire offered to host it at her house, which was a kind gesture, but David couldn't accept it as Roz would have wanted it at her own home.

It was a very quiet and solemn time. Everyone seemed to be very nice to each other. I think it made the family feel very vulnerable, and they valued life much more during this period than ever before. Everyone had so many stories to tell they sat up until the small hours talking Roz-ism's, of which there were plenty.

She had been such an important figurehead for her immediate family and close friends that they all felt a huge hole. David was in a terrible way, and it was difficult to see how he would cope without her. Becky was just crying all the time. She was still inconsolable, and Michael worried how she would ever move on. Stephen just went into himself very deeply. He stopped crying and said very little; he just wanted to be on his own at every opportunity, as for Claire, she had lost a friend and confidante, who opened her up to and taught her about the importance of family first.

R I P. our special friend x

40. Family Updates Two Months After

Two months had passed...

David was not coping, and everyone was worried about him. He never went back to work, never really left the house unless to pray, and turned down every invite for dinner with the family.

The house was a constant reminder of Roz. She was everywhere in every room, in every cupboard. He could not go into his bedroom and slept in Stephen's old room. He went to the synagogue every morning and every evening. He decided to observe the 12 months of mourning. It gave him some comfort for sure, and he was always reminded of Roz. He was left alone in synagogue and never really knew anyone and no one bothered him, which he liked.

Stephen could not get the vision of his mum in a coffin with her body covered with the lid of the coffin open, but her head on show. He tried but could not get that vision out of his head, and he was getting more and more angry towards David for making him do this. He just threw himself into work and again, Abraham was giving him space to grieve and was being amazing, Stephen hardly looked at or touched the baby which was a shame.

Becky was walking around in a daze; her eyes were so sore and bloodshot because she just seemed to cry all the time. She took extended leave and just went from her home to be with her dad, and Michael was not really in the picture. He understood and put no pressure on her, and just worked and came home to be there.

Claire...had all her invites and offers of help turned down by David and the kids. She was still dealing with Tammy, who was calm but not feeling great about herself. Claire was meeting with her lawyer as she was determined to do something about her marriage before Andy did.

Andy was pretty invisible to everyone. He started to travel a bit, but Claire could not care less, so he sort of had carte blanche at the moment. He was back playing golf and doing what he did best: looking after himself.

Michael supported his wife 100% and worked hard to understand the business and deal with tenants who had problems with the properties. He had dealt with maintenance on graves. What could be so different with properties? He never understood. His clients used to be dead, but now they are very much alive.

Tami was coping, though it was a challenge. She spent most of her time at home or in therapy. She continued to see Richard, whom she had met during her therapy sessions. He provided valuable support at this point in her life, and it helped keep her content. Claire kept a watchful eye on her daughter from home, and the situation remained stable.

41. Family Updates Nine Months Later

David…he has recently gone back to work, it was now his place he could lose himself, he often talked about Roz to his customers, had a great picture of her in his cab and it was almost cathartic for him, Michael followed through on his gift to David of a car from the collection he had inherited. He had given David a choice and after refusing many times settled on and agreed to take one of the cars and it was an Aston Martin db7 which he would often take out on a weekend and drive to the coast to breath in the sea air. He had accepted a few dinners at Becky's and that was about as far as he had gone. It had been suggested to him that maybe he should sell the house and buy a flat which at the beginning he flatly refused, he now found himself thinking maybe it was a good idea but as yet he had not decided. So, between the synagogue, the cab, the car and Spurs, he was busy but hated the lonely nights, who knows what the future held for him but he kept hearing Roz say, 'stop being such a drama queen get on with it'. Time will tell.

Becky…threw herself into work, got promoted, and this was her form of therapy. Michael and she were very close, and Becky was now gathering every family photo, every small reminder of her mum and putting it all together to make sure her children would never forget her. It was a project to keep her busy, and it was working. She spoke to her dad every day when he was in the cab with no customers, and sometimes they spoke for hours as her dad worked nights and they could talk until early hours of the morning. How would Becky move on, time would tell.

Stephen was even more conflicted. He found it hard grieving for Roz, so he put it in a box and locked it away. Stephen might come to regret his decision to view Roz in the coffin as he grows older, but for now, he concealed his anger well. He and his father spoke at least twice a week, with David initiating the calls. Stephen was immersed in his demanding work for long hours and didn't particularly enjoy family gatherings that involved reminiscing. His relationship with Abraham remained a challenge, and it was uncertain how long Abraham's patience and support would last. His connection with Rose was distant, and only time will tell. Claire still tried to keep the two families close, but it was very hard as everyone was still hurting so much. Claire was back having fun with her treatments every week, shopping and going out with her friends. She was planning another charity event and was very close with Tami, who was still struggling with many things. She was still seeing Richard, and that was moving along slowly, Claire was preparing her next move with her lawyers, and it was all being discussed every few weeks, and things were taking shape, time would tell.

Andy was having to face the facts that his marriage was probably over, his daughter was like a stranger to him, his son was now working away from the family business, and he had a second family that may not even want him full-time if things went that way. Claire was almost leading a separate life to him, and he had not decided how to play things with his lawyers, but he knew he needed to act before Claire does, time will tell.

Tami appears to be in a good place, as her anxiety hasn't taken a toll on her for the past two months, and her relationship with Richard is enduring, which is a rarity for her. She's started to explore her financial independence and is realising she has the freedom to pursue various opportunities. Her mother remains protective, which Tami appreciates. As for what she will do with her life, only time will tell.

Michael is loving being married to Becky and is just starting to get the hang of things with his newfound responsibility of owning and managing 40 properties. He is thinking of taking on another employee to help with the maintenance and take it back from the managing agents. He's being very supportive of Becky and is enjoying life. Roz once warned Becky that there was something about Michael that she was unsure about, something that she just could not put her finger on, was she right, only time would tell.

42. Friday Night Dinner

12 Months have passed, and very little has changed. Everyone was trying to get used to a new reality and holding their breaths as they took a leap into the next chapter in their lives. The pain of a tragic loss doesn't really go away. It just gets less frequent over time. You go from thinking about that person every minute of every day and one day you will get up, do the normal things in life and realise at the end of that day you never thought about that person. Firstly, you feel guilty and you try to make sure it never happens again. Over time the pain is less and less frequent…it's OK, that's the way it's supposed to happen, that's the way it happens to the majority of people, don't fight it, it will enable you to move forward with your life. Thinking about that person on memorable occasions, and sometimes it will catch you off guard. It just hits you and hits you hard for a day. I truly believe it's the person reminding you or joking around with you that they are still there on your side and fighting for you to have a life.

Claire never gave up trying to get the families together. After 12 months, she failed. Claire does not fail, so she was at home. She made sure Andy, Becky, Michael and Tammy were in. She called them all together and said, "OK, I don't care what you are doing, who you are with or what plans you have. But next Friday you are here for dinner and I am not accepting no for an answer and most importantly I expect the same from David, Stephen, Abraham and Rose we are having our first Friday night dinner since Roz passed. I am not accepting no for an answer…" Then she shut up but never took her eyes off any of them, I think they all thought the same thing, that was very much like Roz…. but, no one would admit it. They all just said, "OK." They carried on what they are doing, Claire said, "Becky, it is your job to get your brother and father here for that night, please tell them and do not accept no for an answer," Becky was quite scared now and said, "OK, leave it with me."

Claire and Romero sat down for an extensive conversation about the meticulous details of setting the table, from the placement of cutlery to the positioning of the Friday night candles. They meticulously reviewed each dish that needed to be served, along with specifics such as the ideal source of each ingredient (with assistance from Becky), how it should be prepared, and, most importantly, how it should taste. Claire emphasised, "You have nine days until next Thursday night to make it absolutely perfect, do you understand?" Romero nodded confidently and replied, "Yes, I understand, and it's quite simple. I can do it." Claire was intrigued and asked, "How do you plan to achieve that? You've never cooked this meal before. How can you possibly pull it off?" Romero smiled and said, "It's simple." "Do you remember when Roz got really sick, but she would not stop Friday night dinners even though she was riddled with pain and could hardly stand up?" "Yes, I remember." "Who do you think she turned to, to help her with the cooking, until I knew how to do it and would prepare it here and take it there so she could heat it and serve it, guilty as charged." Claire looked at him and thought about what he said and replied, "Are you telling me you bought the ingredients, cooked them here, took them to Roz so she could heat everything up and serve it us without us knowing a thing?" "Well yes, that's exactly what I'm saying. Roz made me promise never to tell anyone about it or she would accuse me of some heinous crime and get me put in prison, and you know you didn't argue with Roz." "I don't know whether to fire you or kiss you." "I suggest you kiss me and leave me to get everything ready."

Becky managed to convince her dad to come, and then getting Stephen to come was a no-brainer.

It was Friday at lunchtime, and the preparations were in full swing. Romero was diligently working in the kitchen, Carolina was carefully setting the table, and Claire was overseeing every detail of the plates, cutlery, and napkins to ensure everything was perfect. She felt a mixture of nerves and excitement. Claire decided to leave the Shabbat candles on a lovely silver tray in the kitchen, planning to carry them in when everyone was seated. She had chosen this approach to prevent David from being upset when he sat down, as leaving them on display might be a painful reminder.

The chopped liver was ready to be plated, the chicken soup was made yesterday and was simmering, the chicken was in the oven. The roast potatoes and baked rice were also cooking, the broccoli and peas were ready to boil, the stuffing was in the oven, and the gravy will be last-minute.

The apple cake was ready, and so was the cheesecake and the fresh fruit salad and cream in the fridge.

Claire was getting dressed, Andy was downstairs getting the wine out from the cellar, and Tammy was in her room a little nervous as she had invited Richard for the first time to join them.

Becky arrived first with Michael, then Richard. He was early, which was better, so he never had to walk into everyone already there. Then Stephen and Abraham, with Rose, arrived. They just waited for David as he refused to be collected and wanted to come in his own time. He was standing in the hallway to his house and looking at a picture of Roz. It was taken the first time the Andersons came to dinner before everything went tits up and she looked good. He kissed the photo, and as he was about to leave, he said to her, "Don't worry this will never be as good as when you did it, you were the best, I love you my darling," and he left.

The doorbell rang and for some reason everyone was a little nervous as they all wanted it to be a perfect evening but was it possible? David came in with flowers for Claire and a bottle of good scotch for Anthony. He entered the living room; everyone hugged it out and he got to meet Richard who was also a little nervous. Claire came out of the kitchen and looked very not Claire-like, she was panicking, David noticed it first, he went over to her kissed her and whispered in her ear, "It's OK, breath, I'm sure it will be great," she squeezed his hand and then she said, "OK, everyone can you come into the dining room?" as they all walked in talking to each other there was a sudden silence as they looked at the table and there was some deep breaths being taken, as they all looked around studying the cutlery and the plates and the challah bread on the table sliced up, the cucumbers and strong red horse radish sauce and they all smiled as they saw the ketchup next to where David sits. There was still quiet as they sat down and then Claire said, "OK, everyone, one more thing," and she walked into the kitchen and then came back in, carrying a sliver tray with two candlesticks each with a white candle in, proudly looking up to the sky she put them down and everyone was quiet. Becky was tearful as was Stephen, Tammy, Abraham and Michael. David was looking at his feet to hide the tears that were rolling down his face, then Claire put the tray down and asked Becky to say the pray. Claire had learnt it and was ready to recite it but at the last second, she realised it was not her place she was there to facilitate the whole evening but it was Becky's place. She got up, walked around the table lit the two candles, waving her hands around the top of the flame very slowly three times and the flame lit her face as she looked to the sky and said the prayer. At that moment, David squeezed Claire's hand and leaned over to say, "Thank you; you are the nicest person I know." Claire responded, "Good, because you are going to be coming here every Friday as usual." David simply smiled. As Becky finished the prayer, she said, "Good Shabbas," and everyone very loudly repeated good Shabbas. What followed was everyone speaking over each other, laughing, and passing food across the table. It was at this point that everyone felt Roz's presence, and her smile seemed to shine down on them all. Who would have thought these two unlikely families would come together every Friday to break bread after all that has happened and it all started when two families came together to make a wedding, or did it?

Summary by the Author

This is two normal families, or as my wife would say, "What's normal? definitely not you."

I hope you have fallen in love with the madness of these two families or related to one or more of the characters. I believe there are bits of this that most of us can relate to, and all begin with the trauma of making a wedding.

There is a story to tell going back to before Michael, Becky, Tammy and Stephen were born and whilst they were growing up, some many near coincidences that nearly brought them together through the early years. Also, many stories to tell as the children grow up and become parents themselves and their parents look at the last quarter of their lives and how getting older changes them. I hope you enjoyed getting to know these families. I will soon continue on the journey as we look and deal with their personal challenging times as…

The trauma of pregnancy, birth and young babies.

The trauma of boys and girls becoming teens.

The trauma of becoming parents and becoming a nana and a papa.